She entered his lair...

Kay exited the dark hallway and stepped down the stone stairs that opened into the lovely inner courtyard. Who would have guessed that such a forbidding house could have such a beautiful enclosed garden?

She picked up one of the exotic blossoms of a late-flowering magnolia tree and inhaled its rich fragrance. Suddenly she sensed a movement behind her. She whirled around, finding herself face-to-face with Damian, a man of massive muscle, his ruggedly handsome features transformed by a sizzling, sunlit smile.

"Be careful," his deep voice warned. "A beauty who insists on stealing a flower from the beast's garden must also accept his penalty."

Dear Reader,

Open the gilded doors and step into the world of M.J. Rodgers's JUSTICE INC. A world where principle courts passion. In this Seattle law firm, legal eagles battle headline-stealing cases...and find heart-stealing romance in the bargain.

M.J. Rodgers has become synonymous with the best in romantic mystery. Having written her very first book for Intrigue six years ago, she has gone on to become one of the bestselling and most popular Intrigue authors. Her books are perennial Reviewer's Choice Award winners and last year she received the Career Achievement Award for Romantic Mysteries from *Romantic Times*.

So turn the page and enter the world of JUSTICE INC.

Regards,

Debra Matteucci
Senior Editor and Editorial Coodinator
Harlequin
300 E. 42nd St.
New York, NY 10017

M.J. Rodgers
BEAUTY VS. THE BEAST

TORONTO • NEW YORK • LONDON
AMSTERDAM • PARIS • SYDNEY • HAMBURG
STOCKHOLM • ATHENS • TOKYO • MILAN
MADRID • WARSAW • BUDAPEST • AUCKLAND

This is dedicated to Randall Toye with special thanks for
his vote of confidence in its concept.

ISBN 0-373-22335-8

BEAUTY VS. THE BEAST

Copyright © 1995 by Mary Johnson

Printed in U.S.A.

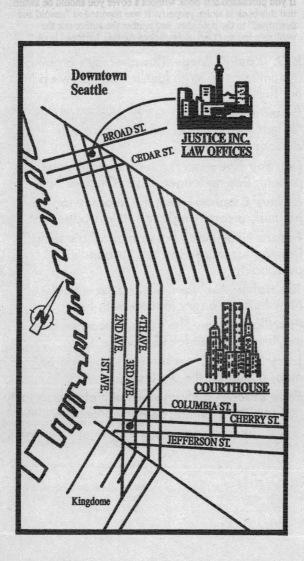

CAST OF CHARACTERS

K.O. (Kay) Kellogg—This attorney's arguing a dynamite case. With luck it won't blow up in her face.

Damian Steele—He's the psychologist who "killed" the nasty personality of a dual-personality patient.

Lee/Roy Nye—Lee is the dual-personality patient; Roy no longer exists. Or does he?

Rodney Croghan—He's the attorney for the plaintiff, a conniving and ruthless opponent.

Fedora Nye—She's the woman who's suing Damian for murdering her husband's personality.

Tim Haley—He was Damian's receptionist. Now he's too angry to work with him.

Priscilla Payton—She's a lady scorned and maybe a lady out for vengeance.

Larry Nye—He's the son of the "murdered" man, a chip off the old block.

Bette Boson—She's another multiple-personality patient with even more severe problems.

ABOUT THE AUTHOR

BEAUTY VS. THE BEAST is the first book in a court-room series by bestselling author M.J. Rodgers. In the next two books, BABY VS. THE BAR and HEART VS. HUMBUG, she will continue to bring you the stories of the dedicated attorneys at Justice Inc., Seattle's legal sleuths.

M.J. is the winner of the *Romantic Times* Career Achievement Award for Romantic Mysteries, their Best Romantic Mystery Award and B. Dalton Bookseller's top-selling Harlequin Intrigue Award. She lives with her family at the base of the Olympic Mountains in Washington State.

Books by M.J. Rodgers

office could have spelled far more serious confrontational disasters.

As he turned to leave, he saw that he had clearly started

with him. Particularly since Priscilla had obviously talked
to Bette before he could, just as she had talked to Tim
Haley.

Prologue

Angry sounds rumbled through the walls.

The little boy rocked sleepily awake as the thunderous sounds shook his small body. His eyes blinked open to darkness.

He burrowed his head beneath his covers, cupping his ears with his palms, trying to block out the sounds. But the violent, unrelenting blows pounded ever more fiercely against his eardrums, making them feel sore and beaten.

He grabbed the pillow and dragged it beneath the covers. He wrapped it around his head to muffle his ears. If he could no longer hear the sounds, maybe he could make them go away.

Please.

But the angry sounds kept getting louder, closer.

He threw the pillow aside and snatched the covers off his head. He dived for the edge of the mattress. His feet tangled in the sheet and blanket. He fell to the floor, kicking and squirming, clumsily trying to free himself.

Frantically, he fought with the bedding and with the tears of terror beading onto his cheeks as the precious seconds slipped away.

And the angry pounding came closer, ever closer.

His tiny fingers clawed at the wood-slat floor as he inched himself beneath his bed. The bulky bedding got caught on the bed frame. He pulled his feet free of it just as the pounding stopped right outside his bedroom door.

He flattened himself beneath the bed as panic welled sick in his stomach and the rough wooden planks scored his delicate cheek.

The door to his bedroom banged open. The hallway light blinded him. He raised a shaking hand to shade his eyes, peering through the slits between his small fingers.

He could see the hideous dark hump swaying in the doorway, so immense its shadow pressed against the walls and climbed to the very ceiling. It was the demon from hell, its eyes glowing red, its rancid stench of smoke and acrid alcohol burning the little boy's sensitive nostrils.

He opened his mouth to scream—great, lung-emptying, panic-packed shrieks that tragically could make no sound at all, except in the deepest and darkest recesses of his mind.

For he knew he could not let the demon hear his screams, or the reasons for them would only get so much worse.

The demon bellowed its angry thunder throughout the boy's small body as it stomped into the room, lifted the empty mattress off the bed and threw it against the wall. This was just the beginning of its search. And the longer it searched and could not find him, the more furious it would get. And the more terrible the punishment would eventually be.

The little boy knew he was worthless and deserved everything he got. He had been told that often enough. He should come out from under the bed now and submit to his punishment.

But the little boy couldn't do it. He just couldn't willingly give up to this angry, hurtful demon. He had to try to escape just one more time.

The demon stomped over to the closet and yanked open the door, growling and kicking and slamming its huge fists against the closet wall when it realized its prey was not there.

The little boy knew his chance had come. He slid out from under the bed and quickly scampered over to the bedroom door.

His heart hammered in his chest as he ran down the hallway as fast as his legs could carry him.

He must hide. But where could he go? He'd been found in the living room behind the couch. He'd been found in the kitchen under the table. He'd even been found in the laundry room at the bottom of the hamper beneath a pile of dirty clothes.

Maybe the demon wouldn't think to look in that old storage shed behind the garage. The little boy jumped uncontrollably as the next angry bellow shook the hallway walls. *It* was coming out of the bedroom.

He had to get away. He could think of nowhere else to go. He would head for the shed.

The little boy's bare feet slapped on the floorboards as he ran for the back door. He grasped the knob and pulled it open. The freezing night air hit him like an icy slap. He held tightly to the rickety banister as he scurried down the porch stairs. But in the panic of his headlong rush, he tripped on the steps and fell face first onto the frozen ground.

He landed hard, the breath knocked from his body. He could hear the demon bellowing once more from inside the house. The little boy gasped for air, forcing himself to lie still against the icy ground, against the chilling terror, until his lungs filled again and his eyes adjusted to the darkness.

He began to make out the faint silhouette of the garage. He got to his hands and knees and crawled beside its rough stucco wall until he reached the old, dilapidated shed behind it. He scrambled to his feet.

His small hands stretched above his head to feel for the rusted iron latch. With all his strength, he pulled the heavy wooden door toward him. He slipped inside the shed and closed the door behind him, hearing the latch click into place.

The shed was absolutely black. The hard earth floor was like ice beneath his bare feet. His knees and palms stung from his fall down the stairs.

The little boy paid no heed to these physical discomforts. He felt his way slowly over the rough-hewn, wood-splintered walls until he had reached the farthermost corner. He leaned his back against it and sunk to the ground.

It took a very long time before his heart stopped pounding against his thin ribs, before his breath stopped wheezing through his small lungs. Finally, he drifted into a blessed numbness, a welcome respite from the ripping terror.

He didn't know how long he huddled there, but gradually he began to feel very cramped and tired and awfully cold. He shifted his position slightly, only to have his bare toes poked by the stiff bristles of a nearby broom. He longed to be stretched out on his bed beneath a warm blanket.

But he knew there were things much worse than being cramped and tired and cold. Much worse.

He could still hear the demon's distant roar as it continued to search the house for him.

He shivered as the cold night breeze whipped through the wooden slats at his back. He could just make out an old tarp shoved against the shed's wall a few feet away. He leaned forward and grasped the tarp's edge and dragged it toward him. He dropped back into his corner and draped the old tarp over his small back and shoulders to keep off the draft.

The tarp was stiff and smelled of paint. He didn't care. For a few precious moments, he almost felt warm. For a few precious moments, he thought he had escaped this night. For a few precious moments...

The back door to the house suddenly slammed. The heavy boots of the demon crunched over the frozen ground as they made their way to the garage, bringing an abrupt end to all the little boy's hopes.

He burrowed his head between his knees as terror once again tore through his heart. *It* would search the garage, and when it didn't find him there, it would be bound to search the old shed behind it.

He should have known the demon would find him. It always found him.

A sob broke through his small throat. No! No! Not again! He must find a way to escape before it came for him. *He must!*

Chapter One

Kay knew he was coming. She stood behind her desk and waited impatiently as she wondered why Adam Justice, her senior partner at the law offices of Justice Inc., had been so mysterious about this new client he was sending her.

The stranger stepped through the open doorway of her walnut-paneled office, halting uncertainly the second he saw her.

"*You're* K. O. Kellogg?"

Kay nodded mutely, at the same time wincing internally at the surprise stamped on his face and in his deep voice. She should be reconciled to both by now. She wasn't.

Still, just as she obviously didn't fit his preconceived idea of a lawyer, he didn't fit her preconceived idea of a psychologist.

His full, unruly, dark brown hair framed a ruggedly square, sun-darkened face. He looked as if he'd be far more at home at the helm of a ship than anchored to an analyst's couch. Yet, in contrast to his rough, outdoorsy features, his dark dress slacks, tan cashmere jacket and open-necked, salmon-colored silk shirt bespoke a man thoroughly at ease in more formal, indoor settings.

"Please come in, Dr. Steele. I've been expecting you."

He closed the door behind him and advanced into the room. His stride was long, muscular and powerful. His face was open, fluid and friendly.

Except, that is, for the sharp assessment in his glinting green eyes. Something about that intense, imposing glint belied the casual countenance of the man.

"I'm only Dr. Steele to my patients," he said. "Call me Damian. And your first name is . . . ?"

Kay leaned across her neat, polished walnut desk to extend her hand. "I'm called Kay."

"Kay," he repeated as his much larger hand engulfed hers and lingered, branding her with its gentle insistence. As she looked into those deep green eyes and felt the claim of his hand, a strange, warm sensation streaked down the back of her thighs.

Kay quickly slipped her eyes and her hand from his and sat down. She knew what that strange sensation was, of course. Her new shoes had to be cutting off the circulation in her legs. She had suspected the heels would be too high. Still, the idea of adding a full three inches to her height had been too enticing to resist.

That would teach her to watch those illogical impulses. As soon as this interview was over, she'd slip her feet into the pair of fuzzy slippers she kept in her drawer. Until then, she'd try to remain seated. She motioned toward one of the walnut-armed chairs in front of her desk.

"Were you expecting a man, Dr. Steele?"

He took the offered chair, but sat on its edge. "No. Your senior partner told me you were a woman."

Kay thought as much. Adam Justice generally cleared that particular obstacle from the start. As for clearing the misleading image of her small size and too youthful face, well, here she was again, beginning the uphill climb. Kay took a deep, resolute breath.

"So, it's my appearance that has caused your . . . surprise."

His eyebrows raised slightly. He obviously had not expected her to address the issue so candidly. The upturn to the corners of his mouth hinted at a small amusement.

"Yes, Kay. You could say your appearance came as somewhat of a surprise."

Well, at least he was open about it.

She felt the frown line forming between her eyebrows. "I hope you're not the kind of man to be unduly influenced by appearances."

He smiled directly at her frown. "I think you'd be safe in assuming I'm not."

He had an inviting, disarming smile—the kind that made one instinctively trust him. Kay did not allow herself to succumb to any such instinct. She rested her hands on her desk and launched into the well-rehearsed litany of her professional credits.

"I've been a practicing attorney for six years, the last five at this firm. I was made a full partner fifteen months ago. Mr. Justice told me that your case involves an unusual civil matter. I've handled many civil matters for this firm, some of which have been most unusual. I've gone to trial on thirty cases and won twenty-nine."

"Adam mentioned you had an impressive trial record."

Kay's forward momentum immediately swerved to this interesting side road. "Adam? I didn't realize you were on a first-name basis with our firm's senior partner. How do you know Adam?"

"We met a few years back."

"Where?"

"Around."

"You're friends?"

"We know each other."

His sentence dropped into a definite and deliberate period. Kay's brief hope of finding out something more personal about Adam Justice took a nosedive. It seemed Dr. Damian Steele was as good at playing mysterious as her firm's senior partner. Yes, that impenetrable glint in those deep green eyes was undoubtedly a warning—this was a man who kept secrets and kept them well.

"I'm glad Adam told you about my trial record. However, he may not have mentioned that I've also negotiated equitable settlements on as many cases that never went to tri—"

"I'm not interested in settling."

The easy smile had quickly left Damian Steele's face. His smooth, deep voice had developed a rough, sharp edge. There was a menacing feel to the glint that now flashed in his eyes. And that's when Kay knew that, charming smile and civilized dress notwithstanding, this man could be dangerous. A half chill, half thrill shot up her spine.

"All right, Dr. Steele, I hear you. You don't want to settle your case."

"Damian, remember?"

The smile was suddenly back, as charming as ever.

"Of course, Damian," she repeated casually. But the sound of his first name passing between her lips set off a warm hum inside her mouth that made her curiously self-conscious.

There was certainly an intriguing mercurial quality to Dr. Damian Steele—open and thoroughly enticing one instant, mysteriously closed and darkly dangerous the next.

Kay cleared her throat and gave herself a moment to whisk away her strangely contrasting and singularly unsettling reactions to this man. She steadied her hands on her desk as she determinedly brought her attention back to the issue at hand.

"Why don't you tell me about your situation? From the beginning, if you please."

He watched her a long moment before leaning back in his chair. Despite his initial surprise at her appearance, he wasn't running for the door. Yet. She followed his lead and relaxed in her chair.

"I'm a psychologist in private practice. Five and a half years ago, a man named Lee Nye came to me plagued by troubling blackouts. In the course of my therapy with Lee, I discovered that living inside him, he had another separate and distinct personality named Roy."

Kay instantly shot forward in her chair. "You mean he's one of those multiple-personality people?"

"Yes."

"Why didn't he just tell you that?"

"He didn't know. Neither of his personalities was aware of the other."

Kay leaned back again, taking a moment to consider his words. Multiple personalities were the latest of the legal hot spots. She'd followed several recent cases with interest.

In those cases, defendants with the disorder claimed that since only one of their multiple personalities committed a crime, their other personalities were blameless and shouldn't be punished. It had become a very sticky legal issue, no doubt about it.

Kay believed that most of these defendants were only doing what defendants had done since the beginning of the trial-by-jury system—latching on to the newest legal loophole that would allow them to get out of taking responsibility for their actions.

She carefully kept the cynicism out of her tone.

"I confess I know very little about this condition. How is it possible for a man to possess two personalities inside him and not know it?"

Damian Steele had been watching her intently with that open face and those secretive eyes. She knew it was impossible, but she had the uncanny feeling that he had been reading her thoughts as easily as a highway sign warning of a divided road ahead.

He raised his hands off the arms of his chair and slowly brought them together. His fingers moved as though to interlace, but instead butted up against one another.

"The two Nye personalities had been living separate mental lives and saw themselves as separate identities. When each personality started to seek control over the consciousness, their identities began to clash."

She leaned forward slightly. "You describe these personalities as having separate identities. Is this multiple-personality phenomenon an intense, extended form of role playing? Like an actor throwing himself into a part so thoroughly, he forgets he's acting?"

"No, Kay. There is no conscious intent to role-play. The divergent and distinct personalities are absolutely real to that person. That's why a clash resulted when these two both sought control over the consciousness."

"How were these personalities able to coexist before without a clash?"

"Lee—the personality I treated—had been submerged for many years while Roy held control over the consciousness. Then Lee began to lay claim to the consciousness approximately six years ago. Lee's emergence caused each of the separate personalities to experience memory blackouts during the time the other took control. After one of these blackouts, Lee would suddenly come to awareness and find himself in a place he didn't recognize, with people he didn't know and with absolutely no memory of the intervening hours, days or maybe even longer periods of time."

"A kind of recurring amnesia."

"Yes."

"And you say the clash between the two personalities began about six years ago because this Lee personality that was subordinated started to come out?"

"Yes."

"Why did Lee start to come out?"

"Because the previously dominant personality—Roy—had been steadily getting weaker over the years, and Lee had been steadily getting stronger."

"Ah, it was like a tug-of-war between them."

"In a manner of speaking. Only, since neither knew about the other, each was tugging, as you put it, against an unknown."

"Tugging against an unknown," Kay repeated, trying out the words in an attempt to better grasp the elusive concept. "I'm striving to relate this to something familiar in my own personal experience, but I confess I'm having trouble finding anything."

"I doubt you ever will. This phenomenon is hard to relate to normal experience. The individual I treated was born LeRoy Lyle Nye on August 20, 1952. That means his body is in its forties. But Lee, the man who came to me for treatment, can remember very little personal history before six years ago."

"Because he only came to life six years ago?"

"In some respects, yes, but he is an adult. He views himself as a man in his early thirties and behaves consistent with that view."

"Surely this Lee personality must have suspected something was amiss when he could only remember back such a short time."

"He thought very little of his past. The present and future claimed his primary focus. His blackout episodes were far more disturbing to him than his lack of earlier personal memories. The latter he accepted as a mere inconvenience."

"He only felt inconvenienced? I would think a normal person would be frantic."

"Because a normal person would feel the loss. But when Lee thought about his lack of memories, which wasn't often, he merely assumed others had the same difficulties remembering as he did."

"Is Lee's reaction typical for someone with his disorder?"

"There is very little that is 'typical' in a multiple-personality case. Each is as individual as the mind from which it evolves. These cases were once thought to be rare. Now, most in the field believe they are far more common than any of us imagined. The literature is growing on the subject, but we still have much to learn about diagnosis and treatment."

"You realize, I expect, that the concept of two separate and distinct personalities existing in the same mind is rather an unusual one for the layperson to envision, much less accept."

His left hand swept across the thick, unruly hair at the side of his head. It was a rough, square hand, a tool for the impatience that she sensed had set it into motion. But it was also a servant to the disciplined mind that returned it to the arm of his chair. As she had earlier sensed, this psychologist could be just as complicated as his subject.

"Kay, multiple personality disorder or MPD still seems like science fiction to many people, even many psychologists. Some postulate that the affected individuals possess

not many personalities, but many fragments of one personality."

"Which approach do you consider more accurate?"

"I'm a pragmatist. I don't fixate on disputing or embracing labels or adhering to hard-and-fast data."

"So how do you approach treatment?"

Damian rested his elbows on the arms of his chair, the
heels of his shoes disappearing into the thick mustard-
colored carpet, his long, lean legs crossing at the ankles.

"I believe achieving results is what is important, not how
the results are achieved. Patients come to me or any psychologist because they want to eliminate their disruptive
feelings or behavior, sometimes both. I try what I believe
will work, and if my method doesn't work, I drop it and try
something else until I find what does work."

"What did you try with Lee when he came to you?"

"Lee wanted to eliminate his disruptive blackouts. Nothing in his present life appeared to be causing them. His lack
of memories strongly pointed to the possibility of past
trauma. I hypnotized him to discover what that past trauma
might be. It was under hypnosis that Roy emerged."

"So up until the time you hypnotized Lee, you didn't
know Roy, the second personality, existed?"

"That's correct. Actually, Roy never came out in my sessions with Lee unless Lee was under hypnosis."

"Are you saying he had to be hypnotized into being
Roy?"

"No. What I'm saying is that under hypnosis, the control Lee exerted over the shared mind was relaxed suffi-
ciently to allow Roy to be called out at will."

"At your will, as opposed to Lee's or Roy's."

"Yes. The first time it happened was quite unexpected. I
had hypnotized Lee and asked him to tell me about his
blackout periods, reasoning that an unconscious part of his
mind must know. And it did. That unconscious part was
Roy."

"He popped up and introduced himself?"

Damian smiled. "Not exactly."

"Then how did you know you were talking to this other personality?"

"Frankly, I didn't know who I was talking to at first. The experience of finding another personality inside one's patient is unnerving. It takes some adjusting and reflection on the part of a therapist not used to the phenomenon."

"Lee was the only multiple case you had seen?"

"At that time, yes. I was eager to get up to speed on proper diagnosis and treatment. After I discovered Roy, I videotaped every subsequent session in order to be certain that I wouldn't miss anything. That proved very fortunate. If I hadn't had the tape to replay for Lee, I doubt he would have believed in the reality of Roy. You see, even people with multiple personalities have difficulty accepting the concept."

Damian smiled at her with warm understanding for her reservations. "I know it must be difficult to take all this in," he said.

Kay found herself wanting to immediately release her skepticism and accept whatever this man said. She caught herself just in time and shook herself mentally. Damn, but this psychologist was good at getting one's defenses down. She'd have to be careful. Very careful.

She sat up straighter in her chair, cleared her throat. "How can a person's mind become separated into these different personalities as you've described?"

"Psychological research connects the development of multiple personalities to a traumatic fragmenting of the core personality."

"And the English version of that translates to...?"

He grinned at her, a very attractive grin.

"Perhaps an analogy would be helpful. If you think of our early-childhood personalities as rough diamonds and life experiences as the diamond cutter, then a multiple-personality individual is the result of life's diamond cutter clearly missing its mark. The personality ends up shattered into pieces—sometimes two, far more often into many different pieces."

"And in the case of your patient, the different fragmented personality piece that emerged as a young child was Roy."

"He was chosen by the mind to exist in the hostile childhood environment."

"What was the hostile environment that fragmented the personality?"

"Roy's mother became pregnant as a young teen. Her parents arranged for the baby to be adopted by a childless couple they knew. However, when Roy was two, his teenage mother kidnapped him from his adoptive parents and fled the state with a guy she had just met. The man physically and emotionally abused the child."

Kay sagged into the back of her chair. She had had to deal firsthand with the emotional devastation of child abuse in her first year as a lawyer in the King County prosecutor's office. The anger and repulsion she'd felt at hearing such stories, along with her frustrated efforts to gather enough evidence to put away so many of the abusers, had finally driven her out of the prosecutor's office and into civil law at a private firm.

She knew she was tough. But she no longer kidded herself that she would ever be tough enough to deal with such horrors and inhumanity with the dispassion the profession demanded. She forcibly refocused her attention to the issue at hand.

"Why didn't the child's mother protect him?"

"I don't know for certain. Maybe due to fear for herself. But by turning her back to the abuse, she contributed to it."

"You say Roy's mother did this. But wasn't she also Lee's mother?"

"Physically, yes. Emotionally, no. Lee remembers little of his childhood. He seems to have nearly total amnesia for his own life events occurring before approximately six years ago."

"But earlier you said that he views himself as a man in his thirties. How can he sense thirty-plus years of existence when he only remembers six?"

"It's like Lee was sitting in front of a window opening to the world. He can tell you about the social and cultural changes that have occurred during most of his lifetime, including names of presidents and world events. He just can't relate them to anything personal that happened to him until about six years ago."

"Because six years ago was when he began to interact with life and not just watch it."

"Yes, very well put, Kay. The Lee personality existed in early childhood only as an observer. He lived in a kind of mental attic where he felt protected and safe. Then six years ago, he came down from his mental attic and began to take over from the Roy personality."

Despite the fact that Kay was still having difficulty getting her mind to accept the bizarre nature of this disorder, she couldn't help but be fascinated by it. Two people inside one mind—each compartmentalized into separate memories and identities. It was literally mind-boggling.

"You said Lee Nye came to you for help. Did Roy Nye also seek help?"

"No. Roy Nye attributed his memory losses to alcoholic stupors."

"And when he learned about Lee?"

"When I showed him the videotape of the sessions with Lee in control, he erupted first into denial, then anger."

"How does he handle the situation now?"

"He doesn't. Roy Nye is dead."

Kay blinked in surprise. "Dead?"

"Yes. He died four years ago. Which brings me to why I'm here, Kay. Mrs. Roy Nye has filed a three-million-dollar wrongful-death lawsuit against me."

"Your patient was married?"

"No, Lee wasn't married. Roy was."

"And Roy's widow blames you for Roy's death?"

"Yes."

"Because of your treatment?"

"Yes."

"Were formal charges ever brought against you in connection with Roy Nye's death?"

"No."

"Did the police ever consider you a suspect?"

"The police were never involved."

"If Roy died of natural causes or an accidental death, how can his wife—"

"Roy died neither by accident nor by natural causes."

Kay leaned her forearms on her desk, trying to bore past the solid wall of secrecy in those deep green eyes.

"Okay, I confess I'm confused. How did Roy Nye die?"

His eyes never left hers. His deep voice did not alter a decibel as he delivered the news.

"I killed him."

Chapter Two

Damian watched his admission rivet Kay's spine into stiff
attention.

He had intentionally shocked her. He wanted to find out
who the woman was inside that delicately petite five-foot
two-inch frame.

From the moment he'd walked into her office, he'd sensed
that Kay Kellogg was nothing like the image she presented.

Not that the image she presented was at all hard to take.
Her long, honey-gold hair strained against its imprison-
ment beneath a silver barrette at the top of her head. Her
eyes floated like plump blueberries in her milk-white face.
She moved as gracefully as a slim willow, her soft voice
sifting through the office like a gentle breeze rustling leaves.

And when she had taken his hand and his body had registered the strong current passing between them, he knew no
woman had ever affected him so immediately or so thoroughly.

No doubt about it. Kay Kellogg possessed that kind of
natural, land-mine femininity that instantly and spontane-
ously detonated deep in a man's body, forcibly reminding
him why he was happy to be a man.

She knew it, too, and the knowledge did not make her
happy. That was evident by her lack of makeup and jewelry
and the formalness and formidability of her dark blue linen
suit and the high collar of her light blue cotton blouse.

She wore her clothes like armor. She was making a mistake. All that starched formality only served to accentuate the soft, beckoning woman beneath.

This valiant need she had to try to hide her femininity was far more disturbing and deadly to Damian than even all that land-mine femininity, because it stirred up all his protective instincts.

She didn't react to his news, except for that initial and instant rigidity of spine. Her eyes remained focused on his, her hands steady, her soft voice absolutely even. She recovered exceptionally fast.

"Are you saying that the police don't know you committed this murder?"

"I don't consider I have committed a murder, Kay."

"You just told me you killed Roy Nye."

"I did."

"Then it was an accident?"

"No, I deliberately set out to do it."

Her eyes still remained glued to his; her composed voice did not falter. He was being deliberately obtuse. Yet she continued to deal with him calmly and coolly. She had an amazingly determined and disciplined mind within that delicate packaging.

"Kay, perhaps the situation will become clearer to you when I say that although Roy Nye is dead, Lee Nye is still very much alive."

The small frown reappeared between her fawn-colored eyebrows. "How can one identity be dead and not the other?"

"Because I consciously sought to extinguish him. I was successful."

"Are you saying you 'killed' the *personality* that was Roy?"

"We term it 'extinguishing' in psychological parlance. Once Lee Nye realized there was another personality inhabiting his body and taking over during the blackout periods, he was eager to be free of him."

"And you agreed?"

"After I got to know Roy. He was in a self-destruct mode, inflicting ever-escalating harm. He was not amenable to change. If he had been allowed to continue, he would have taken Lee with him by killing off their shared physical self, as well as their separate personalities."

"So you're saying that to save Lee, you killed Roy."

"Yes."

"And now Roy's widow is suing you in a wrongful death suit?"

"Yes."

She sat back in her chair and pursed her lips in a moment of quiet contemplation. She had inviting lips—naturally pink and soft-looking. Still, they were deliberately unpainted and she definitely wasn't pursing them in invitation. Good thing, too. Damian resolutely refocused his eyes on her small hands, resting steady and composed on her desk.

"Well, when Adam warned me that your case would be a surprise, he certainly didn't exaggerate. This one is an original. A suit filed on behalf of a widow of a man who isn't even really dead."

"Make no mistake, Kay, Roy is dead. When I was successful in extinguishing him, Lee subsequently divorced Roy's wife and shed all ties with Roy's past, including having his name formally changed from LeRoy to Lee. The two individuals shared a body, but never a life. Roy is, as a matter of record, gone."

"Psychologically speaking, Damian, I bow to your terms. But, legally at least, I think we should begin by attempting to dispute that fact."

Her eyes were bright with possibilities. She tapped her fingers on the desk to an ever-increasing beat. Damian had the strong impression that they were impatiently trying to keep pace with her racing thoughts.

"I assume Mrs. Roy Nye knows all about your treatment of Lee and your part in extinguishing the Roy personality?"

"Yes. Lee fully explained the circumstances in court when he filed for divorce. Mrs. Nye didn't contest the divorce. Lee told me later that she even seemed relieved."

"Then why is she bringing this wrongful-death suit?"

"I don't know."

"You said Lee first came to you five and a half years ago?"

"Yes. I saw him for a year and a half before Roy was extinguished. However, Mrs. Nye didn't file the wrongful-death suit until recently."

"Any idea why she waited this long?"

"No."

"Have you ever met her in person or talked to her over the phone?"

"No."

"Even though you treated her husband?"

"I considered Lee to be my real patient. Her husband, Roy, was a destructive and dysfunctional personality fragment. I feel fortunate that I was successful in extinguishing Roy, thereby freeing Lee to take control of his life."

Damian watched Kay inhale a deep breath and let it out with a shake of her head.

"Well, it's certainly a unique cause of action Mrs. Nye will be bringing to court."

"Will it stand up?"

"Logically, it shouldn't. But with all the crazy things going on in the legal system these days, it's hard to second-guess what a judge will let a jury hear. When were you served papers on this suit?"

"Four months ago."

Her voice rose perceptibly. "*Four months* ago?"

"The pretrial motions are scheduled for this Friday. The trial is scheduled to begin a week from today."

She leaned forward. "*This* Friday? A *week* from today? Why did you wait so long to seek legal representation?"

"I didn't. I've been relying on the lawyer who represents my malpractice insurance company. After months of answering my frequent questions with vague assurances that he had everything under control, he finally called me into his office last week to tell me he was going for an out-of-court settlement.''

"What reason did he give?"

"He said that the publicity a suit like this could generate would only open a Pandora's box of new suits against the psychologists that the insurance company represents."

"Which he naturally wanted to avoid, being their legal representative first and yours second."

"Yes. He was eager to approach the plaintiff with a settlement offer. In fact, he told me there was no way he would let a case like this get anywhere near the publicity of a trial."

"Obviously you disagreed."

"I have no doubt that what I did for Lee Nye was right, Kay. I'm neither apologizing nor paying off."

"I take it the insurance company is no longer in the financial picture?"

"They've told me I'm on my own."

"Without the insurance company's resources, you realize this type of litigation could cost you quite a bit of money?"

"Adam discussed that aspect with me thoroughly. I have no intention of backing down."

He felt her eyes assessing him. No surgeon's knife could have been more precise in its careful probing. Yes, as he suspected from the first, this woman's soft appearance and manner were quite misleading.

"I agree," she said finally. "Backing down only invites others to advance. What we need is a good aggressive line of attack. I already see several possibilities we can pursue."

Damian rose to his feet. He knew he had to stop this before it went any further. His curiosity and strong reaction to her had already let it go on far longer than prudent.

He extended his hand for a shake and set a small smile on his lips.

"I appreciate your listening to my story, but on reconsideration, I would be more comfortable engaging another attorney to represent me in this matter. Thank you for your time. Please send me your bill."

She shot to her feet, but not to take his hand. Blue-white heat flashed in her blueberry eyes.

"You'd be more comfortable with another attorney? How can you possibly make such a decision without first hearing my ideas on the case and my strategy for your defense?"

He let his lips spread into his most soothing, reassuring smile, the one he'd been using for years on agitated patients.

"I'm certain your ideas and strategy are fine. My decision has nothing to do with your legal competency."

She continued to ignore his outstretched hand. She did not return his smile. Her hands balled into fists. She rested her knuckles on the desk and leaned toward him menacingly.

"If you don't doubt my legal competency, why are you dismissing me?"

He dropped his hand since she obviously wasn't going to take it. He tried an earnest look and a calming tone, his most successful combination for difficult-patient situations.

"I don't mean to offend you, Kay. I appreciate your reputation. Please understand that this decision is based purely on a personal idiosyncrasy."

He followed his words with his most winning smile. Once again, she did not smile back.

"Rejection under the vague umbrella of personal idiosyncrasy, is offensive. I would hope you would at least afford me the professional courtesy of saying what you really mean. Don't let my small size delude you. I'm not a child. I'll be thirty in a few months. You don't have to baby me."

Damian's smile faded as his eyebrows rose in surprise for the second time that morning.

So she was demanding the truth from him, was she? All right. He'd give her the truth. He looked her up and down. Deliberately. Not like a psychologist. Like a man.

"I have no illusions about your being a child. Far from it. It is precisely because I find you far too desirable a woman that you will not do. I'm facing a difficult lawsuit. I am not going to risk the possibly disastrous complications of getting personally involved with my attorney while I'm fighting for my professional life. Good morning."

He pivoted sharply on the carpet and strode purposefully toward the door.

Her voice carried quite well considering its innate softness.

"Not so fast, *Dr. Steele.*"

He stopped and swung back to face her, irritated to be so strongly summoned by such a soft, yet clearly minatory, manner. That irritation crept into his words.

"There isn't anything left to say."

She moved quickly around her desk and marched toward him. She stopped directly in front of him, arms crossed over her chest, her chin up, her eyes sparking blue-white fire despite the saccharine smile that drew back her lips.

"I have two things to say. One, it takes two to get involved. And as difficult as it may be for you to imagine, I am fully prepared to struggle against succumbing to your charisma and live up to the ethical standards of my profession."

She was so smug in her sarcasm. So damn smug. His irritation grew.

"I didn't say you couldn't—"

"The second thing I'd like to say is this," she interrupted deliberately, still in that far-too-sweet tone. "If you, a psychologist, cannot control your impulses, then, *Doctor,* perhaps you've been spending your time on the wrong side of the analyst's couch. I can get you the name of a *good* therapist if you don't know one."

Damian clenched his hands at his sides as an unwelcome heat rose in his chest and flared through his nostrils. How dare this pint-size attorney tell him that he needed psychological help and offer to find *him* a good psychologist. His voice lowered into a deadly warning hush.

"I have no trouble controlling my impulses," he said, although at the moment he knew he was having a lot of trouble.

She took another step toward him, obviously ignoring the warning in his tone, her voice still too sweet, her eyes still too blue-white hot.

"Then we have no problem here, do we, Doctor? I will give you my word of honor that I will abide by my ethical code of having no personal involvement with a client, and you will give me your word of honor that you will not fire me for the duration of this case as long as I perform my legal services competently."

Damian watched her silently for a moment, newly stunned by her challenge, wondering how she had managed to maneuver him into this untenable position.

How could he say no? He'd be admitting that he couldn't keep his attraction for her under control. Which was absurd. Of course he could. At the moment, he was far more inclined to wring that slim neck of hers than kiss those soft-looking lips.

"So what's it to be, *Dr. Steele?* Are you going to hire me, or are you going to spend some much-needed time on another analyst's couch?"

She was so damn cool and confident and sure of herself. Behind that soft, feminine facade, he could clearly see a fierce feline with claws and a considerable set of sharp teeth.

What had ever given him the impression that this lady lawyer could be vulnerable?

Damian suddenly found himself smiling, the anger she had provoked in him fading. If she could think this quickly on her feet and prove to be this good an adversary in the courtroom, he'd be foolish not to engage her for his legal defense.

He held out his hand. "All right, Kay. You're hired. And you have my word as a man of honor that I will not fire you for anything other than incompetency."

She closed the small remaining distance between them and took his hand, giving it a good, solid shake, just as she had when they first introduced themselves. A small, triumphant smile lifted the sides of her lips.

"You won't regret it."

On the contrary, Damian was beginning to regret it already. The warmth of her hand was something he could feel right through to his solar plexus. She might be able to disavow the attraction between them, but he couldn't. Her light scent was as addictive as sweet, warm sunshine. She was bright; she was beautiful; she was out of bounds.

A hell of a dangerous combination. Damn. He could see it now. His mistake had been in trying to walk away from her earlier. He should have run.

"So, Kay," Adam Justice began in the Wednesday morning partners' meeting, "I see your case of Nye vs. Steele has already made the local news."

Kay quickly swallowed her sip of licorice-spice herbal tea and set her mug on the oval conference table around which sat the four partners of Justice Inc.—herself, Adam Justice, Marc Truesdale and Octavia Osborne.

Kay swung her body to the right to look into Adam's stone face, as cool and mysterious as his pale eyes and the scar that jagged from his jaw to disappear below his impeccable, starched-white dress shirt.

"Mrs. Nye's tearful interview about the loss of her husband, Roy, was just an overt play for sympathy. The press is obviously giving her airtime only because of the unusual dual-personality feature of her case."

"The news commentator mentioned that Dr. Steele couldn't be reached for comment," Adam said. "Did you advise him to avoid the press?"

"Yes. Pretrial motions are Friday morning. I believe I'll be able to get the case dismissed entirely, in which case Dr. Steele doesn't need to have his face flashed on the screen with that kind of negative publicity."

Adam made a note on his case list, his full head of straight, jet-black hair nodding in silent, sober approval. Adam Justice's reputation as a hard-driving, brilliant attorney was legendary throughout Seattle's legal system.

And his sister, Ariana Justice—better known as AJ—ran a detective firm touted as one of the best in the state.

Yet even after five years of working with the two of them, Kay had learned very little about the human side of either Adam or AJ. Both brother and sister assiduously deflected any and every personal probe.

"What's your angle on dismissal?" Marc Truesdale asked as he grabbed for his second bran muffin from the lazy Susan at the center of the conference table.

Marc was the opposite of Adam, open and easy to get to know. He'd joined the firm just two years before, yet Kay knew far more about him than she suspected she'd ever know about Adam. Marc was overwhelmingly good-looking, oozed charm and was only a few months older than Kay. And despite his reputation for romancing the ladies, Marc always treated her with the strict deference and respect of one colleague for another.

"My argument will be that since no corporal death has in fact occurred, there is no legal basis for a wrongful-death suit."

Marc nodded. "Good logical approach. Think it will work?"

Kay smiled at his question. "I have an ace up my sleeve if it doesn't."

He smiled back. "You always do."

"I had better have on this one. Getting up to speed for a trial by Monday isn't exactly the way I want to spend my weekend."

Octavia Osborne exploded into that rich, throaty, uninhibited laugh that danced around the room and brought out the worst of Kay's envy. At five foot eleven, Octavia was a statuesque redhead whose perfect grooming and gorgeous clothes always exuded the kind of natural flamboyance and woman-of-the-world sophistication that Kay knew she could never emulate. Octavia leaned toward her, a knowing twinkle in her sagacious eyes.

"Come on, Kay. That's just the way you'd like to spend your weekend. Talk about a lady with all work and no play in her life. You turn in almost as many billable hours each month as Adam here, and we all know he eats and sleeps in his office."

Kay shrugged. She didn't take Octavia's observation as a reprimand. On the contrary. She was proud of who she was.

"Okay, I confess. I'm the product of a long line of workaholics. It's in the genes. We Kelloggs enter the world with an inherent proclivity to pounce right from the womb into the work force. We can't help but get excited about our jobs."

Beautifully arched eyebrows rose above Octavia's eyes. She plucked a couple of grapes from the lazy Susan with long, graceful fingers. She reminded Kay of one of those regal and ravishing ladies who graced ancient Grecian urns.

"But even those workaholic parents of yours found time to...ah...get excited about other things, otherwise you wouldn't be here," Octavia's smiling mouth said. "Now, as a fellow partner in this firm, I sincerely appreciate all that hard work of yours that contributes to my paycheck. But as a fellow woman, I'm letting you in on a little secret. Taking time out for some fun can be rewarding, too."

Kay looked away from Octavia's directed glance and fiddled with her file of papers as Damian Steele's ruggedly handsome face unexpectedly and unexplainably materialized in her mind.

Octavia leaned closer, a sweep of an ultralight, ultrasophisticated fragrance advancing before her. "You could always start by asking the sinfully sexy Dr. Steele to show you his couch."

Kay felt the uncomfortable jolt of Octavia's words, so close to her unbidden mental image. Her back straightened as she scrambled to collect her scattered thoughts. "He's a client. You know I would never—"

"Never say never, Kay," Octavia interrupted, holding up an admonishing finger, while at the same time letting the twinkle in her eyes and smile soften her reprimand as she popped the grapes into her mouth.

Kay's shoulders relaxed. Her partner was just being her playful, kidding self. Why was she taking Octavia's jab about Damian Steele so seriously? It wasn't like Kay to be so touchy. No, it wasn't like her at all.

Octavia relaxed back in her chair as a small frown interrupted the smooth surface of her forehead. "I wish I could remember where I heard his name before, though. I've never met him or I'm sure I would have recognized his face when you introduced him around. But his name is definitely familiar. It's maddening not being able to recall."

"So you've been telling us since Monday," Marc said. "Could it be that after catching a glimpse of this Dr. Steele, you're the one who's interested in checking out him and his couch?"

Octavia stretched back in her conference chair. Beneath her long lashes, her eyes glowed in a combination of confidence and amusement.

"*Me?* Interested in a man whose life is devoted to hearing women confess their deepest secrets? Not on your life, Marc. I want a man who is far more fascinated with the woman who reveals nothing."

"Who's opposing counsel?" Adam asked.

The senior partner's question brought Kay's focus back to the case at hand, as he no doubt had intended it should. She turned in his direction.

"Name's Rodney Croghan. Drew a blank with me. Ring a bell for anyone?"

Adam and Octavia both shook their heads.

Marc nearly choked on his last bite of bran muffin. He reached for his cup of coffee to quickly wash it down. "Rodney Croghan? You're sure it's Rodney Croghan?"

"You know him, Marc?" Kay asked, not too surprised that a name that didn't seem familiar to anyone else in the room would register with him. Marc got around.

"I do if there aren't two attorneys with that same name. I was down in Olympia visiting friends a few years ago when a buddy asked me to sit in on a case he was trying. Rodney Croghan, an unknown associate with a big firm, was his legal adversary. My friend thought he had an unbeatable line of attack, everything sewed up tight, no loose ends. Croghan wiped up the courtroom with him."

"Croghan's that good?" Octavia asked as she leaned forward, her interest immediately sparkling in her eyes and tone.

"I think devious would be a more accurate description," Marc said. "Croghan tried some off-the-wall legal shenanigans you wouldn't have believed. Took everyone in the courtroom by surprise. The guy walked a very thin, dangerously high, ethical tightrope during that trial, I can tell you. Made me queasy just watching him."

Kay tapped her fingers on the conference table. "Lawyers generally stay in their hometown where they've established their name and are familiar with the process, people and legal procedures. What is Croghan doing up here in Seattle?"

"Good question," Marc agreed. "Maybe you'd best give AJ a call and start her investigators on a background check of Croghan."

"I'll wait to see how Friday morning goes first before bringing in AJ," Kay said. "I really do expect to get the case dismissed."

"Which judge did you draw?" Adam asked.

"A stodgy one, but that's good. Frederick I. Ingle III."

"Not good," Octavia said, shaking her head.

"Not good?" Kay echoed, clearly surprised. "How can you say that? I had Ingle a couple of years ago in a personal-injury suit and he couldn't have been more by the book. If this Croghan tries any funny legal business, Ingle is just the judge who will slap him into place."

Octavia shook her head. "Maybe a couple of years ago, Kay, but Ingle has expanded his professional horizons. Last month his first novel was published and he's no longer the same man."

"He's written a novel? About what?"

"It's supposed to be based on one of his cases."

"How could his writing a novel about one of his cases cause a problem?"

"Because of what the critics have said about it. They admit his writing is competent but call his main character—who just happens to be a judge—boring, and then added something about if the author was truly writing from real-life experience, he needed to go out and get a new life. They weren't too complimentary about his plot, either. 'Yawning, mundane material,' I think the phrase went.''

"So he didn't produce a legal thriller. I still don't see how that should affect my case before him."

"Ingle has apparently taken the criticism to heart, Kay. He's been seen in some wild getup, scooting around Seattle in a new red Corvette. Inside the courtroom, his legal judgment is taking a similarly...ah...colorful turn."

"How do you mean?"

"He's flat out told parties to suits that they better settle them out of his court because they're simply too 'mundane' for him to have to preside over in a trial. Do you know how delighted he's going to be when he finds out what your case involves?"

Kay took a deep breath and let it out, shaking her head. "Terrific. A shifty lawyer and now a judge in search of the story line for a bestseller. I was feeling pretty good about this case before I came in here this morning."

"You'll handle it," Adam said in his quiet, matter-of-fact way. There was something about the solidness of her senior partner's infrequent but well-timed assurances that always filled Kay with confidence. She found some new starch for her spine as she sent him a small smile.

"Just watch out for Croghan," Marc cautioned.

"I'll try to deflect any legal darts he throws my way."

"Be careful he doesn't do to you what he did to my friend and wait until your back is turned before throwing them."

Kay nodded, a small frown forming between her eyebrows as an unbidden and unsavory image flashed into her mind. She could clearly see her back outlined with several circles of chalk marks, the bull's-eye right between her shoulder blades.

"I'M NOT RELOCATING with you, Dr. Steele," Tim Haley said in a voice cracking with nervous defiance. "I'm going to stay with Dr. Payton."

Surprised, Damian turned toward his receptionist. Tim Haley stood behind his desk, his bespectacled eyes downcast, his freckles suddenly darker against his naturally pale skin, his tall, thin frame visibly quivering like that of a newborn colt.

Damian rested the box of patient files he had just carried out of his office on the edge of the receptionist's desk and faced him. This was very atypical behavior for the shy, willing young man, who always strove so diligently to please. Very atypical.

"Tim, we've been together almost six years. I thought we were a good team. What's wrong?"

Tim's eyes rose briefly to Damian's. The effort to maintain his confrontational pose had set even his normally neat shock of copper hair to shivering on his scalp.

"You know what's wrong," he said, his voice cracking anew.

Damian hadn't known, but he was beginning to get a glimmer. "Tim, it's not what you think. What you overheard—"

Tim's eyes dropped to his desk as he quickly interrupted. "Dr. Payton told me everything. So, it's no use, you see."

Yes, Damian could see. Nothing he could say now would matter to the man. Only thing he could do was to try to leave on as friendly a note as Tim would allow. He extended his hand.

"I'm going to miss you, Tim. Best of luck in everything."

Tim stared at Damian's extended hand, biting his thin lips, quivering again with the conflict of his emotions. As the seconds ticked by and Tim didn't take the proffered hand, Damian realized that Tim would not be able to engage in even this one, last, small gesture of friendship. It would have required that the receptionist leap across the professional and personal chasm that he had so recently and painstakingly dug between them.

Damian dropped his hand and exhaled an internal sigh as he picked up his last box of patient files. He consoled himself with the fact that it could be worse. This last day in his office could have spelled far more serious confrontational disasters.

As he turned to leave, he saw that he had clearly started to count his blessings too soon. Dr. Priscilla Payton stood in the doorway.

He stiffened as he stepped aside to let her pass. "Dr. Payton," he said in as formally polite a tone as he could muster.

Priscilla Payton's dark cap of short, straight, black hair seemed to rise on her head as though electrically charged. She stared at Damian with pupils so dark and enlarged, they looked like aimed bullets.

"Oh, right, it's *Dr. Payton* now."

Damian took a slow, deep breath. "I don't mean to make this difficult for either of us. I thought you weren't going to be in this morning. If I had known you'd be here, I would have cleaned out my office another time."

Her eyes flashed as she spat out the word. "Coward!"

This was not a conversation Damian had any intention of prolonging. "I have to take these files to my car, and I'm due for an important appointment. So, if you'll excuse me—"

"I won't excuse you," Priscilla Payton barked. She not only didn't move from her position in the doorway, she spread her feet to block it further so Damian couldn't get past.

"You want to know why I'm here this morning?" she said. "I'm here because I have an appointment with Bette Boson."

Damian didn't like the sound of this. "Ms. Boson is my patient. How can you have an appointment with her?"

"Because she's not your patient anymore. She was waiting in reception that day when we had our little discussion, remember? She heard it all, every word. You think she'll ever trust you again after what you did to me? You think she'll ever even want to see you again?"

Damian remembered how Bette had nearly run out of the reception area that dreadful day. Maybe he really shouldn't be surprised that she had decided not to continue therapy with him. Particularly since Priscilla had obviously talked to Bette before he could, just as she had talked to Tim Haley.

No use pointing out the total lack of ethics such behavior displayed. Priscilla was, obviously, in no mood to hear it.

"I want her videotapes, Damian."

"Fine," he answered. "I'll pack them up and drop them off here on my way to the lake on Sunday."

"Her videotapes aren't still in your office?"

"I already moved all the videotapes to my home office. Now, if you'll stop blocking the doorway, I'll be on my way."

Priscilla didn't budge. Her hands set on her hips. "I saw Mrs. Nye on the news last night. I hope her attorney creams you in court."

Damian was getting very weary of this vindictive trip Priscilla was on. Very weary. "I expected you to be a little more professional about our differences, Dr. Payton."

"*Me* a little more professional? Ha! Look who's talking."

Enough was enough. Damian's tone descended into an icy hush of warning. "This isn't getting either of us anywhere, Doctor. Move aside."

Her voice rose, even more belligerent and taunting. "What's the matter? Can't face a fight, Damian?"

Damian's jaw clenched. "You know better. If you don't stop blocking the doorway, Dr. Payton, I will physically move you out of the way. You make the choice. You have ten seconds."

Damian watched Priscilla's expression change from one of dare to one of growing disquiet as she read the intent in his eyes. He was not bluffing and she knew it. She scooted nervously out of the way.

"You always resort to violence, don't you, Damian? Don't you?"

Damian didn't waste his time with a retort, nor a backward glance in her direction. He charged through the cleared pathway. He took the hallway in massive strides, shouldered his way through the outer doorway to the parking lot and made a beeline for his forest-green '61 Jaguar coupe, keeping cool in its private parking space beneath the shade of a thickly branched giant madrona tree.

This office complex had been his professional home since he had been lucky enough to find it tucked into a residential section along Lake Union seven years before. It wouldn't be easy to find another that fit his needs so well.

Still, he was going to have to try.

Maybe it was good that this change was being foisted on him. Maybe he'd become too complacent. Maybe he needed a little shaking up.

Well, need it or not, he was certainly getting it. And to think it was only a year ago that he'd refused to be featured in the *Seattle Times* supplement as a prime example of the ruggedly individual and intellectual Pacific Northwest bachelor.

Ruggedly individual? Intellectual? What a joke. It seemed as if lately, all he'd been doing was marching straight into the sea of professional and personal suicide like some brainless lemming. What else could possibly go wrong?

Damian dug into his pants pocket for his key as he approached his car. He opened the driver's side and carefully set the last box of patient records in the back seat. As he straightened up, he noticed a blue envelope beneath the windshield wiper.

He snatched it, expecting it to be yet *another* announcement for yet another new espresso shop. No wonder everyone was sleepless in Seattle. He was just about to throw the blue envelope into a nearby waste bin, when his eyes caught sight of the business card taped to its front.

His business card.

His eyebrows met in a dark frown. This was no casual advertisement. This was from someone who knew him. Damian slit open the sealed envelope and slipped out the single sheet of pale blue paper from inside.

The words on the page were large, blunt and perfectly even. They looked as if they had been formed by someone passing a thick black felt-tip pen over a stencil. He sensed a careful, composed and calm hand had modeled them. The meaning in the words themselves, however, gave him a sense of something quite different.

You are going to pay. I'm going to make sure of it.

Chapter Three

"Dr. Steele, is something wrong?" Kay asked. Over the last week of working closely together, she couldn't remember ever seeing Damian with a frown. "Are you worried about how things will go this morning?"

He was sitting next to her at the defense table in the courtroom, smelling like a hint of spicy after-shave on clean-shaven skin, looking far too good in a single-breasted, Italian cut navy suit, a French-cuffed white shirt and a tie with a subtle geometric pattern. His quick smile showed bright against his summer tan.

"I'm not worried about the suit. I have a good lawyer."

The compliment slipped beneath Kay's careful professional guard. She let out a deep, internal sigh. If he had told her she was attractive, she could have ignored it. But this compliment to her competence managed to find her Achilles' heel.

Maybe it was because so few men had ever really made the effort to see past her outward packaging, and those few who did had not been that complimentary about what they found.

Her eyebrows dived together in a frown. She reminded herself for the millionth time that it did not matter that so many men ended up uncomfortable with her. All that mattered was that she was comfortable with herself.

She was beginning to feel comfortable with this client of hers, too. All week long as they prepared for the preliminary hearing, he had treated her with charming deference and respect, never once getting out of line. That first day in her office, he had said he could control his impulses, and he had certainly proved it this week.

Unless he no longer had those impulses. Well, he wouldn't be the first to be turned off by her once he got to know her.

Now, why did that thought suddenly depress her? Theirs could only be a professional relationship. If he was turned off by her, so much the better.

"I do have a request, however," he said.

"What?"

"I've suffered all week with this Dr. Steele label. Go back to calling me Damian. Don't worry, it doesn't mean I'm getting carried away by your ability and beauty, or that you'll soon be having to fight me off. I promise that as difficult as it is, I'll do my best to be a gentleman."

His smile was dazzling and dynamite. Kay could feel it lighting a fuse at the base of her spine. And she could also feel his attraction for her registering happily—very happily—in every female cell in her body.

She let out another internal sigh. Why did it feel so good to know he was still attracted to her? Damn. This was totally illogical.

She took a deep breath and tried to keep her tone as even and professional as possible as she looked at his ruggedly handsome face.

"Sure, Damian. Not a problem."

But, once again, the sound of his first name passing her lips set off a warm hum inside her mouth that made her self-conscious. She dropped her eyes to the papers on the table in front of her.

Damian smiled as Kay turned away. Always the careful lawyer. She assiduously kept her position on the professional side of the line.

If Damian hadn't been trained to observe and interpret unconscious movements so well, he never would have noted her tugging at her right earlobe whenever he prolonged eye contact, or the way she crossed her legs three different times in succession whenever they sat in proximity to each other.

He knew he disturbed her on a subconscious level and the knowledge excited him. Still, he was content to leave it alone.

No, *content* was the wrong word. *Reconciled* was definitely a more appropriate choice. If he had needed an additional reminder as to why professional relationships had to remain professional, he'd gotten just that on Wednesday in that final confrontation with Dr. Priscilla Payton.

What a mess. Still, as angry as Priscilla was with him, he had a hard time believing she was behind that note he'd found on his car and the second note he'd found in the mail this morning. Surely a psychologist couldn't be that petty and unstable? But if Priscilla wasn't behind it, who was? And why?

"You do seem to be concerned about something," Kay said as her eyes swept his face.

Damian deliberately unfurrowed his forehead and unclenched his jaw. He had no intention of burdening Kay with this. Still, he would have to watch his every facial expression around his attorney. She didn't miss much.

"I'm not fond of waiting," he said to mislead her.

She nodded, accepting his evasion. She'd been perusing the preliminary motion she'd forwarded to the judge earlier that week. She went back to her reading.

She was sitting to his right, looking cool and collected in a blue-mint linen suit. He was close enough to feel her warmth and inhale the light, sweet scent of her skin and hair. She was very alluring. A lot of men must make a play for her. Still, he doubted she had very satisfying or enduring love affairs.

If he had to guess, he'd say that the kind of men who pursued her soft and beckoning femininity soon found themselves unexpectedly coming face-to-face with the strong woman beneath. He also guessed it wouldn't be a happy surprise.

There was just something about a man's short, stubby Y chromosome that had a habit of short-circuiting his brain cells every time he found himself in the presence of such a delectable female. Made it hard for a male to think at all, much less think straight about the fact that the female could be appreciated in ways other than the physical.

Damian found himself staring at the honey-gold strands at the back of her slim white neck. Images of those glistening strands falling long and loose and free across bare, milk-white shoulders stole into his mind. She was so deliciously feminine, so tantalizingly close. He could feel his circuits overloading.

Damn that stubby Y chromosome. He rubbed his suddenly moist palms across his slacks beneath the table. He hoped they'd be able to put this legal suit to bed in the next few minutes.

To bed. Unfortunate phraseology. Freud would have been delighted with the slip and the immediate x-rated images it brought to mind.

Damian tore his eyes from Kay and let them sweep over the large lady clerk and thin lady court reporter, both of whom waited at their positions. Behind the court reporter stood a burly biceped bailiff with a stiff black smudge of a mustache and a grim look. The clerk, court reporter and the bailiff were the only others present in the courtroom.

Damian glanced at his watch, no longer needing to feign impatience. "It's nine twenty-five. Any idea why Mrs. Nye and her attorney aren't here yet?"

"They might be caught in traffic."

Damian's eyebrows rose in amusement. "Traffic? May I remind you, it's a sunny, seventy-degree Friday morning in June in Seattle. The only traffic to speak of is heading out to the recreational areas."

She looked up and flashed him a small rueful smile. "You're right, of course. I spoke without thinking."

Damian liked the way she easily admitted her mistakes, almost as much as he liked her sunny, infrequent smiles. He found himself fascinated by these glimpses of genuine warmth beneath her cool facade. He wondered what she would be like if she ever stepped totally out of her legal persona.

"Do you wish you were heading out to one of those recreational areas for a head start on the weekend, too?" he asked.

She quickly extinguished the smile, reestablishing her emotional distance and refocusing her eyes on her reading. "Not particularly."

"To you, work is fun, isn't it?"

She looked up at him in surprise. "I didn't think you'd..."

Her voice trailed off uncertainly. It wasn't difficult for him to guess what she had left unsaid. "Understand?"

"Yes, that's what I was going to say."

"Then why didn't you?"

"Because, frankly, I didn't think a psychologist could ever view work as fun."

"I often view my work as fun, Kay. Exploring the mind is an exciting adventure. And helping people to get in touch with their happier feelings is the greatest high I know."

Her eyes shone as she looked off into a mental distance. "I know that high. Sometimes when I'm addressing a jury, and I know the logic of my argument is indisputable, and I can see the understanding dawning on their faces, it's like— it's like my birthday and Christmas and the Fourth of July all rolled into one."

"Looking for that high in your work is what makes you good at it."

Her returning smile was small but possessed genuine warmth. Then she began to look uncomfortable at the prolonged eye contact and tugged at her right earlobe. Damn, it was an adorable earlobe and she looked adorable tugging at it.

"Is your first name really Kay, or does the K.O. stand for something else?"

"It stands for something else."

"What?"

"Sorry, but I limit the number of people who know that secret to my three closest friends—all of whom have given me their solemn vow of silence in a blood pact."

He grinned. "It's that bad, huh?"

She chuckled. "Worse."

"You were named after a mad aunt?"

Her chuckle deepened. "Good guess. Actually, I was named *by* a mad aunt."

"I have to hear this story."

"No. Really. I'd rather not go into it."

"But you must. I insist."

"Are all you psychologists so inquisitive?"

"Are all you lawyers so tight-lipped? Come on. You don't have to tell me what the K.O. stands for. Just give me the rest of the story."

Kay smiled in good natured defeat. "Okay. Edited version. My mother's small like me. Her doctor warned her that there were bound to be complications in any pregnancy. She's a medical researcher herself and knew to take the warning seriously. She planned me carefully, even scheduling her delivery for when my dad would be back from his engineering job in Saudi Arabia. Unfortunately, I decided to be born at seven months and threw off all her careful planning. Caught unawares and out of the range of immediate medical attention, she . . . lapsed into a coma."

Her voice had dropped and gotten even softer than usual with that last detail. As if of its own accord, his hand covered hers. "But she did eventually get medical attention and you both came out of it all right?"

"Yes, but because of the delay, she was unconscious for several days. With my father out of the country, that left my aunt, Loony Luddie, the only one available to put a name on my birth certificate."

"*Loony* Luddie?"

"Not that Aunt Luddie's really loony, you understand. She's actually a sweetie. It's just that she has a very simple and rather lighthearted view of life."

"So your name ended up reflecting that simple, lighthearted view?"

"You could say that."

"Of course!" Damian exclaimed, catching on. "K.O. aren't initials for a girl's name. Your loony Aunt Luddie named you K.O. because you knocked out your mother when you were born!''

That small frown reappeared between her eyebrows. ''Damn it, Dr. Damian Steele, you are entirely too clever.''

Damian chuckled at her peeved response to his accurate guess. ''So, now that I know, will you rely on my discretion, or shall we cut wrists and join our blood in a solemn pact of secrecy?''

She smiled as their eyes met for the warmth of a moment. Then she withdrew her hand uneasily from beneath his and dropped her eyes again to the papers on the table, tugging at her right earlobe once more.

Damian could feel the residual warmth of her hand and her smile. She got more alluring by the minute, inside and out. Too bad things were the way they were. On the other hand, maybe it was just as well. Kay didn't strike him as the casual kind, and he wasn't interested in a commitment.

He resolutely rested his gaze on the burly bailiff, who was now pacing in front of the closed door to the judge's chambers, as the second hand on Damian's watch wound down to the half hour.

''Could this Croghan be attempting some legal tactic by being late?''

Kay kept her eyes on her papers this time. ''Can't think of what he could hope to gain. There are neither jury nor spectators present to impress. And if he ends up making his entrance after the judge, I very much doubt the kind of impression he's likely to leave on His Honor will be a beneficial one. Ingle should emerge any second now.''

Right on cue, the big bailiff straightened as the door to the judge's chambers opened. The bailiff's voice rose in a squeaky tenor, quite in contrast with his bulk. ''All rise and come to order. The court of Judge Frederick I. Ingle III is now in session.''

Damian got to his feet beside Kay as His Honor exited his private chambers. Ingle wore the traditional black robe of his exalted position. But that's all that he wore that was traditional.

On the judge's feet were white tennis shoes with fluorescent orange laces. A gold loop dangled from his left earlobe, while a diamond stud flashed from his right nostril. A stiff, white mohawk bifurcated his otherwise shiny skull.

None of the courtroom personnel paid any notice to His Honor's unusual appearance. They had, obviously, already been initiated. Ingle perched upon his chair with a black-winged sweep. He wore a defiant smirk as he sent Kay and Damian an amused, piercing stare, as though daring them to say something about his getup.

Damian had to stifle a smile. He heard Kay clearing her throat beside him and guessed she was having to do the same thing.

Kay had filled him in on the judge's reaction to the critical reviews his novel had received. Damian understood that Ingle was probably attempting to put some color into his life with this unusual garb.

The judge's eyes swung to the plaintiff's table, which stood empty. "Where is the—"

"Right here, Your Honor," an industrial-size voice yelled from the back of the courtroom.

Damian swung around to see the rear doors bang open as a large, barrel-chested man with a bubble of black hair and a neat-as-a-pin, full black beard crashed into the courtroom.

Crashed was definitely the word. The doors whacked against the walls, vibrating from the force of being shoved so violently apart. The newcomer strutted down the aisle like the ringmaster of a circus.

He looked every bit the part, too. He wore a red cape over an improbable double-breasted, three-piece white suit, from which dangled an enormous gold pocket watch and chain. Golden rings glistened from every finger.

His dress and manner were so startling that it took a moment for Damian to notice the woman the lawyer had in tow. She was plump, looked fifty-something, with a wide face, short neck, thin, straggly gray-brown hair and a somewhat bewildered look in her large, faded brown eyes.

Damian immediately recognized Mrs. Fedora Nye from her interview on the evening news a few days ago.

"Your Honor," the bearded man began as he proceeded to the front of the courtroom. "I am Rodney Croghan, representing Mrs. Fedora Nye, the plaintiff in this very serious matter before you this morning. Please excuse our slightly tardy entrance, but we were meeting with the press."

"The press?" Judge Ingle repeated, his voice rising in obvious interest. His Honor had apparently missed the TV news coverage.

Croghan had reached the plaintiff's table. He withdrew Mrs. Nye's limp hand from the crook of his arm and beamed at the bench with a full set of flashing teeth.

"Yes, Your Honor. The press is very interested in this case."

He paused to untie the string at the top of his cape and then to whisk off the garment with a dramatic sweep that set his gold pocket watch to swinging and clanging against his belt buckle.

Between this attorney and this judge, Damian knew he would be hard-pressed to decide which one displayed the most obsessive need to be different, to be noticed.

"The press is interested in this case?" Ingle asked.

"I was just meeting with a local station about the possibility of filming the trial and broadcasting it live," Croghan's all-too-loud voice announced.

Damian watched as the judge's bushy eyebrows rose in even more interest. "Broadcasting it live, you say? Well, well. One of my cases on television."

"Your Honor," Kay interjected in a soft yet emphatic tone. "May I suggest that any discussion of press coverage is still premature? After all, there is still a pretrial motion I've filed on behalf of my client in this matter that must be addressed."

Ingle turned to her, wearing the expression of a day-dreaming schoolboy whose attention was being forcibly brought back to his class work.

"Yes," he admitted somewhat grudgingly. "Defense has filed a motion to dismiss. Ms. Kellogg, I have not had time to review the lawyers' briefs on this case. Please succinctly state your position for the record.''

"Yes, Your Honor. Mrs. Nye is suing Dr. Steele for the wrongful death of her husband. In point of fact, however, her husband is not dead.''

Croghan pounded his fist on the table before him. "The plaintiff contends that Mrs. Nye's husband *is* dead, Your Honor!''

Kay jumped, obviously startled. Damian certainly understood. He was more than a bit startled himself.

Ingle, however, simply raised his hand, looking more pleased than perturbed by the unprofessional pounding. Damian wondered if the judge was making mental notes to use Croghan as a character in his next book.

"You'll have a chance to speak, Mr. Croghan. Go on, Ms. Kellogg.''

"Thank you, Your Honor,'' Kay said. "Before you is a copy of a name change approved by a Seattle court. As you can see, the man previously known as LeRoy Nye, the man to whom the plaintiff was married, legally changed his name to Lee Nye three years and five months ago. Lee Nye is very much alive. If necessary, the defense will be happy to produce him to prove that fact. As I said before, there is no basis for a wrongful-death suit, since there has been no death.''

"Your Honor—''

Ingle held up his hand. "A moment, Mr. Croghan. Give me a chance to review this motion.''

Ingle quickly scanned the documents that Kay had pointed out. A frown cut into his forehead. "Ms. Kellogg appears to be correct about this name change. Mr. Croghan, I fail to see—''

"Your Honor, the defense attorney is trying to mislead this court. She knows perfectly well that we're dealing with a dual-personality individual. The truth is that even though the body that Roy Nye once possessed is still walking on this earth, Roy's personality—what distinguished Roy Nye as a man like you or me—is dead. He was killed by Dr. Damian Steele.''

Ingle leaned over his bench, his interest clearly piqued. "Mr. Croghan, am I to understand that Mrs. Nye is suing this psychologist because he did away with her husband's half of a dual-personality patient?"

"Exactly, Your Honor. You've stated the matter perfectly."

Ingle leaned back, his smirk returning. "Hmm. Nothing mundane about this cause of action," he mumbled as though to himself. "Is this true, Ms. Kellogg?"

"Your Honor, Lee Nye—not Roy Nye—was the patient who came to Dr. Steele for treatment. The Roy manifestation was only a dysfunctional personality fragment that—"

Croghan banged on the table, interrupting once again. "Your Honor, I protest! That man's attorney just called my client's husband a dysfunctional fragment!"

"Your Honor," Kay began again, "Mr. Croghan's outbursts are disruptive to—"

Croghan's fist hit the table yet again. "Disruptive nothing! We have a right to be furious! This so-called psychologist thought of Roy Nye as only a dysfunctional fragment. We have it on record now!"

"Your Honor," Kay said in a voice that sounded as if it was rapidly losing patience. "I appeal to you. It is very difficult to state the defendant's position while the plaintiff's attorney continues to interrupt with these pounding theatrics. I respectfully ask the court to admonish Mr. Croghan—"

"Yes, yes," the judge interrupted. "A little less noise, Mr. Croghan," he said without any real enthusiasm for the censure.

"Now, Ms. Kellogg," the judge continued, "do I understand the defense's position correctly? Is it your contention that Roy Nye was only a dysfunctional personality fragment and, therefore, Dr. Steele had a right to eliminate him?"

"Your Honor, I am not a psychologist, so it would be inappropriate for me to make any such contention, just as it would be inappropriate for this court to attempt to do so. The real issue—the *legal* issue—facing us this morning is whether or not a man has died. I have presented documentation to show that he has not.''

"Roy Nye is dead, Your Honor!" Croghan bellowed again. "Dr. Damian Steele psychologically murdered him!"

Ingle nodded appreciatively, his dark eyes as shiny as fresh fountain ink waiting for the dip of a feathery writing quill. "A psychological murder, eh? I like the sound of that. What do you say, Ms. Kellogg? Did your client psychologically murder Roy Nye?"

"Your Honor, despite the natural human titillation and intellectual draw of such a question, it is clearly not one that can be answered by lawyers. A debate over whether a man can be psychologically murdered, as the plaintiff claims, does not fall within the purview of the legal system.''

Again Croghan shouted. "Your Honor, I protest! Defense counsel is trying to cloud the issue."

"No, Mr. Croghan, you are the one filling the air with the foggy fumes of rhetoric in order to try to block out the clarity of reason," Kay said quietly, but firmly. "This is not a legal matter and you know it."

"It is a legal matter! If a medical doctor's malpractice results in death to his patient, the avenue of financial redress for the family is the court. This is no different. Dr. Damian Steele is a psychologist who deliberately performed psychosurgery to cut Roy Nye out of his own life. Mrs. Nye's only course of redress for the loss of her husband is this court. Her case deserves to be heard!"

Ingle ran the palm of his hand over his mohawk appreciatively. "Hmm. I like your analogy to a medical doctor."

"Except that logically and legally it doesn't hold up," Kay quickly interjected. "No medical definition has ever recognized death as occurring with the removal of a dysfunctional personality part—"

"The defense attorney is wrong, Your Honor! Brain-dead is legally dead!"

Kay turned to Croghan. "You know perfectly well that Lee Nye is not brain-dead. He is a functioning—"

"But he is not Roy! It is not a man's body that defines him, but his thoughts, his emotions!" Croghan's arms made great circles around him, building momentum before pointing accusingly at Damian. "Roy Nye's essence is gone—murdered by that man!"

"Your Honor, there are absolutely no legal grounds—"

Ingle's hands came up. "Yes, yes, Ms. Kellogg. You are right about there being no legal precedent for Mrs. Nye's unusual cause of action. But it's a damn interesting cause of action, you must agree. Hell, I can't wait to see what the cri—uh . . . I mean, the jury will make of this one."

Ingle picked up his gavel and held it high. "Motion to dismiss due to lack of cause denied." He rapped the gavel once, its vibration bouncing ominously off the walls of the mostly empty courtroom.

Damian felt the legal blow of the judge's decision. But Kay seemed amazingly calm and collected in its wake. Without hesitation, she walked up to the judge's podium, papers in hand.

"Your Honor, this is a motion to dismiss Mrs. Fedora Nye's suit based on the fact that the plaintiff's petition for redress was filed a month after the three-year statute of limitations."

Croghan was instantly shouting again. "I protest, Your Honor! Washington's wrongful-death statute does not contain an express statute of limitations."

Kay's soft voice retained its elegant calm. "Your Honor, Mr. Croghan is in error. The statute of limitations is provided in the Washington Revised Code, which sets forth time limitations for commencing various forms of legal actions. A three-year statute of limitations is applicable to a personal-injury suit. Lee Nye legally eliminated the Roy part of his name three years and five months ago, yet it wasn't until four months ago—a full month after the three-year filing deadline—that Mrs. Nye commenced her personal-injury suit against Dr. Steele for the wrongful death of her husband."

Ingle's forehead frowned under the clear logic of Kay's thrust. He glanced at Croghan hopefully. Croghan couldn't have missed the fact that the judge was rooting for him. And he was ready with his rebuttal.

"Your Honor, Mrs. Nye did not discover that her husband—I mean, Lee Nye—had changed his name from LeRoy until at least six months after the fact. That puts the filing of her suit well within three years of learning of the legal name change."

Damian caught Fedora Nye looking up quizzically at Croghan. She obviously was surprised to learn that she didn't know of the name change until six months after the fact.

Kay shook her head much like a tired but patient parent. "Your Honor, I gave the official name-change date as the last possible time that Lee was still in any way identified by the Roy name. In truth, the plaintiff's husband officially divorced her in court four years ago, giving as his reason the fact that the Roy personality no longer existed and he wished to legally sever all ties to the man's life. As Mrs. Nye officially learned this in their divorce proceedings four years ago, how can her attorney claim she didn't know that her husband was gone until nearly a full year later?"

"Because my client's religion does not recognize divorce," Croghan rebutted in his louder-than-life voice. "In the eyes of God, Fedora was still married to Roy and hoped for his return to her and their children. It wasn't until she learned of the legal name change—months after it took effect—that she realized Roy was gone forever from her life, a victim of *that* man."

Croghan was back to dramatics, pointing his finger in Damian's direction. Ingle once again picked up his gavel.

"Applying the discovery rule to this case, I find that the statute of limitations for filing the wrongful-death action did not commence until Roy Nye's statutory beneficiary, Mrs. Fedora Nye, discovered all the elements for her cause of action, to wit, that her husband's name had been changed. Motion to dismiss based on a tardy filing denied."

A second rap and it was official. They were going to trial.

Damian was surprised to realize that he was as disappointed for Kay as he was for himself. He had no doubt that her arguments had been legally sound, and the only reason they were going to trial was that this judge was determined to gather material for his next novel. Still, as Damian glanced at his attorney, he was equally surprised to see that no defeat marred her face.

"Your Honor," Kay said. "I respectfully request a two-week continuance. As I have only received Dr. Steele's case this last Monday, I am hardly prepared to—"

"Save your breath, Ms. Kellogg," Ingle interrupted. "I'm not going to let your client's dissatisfaction with prior legal representation delay this trial. I've had defendants play that game with me before. They change counsel every week and each new attorney demands a continuance. No. We will begin jury selection in this matter Monday morning."

Once again, Kay spoke up. "Your Honor, the defense formally requests that all cameras and live media coverage be barred from the courtroom for the duration of this trial."

"I protest, Your Honor," Croghan immediately countered. "Trials are meant to be free and open to all the citizens—"

This time it was Kay who pounded her hand on her table, much to the surprise of Croghan, the judge and Damian—who joined the other men in openly staring at her.

In that resulting shocked silence, her soft voice carried very well. "Your Honor, I will not allow the plaintiff's lawyer to turn this courtroom into a three-ring circus for live-action news. Dr. Steele's spotless reputation and professional standing will be protected. Because if they are not, I promise that when we win this case—and we will win it—we will be filing a lawsuit against Rodney Croghan, his client and any and all other parties who would dare sanction such slander."

Kay had made it clear that she meant Judge Frederick I. Ingle III as one of those other parties. Damian was amazed at the real threat that gentle voice could portray. And, he was even more amazed when he watched her smile sweetly at the judge after making her threat. The lady behind those bright blueberry eyes was just full of unexpected dimensions. He had yet to find one that disappointed him.

Judge Ingle didn't seem all that disappointed, either. He looked at Kay as if with new appreciation for her fighting spirit. Then he raised his gavel, once again.

"No filming inside the courtroom," he said simply. He followed his proclamation with a short rap.

"But, Your Honor—"

"Come now, Mr. Croghan," Ingle interrupted. "With the kind of sensationalism this case will engender, you won't be able to keep the news hounds at bay. Now, you two, listen up, because we play by the Marquis of Ingle's rules in this court. I want a good fight, a clean fight. You'll get no interference from the bench for surprise punches, but keep them in the legal zones. Nine o'clock Monday morning we'll begin to impanel the jury. By ten o'clock Tuesday morning, I expect each of you to be ready to come out from your corners swinging your introductory remarks. May the best lawyer win. Court's adjourned."

"DAMN INGLE and his sudden need for literary acclaim," Kay lamented. "His allowing the case to be heard was always a possibility, but his accepting Croghan's feeble argument to extend the statute of limitations for filing was ludicrous, absolutely ludicrous. He's just looking for colorful grist for the milling of his next novel. This case should never be going to trial."

Kay threw the words over her shoulder as she charged down the King County Courthouse stairwell, doing her best to physically work off her anger. They had seven more flights to go and she knew she was going to need every one.

She heard Damian's reply from behind her as he kept pace with her downward plunge. "At least you got the media barred."

"From filming in the courtroom only. They still can have reporters flooding the spectator area. And you can bet Croghan is going to make sure they do. This is just the kind of unusual case they love to sensationalize. In addition to everything else, we're going to have to be prepared for the press."

"Are you really not ready to start Monday?"

"It's certainly not when I would have chosen to begin. But we'll manage. What will be critical is lining up defense witnesses in time."

"How can I help?"

"You could start by contacting those two psychologists you told me about earlier this week, the ones you consulted with on Lee's case. See if both will be available to appear in court next week."

"What day?"

"Soonest would be Thursday. As you heard, Monday will be taken up with jury selection. Tuesday and Wednesday will most likely be the days when Croghan will be presenting the plaintiff's case. He gave me a long list of potential witnesses, one hundred in all."

"A hundred witnesses? You must be kidding."

"No, but he is. It's a ploy to try to overwhelm us, to use up all our energy tracking down these people to find out what they could possibly have to say. He probably won't be calling more thàn a handful. Still, we have a full weekend ahead preparing even for that handful."

"How can we know which ones will be included in that group?"

"We can't know for certain. That's why he made the list so long. Try to see if the two psychologists can keep Thursday and Friday open."

"Anything else?"

"Yes. Croghan has a psychologist on his witness list, a Dr. Upton Van Pratt. I doubt he's a red herring. Recognize the name?"

"Upton Van Pratt is a past president of the American Psychological Association."

"Damn. That alone will give him clout in the jury's eyes. What else do you know about him?"

"If memory serves, I believe he's retired now. I'm surprised he's willing to testify in a case like this considering his standing. I'll see what I can find out."

"That'll be helpful. I'll also need a list of any books or articles he might have written."

Kay checked her watch as she continued her trajectory down the last flight of stairs. "I have to talk to Lee Nye right away. This afternoon, if possible. Tomorrow, at the latest. Can you set it up for me?"

"Today is probably impossible. I'll see what I can do for tomorrow. Your office?"

"Yes. The psychologists are important, but at the moment, Lee is our key defense witness. You're sure he's willing to testify on your behalf?"

"Last time I spoke to him. I can't imagine anything that would have changed his mind."

"How does he come across?"

"What do you mean?"

"I mean, do you think a jury will consider him a credible witness?"

"That's hard to say."

Kay came to an abrupt stop on the stairs and whirled. She hadn't realized how closely Damian had been following her until they collided. He grabbed her shoulders to steady them both.

Kay felt the warm strength of his hands. She smelled the exciting clean scent of his after-shave. He felt good and he smelled good, and she knew the sudden breathlessness in her body had absolutely nothing to do with her rapid descent on the stairs.

They were so close, she could feel the warmth of his breath on her forehead. He was looking down at her, his thick, rich, dark brown hair haloed by the subdued overhead lights, the strong planes of his face shadowed, his eyes mere glints of green.

The blood began to beat far too loudly against her eardrums, silencing her fading thoughts. She drifted closer to him as though drawn by the insistent pull of some invisible magnet, her senses swimming with the drawing heat and scent of him.

Then, suddenly, the door to the upper floor was pushed open and voices rushed into the stairwell as the echo of several pairs of feet clattered above them, climbing to the next floor.

Kay started at the noise. The rational part of her mind
came to as though it had been in a trance. She was surprised and shocked to find herself so close to her client.

She immediately leaned back, slipped her shoulders from
beneath his hands and descended the next step. He did
nothing to stop her retreat. Nor did he advance. He just
stood there watching her with those glinting eyes.

Kay looked away and tried to collect her jumbled
thoughts. Damn, what had they been discussing? She had
to think. Ingle was making the case go to trial. She had to
have everything ready by Monday. The press. The psychologists. Lee. Yes, that was it. Lee.

She looked back at the man waiting on the stair above her
and schooled her voice into its most professional aplomb.

"You're being deliberately evasive about Lee. Why?"

He leaned his elbow against the stairwell banister and
smiled down at her, displaying all the relaxed composure she
was currently missing within herself.

"You're right, Kay. Possibly, I should have told you this
sooner, but I'd hoped for the suit to be dismissed this
morning and, in that event, I believed telling you wouldn't
be necessary."

As always, Kay did her best not to succumb to the infec-
tiousness of his smile and to concentrate instead on the import of his words.

"What have you kept from me?"

"Lee Nye is a bit . . . unusual."

"Unusual? How do you mean, unusual?"

"I don't want to prejudice your thinking. I'd rather you
met him and made up your own mind."

Kay turned to descend the final few stairs. A bit . . .
unusual. She didn't like the sound of it. She didn't like the
sound of it at all.

*THE ATTIC BEGAN to lighten a bit. Lee Nye, the little boy who
had been sleeping for such a long time, opened his eyes and
realized that something was nudging him awake. He didn't
quite know what it was, but the gentle mental poke was un-
mistakable. He yawned and stretched and got out of his nice*

*warm bed to pad over to the narrow attic window. He
perched his chin on the sill to see what was going on.*

*The objects were even clearer than last time. The colors
even more vibrant. He'd never felt so... close to the world
below before.*

*When he'd first looked out his attic window, it had been
so fuzzy. The objects and people moved as though they were
simply dark shadows against a gray sheet. But not today.
Today things were so clear, so real.*

*He stepped back from the window. Sometimes, the real-
ness disturbed him. He wasn't certain he wanted to look.*

*He remembered a long time ago he had looked out his
attic window and a little boy with a sad face had looked up
at him as though he were asking him to come out to play. He
didn't think anyone down there could see him until that little boy had looked directly up at him.*

That, too, had been too real.

*He hadn't gone down to play, of course. He didn't know
the little boy. And why would he have wanted to leave his
attic, anyway?*

*He moved toward the window again, pressed his nose
against the pane. Once again, the world below flashed clear
and close.*

*It seemed so chaotic down there. At least the people were.
Irrational. Loud. Even violent. Some things were interesting, though. Some things he liked to watch.*

But nothing that was going on today.

*The little boy stepped back from the window again. He
walked over to his desk and took out a pencil and paper
from the drawer. He sat down and began to write down all
the fascinating numbers that had started to pop into his
head.*

*He liked numbers. He added them and subtracted them
and multiplied them and squared them and strung them into
equations. The more complex the equations became, the
more they appealed to the little boy.*

*Yes, he liked playing with his numbers up in his cozy at-
tic. No matter what happened down there in the outside*

world, he could always do just exactly what he wished up here in his attic.

Maybe when he was older and bigger and playing with the numbers no longer amused him so much, he might go down and see what was really going on in that world out there and find those interesting things that sometimes flashed by.

Maybe.

Chapter Four

"Lee Nye, this is my attorney, Ms. Kellogg."

Lee stood before Kay—a medium-size man with medium brown hair and medium brown eyes. He wore a carefully cut light brown suit, a shade darker tie, neat hair and the blandest look on the blandest face Kay had ever seen. There was absolutely, positively, nothing remarkable about him, Kay thought. He was the kind of man you passed on the street every day and never noticed.

Kay felt immediate relief. After Damian's cryptic statement yesterday about his multiple personality patient being unusual, her imagination had been toying with the possibility of coming face-to-face with a multiheaded Hydra.

She smiled and held out her hand.

Lee's return smile was anemic, his shake barely perceptible. Kay reclaimed her hand. She gestured to one of the chairs in front of her desk.

Lee moved to the offered chair and sat down with what looked like mechanical obedience.

Kay felt a slight twinge of unease. She circled her desk and sat down as Damian quietly moved the chair next to Lee closer to the far wall. He purposely sat away from them. Kay suspected that he wanted to make himself unobtrusive, so Lee would give her his full attention.

"I very much appreciate your making time for me on a Saturday," Kay said, once again smiling at the man, trying to break through the bland barrier that seemed to surround him.

His return smile was even less noticeable this time. "It's just another workday for me—and a busy one—but Dr. Steele assured me you wouldn't be too demanding. He knows my time is valuable," Lee said.

Lee looked at his wristwatch as though to emphasize the latter, although there had been no hint of impatience in his voice. As a matter of fact, nothing about his body language gave the impression that he was in a hurry.

Kay was definitely confused by the signals she was receiving. She decided for the moment to just put them aside. "Let's get right to it then, Mr. Nye. Do you mind if I turn on this audiotape and use it as my recorder? I find it so much less distracting than taking notes."

"I don't mind." He had answered without hesitation. His cooperation seemed complete, his attention politely focused.

Kay pressed the button, waited for the tape to move past the leader, and then began.

"Mr. Nye, I assume you are aware that Mrs. Fedora Nye has brought a wrongful-death suit against Dr. Steele?"

"Dr. Steele explained this to me."

"Did he also explain that we would like you to testify on his behalf Thursday or Friday of next week?"

"Yes. That will not be a problem."

"That's good to hear. We both appreciate your cooperation. Now, just a few personal questions, if you don't mind?"

"I don't mind."

"Where do you live?"

"I lease an apartment at 1401 Boren Avenue in Seattle."

"How long have you lived there?"

"About two years."

"Are you married?"

"No."

"Engaged?"

"No."

"Do you have a significant other in your life?"

"Significant other? You mean a romantic interest?"

"Yes."

"No. I have no time for that."

Nor inclination, it appeared from the quick assurance of his response. "I'd like to talk to you about some things that might come up in your testimony next week."

"Fine."

"I understand you first came to Dr. Steele five and a half years ago, is that correct?"

"Yes."

"Are you still his patient?"

"No."

"Why not?"

"He cured me of my problem. I have no reason to see him anymore."

"You said he cured you of your problem. What was your problem?"

"I had recurring blackouts. Dr. Steele stopped them."

"Do you understand how he did this?"

"Yes. He found someone else living inside me. He got rid of him." No inflection disrupted the man's matter-of-fact tone.

"What do you know about this other personality?"

"Only what I learned on the videotapes Dr. Steele showed me."

"And what did you learn from those videotapes?"

"The personality called himself Roy. He was totally unlike me, yet he was in possession of my face and body. It was most unsettling."

Except Kay could clearly tell Lee didn't look or sound unsettled at all. He could just as easily have been reading the ingredients off a cereal box as admitting to seeing a videotape of another personality inhabiting his body. Kay shifted uneasily in her chair.

"What were the effects of these blackouts on your life?"

"The blackouts interfered with my work. I never knew when they would occur."

"Can you give me a specific example of such an incident?"

"I was in the middle of putting samples into a package to mail to a client. The next thing I knew, I opened my eyes to find a large alley rat biting my fingers. I looked at my watch and discovered that nearly twelve hours had passed. It was the middle of the night. I was dirty and smelling of alcohol, lying in a stinking alley on the other side of town, with absolutely no memory of how I got there."

As horrible as this experience must have been, Lee's physical and verbal calm remained unchallenged throughout its recitation.

Kay decided to suggest a little emotion to see what would happen. "That must have been frightening."

Lee maintained his bland composure. "It was most... disruptive."

"Were the other incidents similar?"

"Some were. Some weren't."

"Can you describe some of the others?"

"Roy would get into drunken fights in bars. He would pass out. I would then wake up on the barroom floor a moment later with the consequences."

"You mean you would wake up drunk?"

"Drunk? Of course not. I never drink."

Kay shook her head at this incongruity and put it aside to deal with later. "Then what were these consequences you spoke of, Mr. Nye?"

"My eyes would open to see angry, drunken people beating me. I had a broken nose and several groin injuries once and, another time, a broken wrist that required a cast for six weeks. Several times, I had to go to work with one or two black eyes."

"That must have been dreadful, not to mention very painful."

"It was most unpleasant."

Just unpleasant? Was this man a master of understatement, or what? "How did you explain these injuries to your employer?"

"I couldn't explain how I had awakened to find myself in a bar. I couldn't explain why these people were angry at me. Since I didn't know about Roy, I had no explanations whatsoever. It was my employer who finally urged me to seek treatment.''

''Your employer sounds very caring.''

''He knew I was a good worker. He didn't want to lose me. He sent me to a company doctor.''

''So you first went to a medical doctor?''

''Yes. His tests ruled out brain tumors and other such possibilities. He gave me Dr. Steele's telephone number and urged me to call.''

''How did you feel about being referred to a psychologist?''

''What do you mean?''

''Did it upset you that your problem might be mental?''

''I knew my problem was not mental. It was the blackouts and what happened during those times.''

''I . . . see,'' Kay said, not really seeing at all. ''And when you discovered that Roy took over during those blackout periods, was it your idea or was it Dr. Steele's idea to try to extinguish Roy from your life?''

''I told Dr. Steele I wished to be rid of the disruptive blackouts and their cause. Dr. Steele agreed after a time.''

''Are you happy that Dr. Steele extinguished Roy?''

''I will always be thankful. If Dr. Steele had not gotten rid of him, I believe that Roy would have eventually killed himself and me.''

Kay would have felt a lot better about Lee's words if his expression hadn't remained so deadpan and his tone so lifeless.

''Earlier you said you'd been mailing out some samples to a client when suddenly you blacked out. Is that the work you typically perform for your employer?''

''I was a mail clerk at a local marketing firm. Putting together and mailing the material for product presentations was my primary function. I no longer work for that company. I started my own firm three years ago.''

Kay was surprised. ''Your own firm? What kind of firm?''

''Marketing, the same type as the one I worked for. Now my company is almost as big as the one I left. I'm opening satellite offices in Portland and San Francisco later this year."

Kay sent a big smile to accompany her words. "After only three years? That's very impressive, Mr. Nye. You must possess a strong entrepreneurial spirit."

For the first time since the interview began, Kay thought she saw a small ripple of feeling cross Lee Nye's impassive face.

"I like...numbers. That's all it is, really. Meeting the challenge of positioning products correctly just involves some calculations. It all comes down to finding the right equation."

"The right equation?" Kay echoed.

Lee held out his left hand, palm up. "On one end, the producer." He held out his right hand, palm up. "On the other end, the consumer." He leaned forward until his body was between his hands. "I am in the middle—the equal sign."

"You see yourself as an equal sign?"

"A part of the right equation. I am the thing that makes the system equate properly. You understand?"

The *thing* that makes the system equate properly. Kay understood all right. She only wished she didn't.

DAMIAN WATCHED Kay get up to pace her office the second after Lee left. A frown drew her eyebrows together.

"Lee is obviously willing to testify on your behalf," she began. "He articulates well. He says all the right things. I don't think there's a lawyer alive who could get him riled on the stand. And his business acumen says much for his successful integration into society since Roy was extinguished."

The "but" was there at the end of her sentence, despite the fact that she hadn't given it voice. Damian was pretty sure that, considering who the lady was, she wouldn't be able to keep it unspoken much longer. He waited.

She stopped her pacing after a moment and turned to face him. "No one is going to believe that this Roy could have drunk himself senseless, only for Lee to wake a moment later perfectly sober. That's just not physically possible."

"It happens with multiple personalities, Kay, and it's only one of the mind-bending realities that have been documented many times with these people."

"One personality getting drunk while another stays sober?"

"Absolutely. When the personalities are aware of one another, sometimes they'll get together and decide who will be the nondrinking designated driver, and then the rest will go ahead and drink whatever they want."

"And you're telling me the personality that drives them home is sober?"

"Yes."

"That flies in the face of all logic."

"These cases frequently do. Depending on which personality of a multiple is controlling the mind, even such verifiable medical conditions as allergic skin rashes, cysts, tumors, tuberculosis, even symptoms of pregnancy have been diagnosed only to disappear when another personality takes over."

"That's incredible."

"So are the brain wave patterns that change dramatically when a different personality is in charge of the consciousness. All of which tells us we know next to nothing about the synergy between mind and body."

"You say this has been documented?"

"There are dozens of case histories you can introduce to help substantiate Lee's experiences and perceptions."

Kay took a deep breath and let it out. "No, I doubt if anything could help."

"Kay? What is it?"

"It was...unnerving. Lee talked about being saddled with the Roy personality as though Roy had been an annoying cough. When he described waking up to a rat biting his fingers in some stinking alley with no idea how he got there, it was with the same mild irritation that someone would express because the waiter brought the wrong soup."

She swung around and headed for her desk. "You said Lee was unusual. You didn't say he possessed about as much human warmth as cottage cheese."

Damian understood her reaction. At one time, it had been his, too, before he had grasped what had happened to this individual. Now he was filled with awe for the resilience of the human spirit.

"Kay, this might take some time for you to fully appreciate, but Lee's unusualness stems from the dissociation his mind went through."

"Dissociation?"

"What we talked about briefly the first day I came to your office. As a helpless child, this individual was subjected to severe mental and physical abuse from which he could not escape. He could have gone insane. Instead, his mind mastered the ability to create different personalities that protected themselves from both the memories and the feelings of the abuse."

"You mean this blandness is because he doesn't feel anything?"

"The Lee personality expresses annoyance and impatience and mild appreciation. But he's removed from any deeper feelings of anger or pain or pleasure."

"How can someone remove himself from feelings?"

"Multiple-personality people often possess superior intelligence. Their minds can do many things that are hard for the rest of us to understand. How they do these things, we're still not sure."

"But what about all the positive emotions, like joy and wonder? Why would Lee dissociate them?"

"If you're going to give up deep feelings, it's generally an all-or-nothing thing."

"But, Damian, to *willingly* give up emotions?"

"We don't know that *will* has anything to do with the mind splitting into multiple personalities and dissociating from emotion. I believe that, quite apart from will, the split may be a creative and inborn survival mechanism of these highly intelligent people."

"But how could such an intelligent child give up joy?"

"He lived a nightmare of horrendous abuse. For him, giving up joy might not have been much of a sacrifice."

Her mouth tightened. "That's so damn . . . tragic."

Damian could tell her heart had trouble with these things, despite how disciplined she had trained her mind to be. He was glad she had this trouble. A person too removed from the pain of others was too much in danger of being removed from his or her own humanity.

He smiled at the small frown that had reappeared between her light-colored eyebrows. "Society has never properly acknowledged the importance of the parenting role. Otherwise, it would be awarding the million-dollar contracts to the exceptional mothers and fathers—not the football players and movie stars."

Her eyes gazed into his for a long moment before she said anything. When she finally did, the corners of her lips had risen ever so gently into a smile.

"There may be something to say about psychologists running the country for a while."

He smiled back. "Considering that comes from a member of the profession that does run the country, I take that as a high compliment."

Her smile expanded until it lit up the room with warmth. He basked in its glow as he let his mind toy with some of the more interesting nonverbal ways he'd like to bring out that smile. She looked away, obviously uncomfortable with the moment of intimacy and prolonged eye contact that had grown between them.

He watched her with some amusement and more than a bit of regret that he could do nothing about that unconscious tugging at her right earlobe. He wondered if she knew how close she'd come to kissing him on that stairwell yesterday.

No, probably not. He doubted whether she understood that she shared a small but significant similarity with Lee. She, too, was denying her deeper emotions and needs, pretending they didn't matter and that she could do without them. He wondered, not for the first time, just how much woman hid beneath that all-business suit and that sharp, logical mind.

"Did you ever talk to Lee about his stunted emotions?"

Damian reluctantly refocused his thoughts to their conversation. "Extensively, both before and after I was successful in extinguishing Roy."

"But you couldn't help him?"

"Before Roy was extinguished, Lee could concentrate on nothing but getting rid of the disruptive personality. Afterward, he told me I had cured him of his blackout episodes and that was all that was necessary."

"And I just bet he told you with that same deadpan face and voice."

Damian nodded. "Lee told me quite matter-of-factly that he didn't need any deeper emotions. He was doing fine without them."

"Is this lack of emotional depth common in a multiple-personality patient?"

"It's not atypical for one or more of the personalities to have rejected emotions."

"Had Roy?"

"No, quite the contrary. He was a bundle of intense negative emotions, very close to the surface and, for the most part, violent and spontaneous."

"Spontaneity," Kay said. "Yes, that's another thing Lee lacks. Well, there goes our star defense witness."

Her comment surprised him. "You're not going to put Lee on the stand?"

"Damian, a good witness must possess many qualities, the most important of which are likability and believability. Lee says all the right things, but without the expression of the normal human emotions to underlie the recitation of his harrowing experiences, a jury would never sympathize with him."

"I see the difficulty. But you said yourself that his testimony was a vital component to my defense."

"Believe me, *not* putting him on the stand is now far more vital to your defense."

Damian sat on the edge of her desk. "Why don't I take the stand before Lee and explain his emotional dissociation. I'm sure I could get the jury to understand the circumstances that have made him the way he is."

"Possibly. But I'm not sure I want even you to take the stand."

This surprised Damian even more. "You don't want me to take the stand? I would think that the jury would expect me to tell my side of the story."

"The problem is, you wouldn't just be giving your side of the story and explaining what brought you to your decision about extinguishing Roy. You would be cross-examined by Croghan. And he'd do his best to paint you as some quack or psychotic doctor."

"I can handle myself."

"Damian, I know that. But when a defendant takes the stand, no matter how articulate and innocent he is, his testimony is tainted in the mind of the jurors simply by the fact that he is the accused. I would much prefer to have other credible people in your profession testify to your competence and the solidness of your treatment procedure with Lee."

"You want others to validate my actions so I don't look defensive."

"Exactly. And speaking of defensive, you haven't ever been involved with the police—arrested, sued or anything like that, have you?"

"No."

"Good. Because you can bet if you had been, Croghan would find out and make sure the jury learned of it."

"Even if it had nothing to do with this case?"

"Especially if it had nothing to do with this case. No, if it's at all possible, I'd like to keep you off the stand and get the other psychologists to support your treatment method. They will, won't they?"

"I fully expect them to, despite the fact that they never actually met Lee or Roy in person."

"They didn't? But I thought you said earlier this week that the two psychologists whose names you gave me were familiar with the case?"

"We went over the particulars in depth. They didn't actually interview the patient."

"But they concurred with your treatment based on the data you shared?"

"Yes."

Kay recircled her desk and opened her file folder on the case. "Have you been able to reach either of them yet?"

"First one on the list, Dr. Jerry Tummel, said he'll be happy to testify, although he'd like at least two days' notice before he has to appear."

"That shouldn't be a problem. When can he come to the office for a preliminary interview?"

"He's booked solid during the days but told me he would try to make himself available for an evening get-together. He's promised to call me tomorrow to set it up. I've listed his credentials and publishing credits for you there," he said, pointing to the file.

"Impressive. What about the other psychologist, Dr. Pat Fetter?"

"Pat is a specialist in multiple personality, and is even in the process of writing a book about it. Unfortunately, at the moment, she's incognito conducting a two-week, multiple-personality treatment session in some undisclosed, rural town in Idaho. She's kept it hush-hush because several multiples are attending and she doesn't want them bothered by the press. Her receptionist says there's no phone to reach her on, and she has to rely on Pat calling in for messages."

"That's tough. We really should have two psychologists to help counteract what Dr. Van Pratt is going to say."

"You know what Van Pratt is going to say?"

"I know it won't agree with your treatment of the case, otherwise Croghan wouldn't be calling him to the stand. With your help, I'm going to have to find out everything I can about the man. I have to be ready to counteract and thoroughly discredit his testimony."

"Wouldn't it be enough to just shed doubt? After all, the burden of proof rests with Croghan. He's the one who must prove his case beyond a reasonable doubt in the minds of all the jurors."

"That's criminal law, Damian. In civil law, it's the preponderance of evidence that prevails. If the majority of the jurors decides that the evidence is even slightly tipped in Mrs. Nye's favor, then they're going to find for her and award her damages accordingly."

"So we have to weight the scales in our favor."

"That's the game plan, and the play is to discredit Dr. Van Pratt at every turn. The jury cannot be allowed to believe anything but that extinguishing Roy was the appropriate thing to do. I have to be ready for whoever Croghan puts up on the stand and for whatever they're going to say."

Damian glanced down the witness list. "He's got Mrs. Nye and her two children listed. You really think they'll all testify?"

"Yes. He's even listed them twice."

"Twice?"

"Yes, look again on this fourth page. See? On the first page, they are shown as Fedora Nye, Larry Nye and Rosy Nye. On the fourth page, they're listed again with only their first initial—F. Nye, L. Nye and R. Nye."

"Just to pad the list to make it look overwhelmingly long."

"It's long enough even without that duplication."

"Who else on this list will he actually call besides the Nyes and Dr. Van Pratt?"

"Maybe you can help answer that question. Take a quick look and let me know if any of the names sound familiar."

Damian paused for a quick perusal. "No. Nothing jumps out."

"The Nyes and the doctor may be all he figures he has to put up there, particularly if the prospective jurors have seen any of the news broadcasts of the grieving widow. He obviously got her the airtime to sway whatever minds he could. My first job on Monday will be to find jurors who..."

Kay stopped speaking abruptly when a tall, striking woman with long black hair, dressed in a blue and gray jogging suit, suddenly stepped into the office.

The newcomer's voice was very deep and husky. "Kay, I have to talk to you. Oh, sorry. Didn't know you weren't in here alone."

"Not a problem, AJ. Come on in. Damian, this is Ariana Justice—better known as AJ—the head of a private investigation firm we use. AJ, my client Dr. Damian Steele."

AJ stepped forward and Damian felt the strong, solid shake of her hand. She certainly shared her brother's dark good looks. She also shared the detached, mirrorlike aloofness in her pale blue eyes. Their reflective stare was even more disturbing to Damian than when he had first seen its like in Adam Justice's eyes many years ago, when they'd met.

"If it's something urgent, AJ," Kay said, "I'm sure Dr. Steele won't mind if I step outside with you for a moment."

"We might as well talk right here," AJ said as she turned back to Kay. "This concerns Dr. Steele, too."

"Something about the case?" Kay asked.

AJ slipped into the nearest chair. Her movements reminded Damian of a very supple and alert dancer, waiting for the next cue, never quite at rest. She looked from Damian to Kay.

"Yes, you could say that. I have some bad news and some worse news. Which one do you want to hear first?"

Damian watched Kay as she faced the private investigator. Her expression retained its cool calm, her voice did not waver. But he could see the almost imperceptible straightening of her spine, as though she were preparing herself for the blow.

"Let's work up to this. Give me the bad first."

"My investigators have discovered that a week ago, Croghan met with the executive producer at a local Seattle television station. Croghan promised the producer exclusive rights to Mrs. Nye's story for a future made-for-TV movie. In exchange, the producer is gearing up to make the trial an ongoing fifteen-minute special every night, to be discussed by a four-member legal panel on their local news segment."

Kay slowly and stiffly circled her desk and reclaimed her chair. She sat on its edge, that small characteristic frown drawing her eyebrows together again.

"And with Croghan making the deal, you can bet he'll do everything he can to slant the coverage in favor of Mrs. Nye."

"And knowing human nature, you can also just bet one or more of the jurors is going to have to peek at the coverage of a trial they're sitting on," Damian said. "What can we do about it?"

AJ shrugged her limber dancer's shoulders. "It's in your bailiwick now, Kay."

She nodded. "The logical thing to do is to try to sequester the jury, but even in his sane days, Ingle would never sequester a jury. Refers to it as locking up the good citizens like they were the criminals."

She exhaled as though coming to an unsatisfactory decision. "We'll just have to persuade the judge to admonish the jury so strongly that he makes them afraid to watch. Only, with Judge Ingle's own current fascination with this circus, I doubt any admonition coming from him will sound all that genuine. Good heavens, AJ, if that's only the bad news, what's the worst?"

"You ready?"

"Probably not, but you'd better go ahead, anyway."

"Croghan got the TV producer to approach Judge Ingle this morning and ask him to write the script for the made-for-TV movie."

Kay lunged forward. "You can't be serious. But that's clearly a conflict of interest!"

AJ shook her long, dark mane. "You'd never get it to stick. Ingle is playing it smart. He says he won't talk a deal until the case is over. And there's no evidence he even knows that Croghan put the producer up to it. Just like there's no proof that Croghan deliberately finagled the case into Ingle's courtroom by delaying several documents and making sure they arrived at the precise moment the clerk was ready to assign the next case to Ingle.''

"Croghan did that? But how?''

"Same way Marc Truesdale has gotten his cases before a particular judge—by knowing the clerk's procedures, the percentages and playing them both.''

"Marc does that? Why, that scoundrel. No wonder he's always winning those hopeless cases.''

"Playing the percentages and throwing in a little legal finesse goes a long way sometimes,'' AJ agreed.

Kay's fingers tapped on her desktop to a rapid mental march. "So Croghan knew all about Ingle's book and its critical reviews. He finagled the case into the judge's court, guessing that Ingle would be delighted to have a juicy case to preside over and, subsequently, write about. And he guessed right. Damn. So far, Croghan's every step has been carefully calculated.''

"So it would seem,'' AJ said as she glided to her feet.

"Why did he leave Olympia to practice up here in Seattle?'' Kay asked.

AJ paused at the door and turned. "He's done some moonlighting over the last few years in the courts up here. Word is, he finally left the big firm he was with in Olympia to open his own Seattle office where he could be his own boss. He's obviously out to make a name for himself. Be careful of him, Kay. He's slippery and he's sharp. There's no telling what else he's going to pull. Don't hold anything back.''

"AJ's RIGHT. I can't hold anything back, Damian.''

Kay tapped her fingers on her desk as her mind raced. The fallout from AJ's two bombs still mushroomed in her thoughts, despite the fact that the private investigator had left several minutes ago.

Damian draped a long leg over the edge of her desk as he rested against its side. "I still think you should put me on the stand and then Lee. If the jury just understands—''

"You, I'll consider, but never Lee," Kay interrupted. "I don't know what a jury would make of him, but I suspect they'd decide you'd extinguished the wrong personality."

"They wouldn't if they had met Roy."

Damian's words struck like a bolt of bright lightning through all the gray fallout clouds in Kay's mind. She shot to her feet and faced him, feeling newly charged.

"Then let's let the jury meet Roy."

"Meet Roy? Kay, you know Roy's gone. You're not making sense."

"The videotapes, Damian. Let's show them the videotapes of Roy."

"No. Absolutely not."

"Why not?"

"Patient confidentiality prohibits it."

"What patient confidentiality? Roy wasn't your patient."

"The mind that contained him was."

"Are you saying you don't have Lee's approval to share those tapes?"

"I have Lee's approval to share the tapes. He signed a release at the beginning of our sessions together."

"Well, then, I don't understand—"

"I asked him to sign the release so that I could show the tapes to other psychologists with years of training in treating multiple personality disorder. Kay, there are very sensitive issues at stake here. I'll continue to discuss the case with you in general terms, but the specifics must remain protected under the confidentiality oath between doctor and patient."

"All right, I'll look at the tapes first and see what—"

"No."

"No?"

"The confidentiality oath between doctor and patient—"

"Is no less than that between lawyer and client," Kay interrupted. "Were I to repeat any privileged communication between us, I would be disbarred and lose my license to practice. What's more, nothing I divulged could ever be used in court. By law, it would be inadmissible evidence.''

"There are other considerations. Without psychological training, it would be difficult for you to understand—"

"View the tapes with me then. Explain what I don't understand."

She watched as Damian swept his broad, strong hand to the back of his neck and rubbed it as though trying to ease a pain there. "It's more than just understanding."

She went to his side, put a hand on his forearm and felt the instant tightening of the steel muscles beneath.

"Damian, help me out on this. You heard what AJ said. Croghan is devious and he is determined. I have to have something concrete to show the jury—"

"I repeat, the jury can never see those tapes, Kay."

"But *I* have to see them."

"Why? I've told you everything that is germane to the two personalities."

"From a psychological standpoint, I have no doubt. But how can you know what's germane from a legal standpoint? There may be something I can use that you would never have thought of. I can't go into court on Monday with any blinders on. I must fully understand who Roy Nye was in order to properly defend your decision to extinguish him. To do that, I must see those tapes."

"You don't know what's on those tapes, Kay."

"That's why I have to see them."

"I strongly advise against this."

Kay increased the pressure on his forearm. "Damian, it's the only way. Unless I can see this personality—Roy—for myself, how can I adequately describe him to a jury?"

Damian exhaled a weary breath. "I'll probably regret this."

"I've given you my word that I will not repeat what's on those tapes without your approval. What else is causing you concern?"

"That you aren't prepared for what you're about to see."

There was something about the hard look in Damian's eyes and the hard edge in his voice that gave Kay a small shiver. For the first time since the brilliant thought had occurred to her, Kay wondered whether it was so brilliant, after all.

Chapter Five

Kay parked her new blue Camry behind Damian's vintage green Jaguar and wondered what they were doing in this residential section of Seattle. She followed Damian around a riotous growth of fifty-foot Douglas firs, only to be almost immediately confronted by a huge, towering, gray Gothic house, encased in broad and batten wood cladding, gable dormers, thorny pinnacles and even a castellated tower.

It looked like something out of Grimm's fairy tales. Very grim.

"I thought we were going to your office to view those videotapes?"

"My home is also my office these days."

Kay gazed up at the Gothic monstrosity before her. His home? This outwardly well-balanced, charming psychologist? It seemed rather incongruous. Still, in a strange way, it also seemed to fit something in him—something Kay had sensed from the first, something dark that dwelt behind those secretive eyes. Or was she just being fanciful?

A blue envelope had been taped to the heavy paneled front door. Kay didn't get a chance to see if anything was written on it. As soon as Damian spied it, he snatched it and shoved it into his pocket. He fitted his key into the massive door and turned the lock. It swung open to the accompaniment of a loud, squeaky-hinged protest.

Kay stiffened. Last time she'd heard that kind of ominous sound, the actors on-screen had just walked into a haunted house where they were suddenly attacked with a hatchet. Not a comforting memory to spring up at this moment.

Kay hesitantly followed Damian inside. She trod carefully across the stone-floor coldness of the age-darkened entry hall. A hollow-eyed, enormous old suit of armor, anchored by a heavy metal chain to the stone wall, held a battle-ax clutched in its iron hand like a sentry ready to split open the head of any intruder.

Kay shivered involuntarily as she gave the old armor a wide berth.

Her detour took her to Damian's side and for the first time she saw what lay ahead. She stopped in her tracks. She simply could not believe her eyes.

"My office is this way," Damian said as he veered right down a narrow and equally dark hallway.

Kay did not follow this time. She proceeded straight ahead, her attention totally captured and drawn to the vision she was certain would vanish any moment.

Because it was a lovely, impossible vision.

Sunlight poured down on glistening blue fountains. Fuchia foxgloves towered amidst purple-leafed hazelnut, white catmint, yellow euphorbia, and blue iris with the fragrance of lavender springing out of the heart-shaped leaflets of an epimedium evergreen ground cover. The tops of tall, golden-black locust trees swayed in a gentle breeze.

She exited the dark hallway and stepped down the three stone stairs that opened into the lovely inner courtyard and garden. Immediately, the warm afternoon sun caressed her hands and face and hair, as bees hummed past on their way to the fragrant flowers. The song of birds flitted through the tallest of the trees, the babble of the water laughed as it danced over a crystal rock wall.

Dear heavens, it was real. Who would have guessed that such a sinister-looking, forbidding house could have such a beautiful enclosed garden. Kay wondered if this was how

Alice had felt when she fell down the dark rabbit hole and got her first sight of Wonderland.

She scurried across a bridge that spanned a bubbling pond full of fat, foot-long goldfish, and then she ducked into the cool shade of a grotto on the other side. She circled it to find yet another fountain and the prodigious exotic blossoms of a late-flowering magnolia tree, bending gently toward a carpet of emerald green clover.

She picked one of the globular flowers and inhaled its rich fragrance. She rubbed its soft petals against her cheek.

Suddenly, she sensed movement behind her. She whirled, finding herself face-to-face with the master of this horrible house and gorgeous garden, a man of massive, beastlike muscles, his rugged features transformed by a sizzling, sun-lit smile.

"Be careful," his deep voice warned. "A beauty who insists on stealing a flower from the beast's garden must also accept his penalty."

Kay smiled. She had obviously been dwelling on the wrong fairy tale.

She tossed the flower to him. Lightning fast, his hand flew up and caught it. He held it out to her again, a light of daring in his eyes. She allowed herself to be swept along on this mood of mild enchantment.

"Not so fast. What penalty will you impose for this one flower, Mr. Beast?"

He pretended to be weighing the matter. The bright sunlight disappeared in his dark brown hair, his green eyes glowed just a shade darker than the lush clover at their feet.

"What else but to forever be captured in my garden?"

Kay inhaled deeply of the warmth and the scent of sweet flowers as she accepted the magnolia blossom from his hand.

"Not a bad sentence. This is absolutely lovely. And so unexpected."

"Grandmother's doing. Grandfather insisted on building a replica of the Gothic home his grandfather had owned back in the old country. To counteract the severity of its architecture, grandmother began this garden. But the deer kept jumping the fence and eating the plants, and the neighbors' dogs kept burrowing under the fence to dig up grandmother's prize posies. So she finally convinced my grandfather to have a giant rock wall built to enclose and protect her garden.''

Kay twirled around, trying to get a feel for the garden's size. She was surprised to see the huge thistle climbing the rock wall on its perimeter, until she saw the bright yellow finches flittering above its purple flowers. Yes, she'd let thistle grow, too, to attract those lovely birds.

"I'd like to meet your grandparents."

"They're both gone."

Kay turned back to Damian. "I'm sorry."

He was looking at the garden, his expression even, his gaze lost in a distance of memories.

"Me, too," he said simply. "But they went together and that's what they wanted."

Kay didn't know why a small lump formed in her throat. Maybe because the casual way Damian had said the words had conveyed a feeling that was not casual at all.

She waved a hand back at the Gothic structure behind them. "The house seems huge."

He looked at her. "It's uninspired and unwieldy and, for the most part, cold and uncomfortable. In other words, a typical beast's lair. Come on. I'll show you around."

He hadn't exaggerated about the house. In contrast to the light, warmth and lushness of the garden, it was dark and cold and pedestrian-plain—stone floors, dingy gray walls. At least the walls facing the inner courtyard and garden were dressed with slim, pointed-arch windows that let in the light and the view.

The corner room that Damian had converted into his office opened on two sides to the garden and sported an enormous skylight that flooded the room with more of the outdoors.

Kay noted that the room's bamboo-and-wicker desk, divan and chairs blended beautifully to promote a light, tropical casualness quite at odds with the heavy architecture and ponderous furniture throughout the rest of the house.

Dozens of unusual objects sat on wicker and glass shelving units. One piece stood out in a special place of honor. Kay studied the foot-long, canoe-shaped craft.

"Is this a kayak?"

"Yes. This particular replica is an ancient and genuine piece of art. When the earliest peoples of Alaska and Greenland made the kayak to navigate the icy waters, they fashioned it out of animal skins like this one."

"So this is like a model they made for the larger craft?"

He nodded. "I brought it back from a trip to Alaska a few years ago. All the stuff in this room are souvenirs from one trip or another to places where I can paddle. Seeing the world by kayak is one of my favorite ways to relax. Gives you a good workout, too. The tapes are over here."

Kay turned around to see Damian approaching a light teak-paneled wall on which hung dozens of primitive masks and a single shield. When he touched something in the center of the shield, the wall opened to reveal a very large filing room. One wall was filled with videotapes.

"You tape all your sessions?" Kay asked.

"A multiple-personality case is the only type I have reason to videotape."

"These are all Lee's tapes?"

"No. I've been treating another multiple personality over this last year. Or at least I was. She's decided to see another analyst. I'll be boxing up her videotapes tomorrow morning and dropping them off at the analyst's office. These fifteen tapes are Lee's. Each contains six, sequential, one-hour sessions, except the last tape, which contains only the final one-hour session I saw Lee. Roy was no longer present at that time."

Kay quickly did the math. "That's eighty-five hours."

"I treated Lee for a year and a half. I believe I mentioned that."

She sighed. "So you did. Well, we'd best get started. Where's your TV and VCR?"

"Next room. It's a dark cubbyhole I call a den, but it has a comfortable sofa. Just give me a minute to check my messages."

He handed her the tapes, closed the hidden file room and made for his bamboo-and-wicker desk. He had two answering machines on it. He pressed the message key for the first one, and, as Kay meandered toward the den, she heard a message from a male patient who wanted to change his appointment time.

Kay then glanced over her shoulder and saw Damian press the message key for the second answering machine. This message sounded far different. Kay couldn't tell if it was a man's or woman's voice, young or old. It was low, breathy, almost inhuman.

"I know you're not there. I know exactly where you are. I always do. I always will."

A dial tone followed this strange message. Kay looked back at Damian to see his reaction. His rugged face was a stone mask. Only the chilling glint in his eyes betrayed him. He must have felt her scrutiny, because he suddenly looked over at her. His voice was uncharacteristically distant, cool.

"You go ahead. I'll be with you shortly."

Whatever the cryptic message meant, he obviously didn't mean to share his interpretation with her. Kay slipped into the next room. The den was as described—a dark hole with dingy walls. A television stood against one wall, a makeshift cabinet next to it, which contained the VCR and more tapes.

The ugly, overstuffed, red-checkered couch was also as described—soft and as comfortable as a pillow. Kay sank into it and contemplated the fifteen tapes in her lap. She'd never have time to view eighty-five hours' worth. She was definitely going to have to rely on Damian to direct her to the most important ones.

He walked into the small den a moment later.

"I've faxed a note to my favorite librarian asking her to do some sleuthing on any books or articles that Dr. Van Pratt may have authored. Knowing her, I'll probably have a return fax by morning. You ready to get started on these?"

She pointed to what appeared to be just a jumble of alphanumeric entries on the labels. "Is this some secret code?"

He smiled at her, the chilling glint now gone from his eyes. "Known only by those who ordered the official psychologist's decoder ring."

The charming beast was back at ease and in command of his lair. Kay deliberately looked away from that infectious smile.

"Which one of these is the session where Roy first came out?"

Damian plucked a tape off her lap and walked over to the VCR where he slipped it in. He picked up the remote control and returned to the couch.

"I didn't record the first time Roy appeared, because I had no idea Roy was there. I put in the next session, the first one I taped. It takes place two days after Roy first appeared."

"How long had you been in therapy with Lee at this point?"

"About three months, with a standing appointment for one hour every Wednesday afternoon."

"What had you and he accomplished so far?"

Damian sat next to her on the couch, stretched out his long legs and leaned his arm over the back. Kay was immediately distracted by the warmth of his body and the proximity of his arm to her shoulders. He smelled so good. Damn, he always smelled so good.

"We'd been getting to know each other."

Kay set the other tapes on the couch beside her, trying to keep her mind on business and irritated to find her thoughts so easily distracted around this sensually exciting man.

"Just getting to know each other?" she repeated.

"No *just* about it," Damian replied.

He was looking at her intently, his manner and tone gentle. "Multiple personalities have a big problem with trust, since theirs has been so completely violated. They're not the only ones with this difficulty, Kay. Many of us have stopped trusting ourselves and others. Yet in order for therapy to work, or any relationship, for that matter, the two people involved must trust their emotions, themselves, each other."

Kay found herself taking his comments far too personally. She let out an internal sigh. Damn, it was hard not to take this man personally. She had to be on her guard every minute.

"Such trust begins with knowledge," Damian went on. "Both therapist and patient have to have a feel for how the other thinks and reacts. At this point in our relationship, Lee was ready to believe that I really wanted to help him. I was ready to believe that he really wanted to help himself."

"And you hypnotized him and out came Roy."

"And that was something neither of us was ready to believe."

"What about Roy?"

"I questioned him as long as he let me. The session ended abruptly with him stalking out."

"Roy stalked out? What happened to Lee?"

"He was missing for the rest of that day and night. He had total amnesia from the moment I hypnotized him. I asked Lee to come back the next day for another session and took the time in between to consult with a colleague."

"Which colleague?"

"Dr. Jerry Tummel."

"So he was in on this from the beginning?"

"As a consultant. He'd handled two multiples before, so I reasoned that if Lee indeed was one, Jerry might be able to say for certain. Jerry confirmed that the blackouts, the amnesia regarding childhood events and the ability to be easily hypnotized were all clear signs that Lee was a multiple."

"Easily hypnotized? That's a sign?"

"Yes. It's believed by some that the creation of separate personalities is a form of self-hypnosis that multiples learn very early. Their other personalities are altered states of consciousness, induced by hypnosis. Multiples are very adept at the process."

"How could you tell when Lee became Roy?"

"I could give you a list of subtle and not so subtle differences between the two, but I think it would be easiest if you just watched the tape. You'll see what I mean."

Damian switched on the television by remote control and pressed the play button on the VCR. Kay settled back in the comfortable couch, attentive and expectant.

Lee's bland face and voice filled the screen as he sat in a brown leather lounge chair. Behind him to the left was a shelf of books, and to the right was a window with a view of trees. Kay guessed this had been Damian's office before he started to practice out of his home.

"No, Dr. Steele. I don't mind that you've decided to tape our sessions," Lee was saying.

"That's good, Lee," Damian answered on the tape. *"I think it will be a big help to me. You remember I asked to hypnotize you the day before yesterday?"*

"Yes. I lost time."

"Do you mind if I try to hypnotize you again today?"

"No. What do you wish me to do?"

"Just as I suggested before. Lean back in the chair. That's right. Get comfortable. Close your eyes. Do you feel relaxed?"

"Yes. But it makes me ... uneasy."

"What is making you uneasy?"

"The relaxation. I feel I might ..."

"Yes?"

"Lose time. I'm ... uneasy about it."

"You don't need to feel uneasy. I'm here and I won't let you lose too much time. I want to know for certain what happens when you lose this time. Now, here's what I want you to do. I'm going to put you in a very relaxed state and send you somewhere else in your mind. But when I call your name, you will instantly come back and speak to me. Do you understand?"

"Yes."

"Good. Remember, the moment I call your name, you will come instantly back from where I send you."

"All right."

"Now you may relax. Imagine yourself lying on your back on a warm sandy beach, the waves lapping gently against the shore. The sun is high in the sky. A light breeze

drifts over your face. Can you feel the warm sand against your skin?"

"Yes. The air smells salty. It's relaxing."

"Yes, very relaxing. Now let your body go loose."

Everything about Lee's taped image seemed to go slack all at once. Kay watched as Damian appeared on camera and lifted Lee's right arm. He let go of it and it dropped like a lead pipe onto the chair. The man had become hypnotized in less than thirty seconds. It seemed incredible. Goose bumps collected on Kay's arms.

"Did he go under that quickly the first time?" she asked, her eyes still glued to the TV.

"Yes," Damian answered.

Damian's taped image disappeared out of the picture and his voice spoke to the man in that same steady conversational tone.

"I would like to speak with Roy. Roy, are you there?"

Nothing seemed to be happening. Lee's body remained slack and relaxed. The only change Kay could detect was the slight movement of his eyes beneath his closed lids, as though he might be dreaming.

Then suddenly, the man in the lounge chair sat up, his facial expression contorting as his forehead and lips twisted downward. His shoulders rose toward his ears, his hands latched on to the chair arms like claws. His eyes slid open wide, and Kay noticed how bloodshot they were. Almost immediately, they were reduced to mere slits, darting around the room suspiciously. When he spied Damian, his voice rasped in a gruff, unfamiliar tone.

"Wha' youse want?"

The transformation was like nothing Kay had ever witnessed before. Apart from general size and coloring, and the fact that he was wearing the same clothes, this jumpy, snake-eyed individual looked and sounded nothing like the bland Lee. One didn't pass this man unnoticed on the street. One noticed this man immediately and purposely crossed the street to avoid him.

An icy chill shot between Kay's shoulder blades.

"Do you know who I am, Roy?" Damian's voice.

"Yeah, you're that shrink. The one who ain't got no cigarettes or booze, just lotsa questions."

"That's right, Roy. Do you mind if I ask you a few more questions?"

"Wha' questions?"

"I want to know about Lee Nye."

"Look, I told youse before. I don't know no Lee Nye. If he's in some trouble, I wasn't in on it, see?"

"Lee isn't in any trouble, Roy. He's a patient of mine."

Kay watched the sneering man lean back in his chair, still clutching its arms, still leery and wary.

"And youse say he ain't in no trouble. You think bein' loony ain't trouble?"

"Not everyone who comes into a psychologist's office is loony, Roy. You're here."

Roy's wary unease sharpened as a frown furrowed his forehead. *"Wha' the hell am I doing here, anyway?"*

"You came to tell me about yourself."

"Yeah, well, if that's true, why did youse seem so surprised to see me last time?"

"Because I wasn't expecting you the last time. When were you born, Roy?"

Roy sat back, somewhat less wary, a bit more cocky and belligerent looking. *"Youse don't know nothing about me."*

"That's right, I don't. That's why I'm asking questions. I'd like to know about you. When were you born?" Damian repeated.

Kay didn't like what passed for a smile on Roy's face. It had a slimy look to it.

"I wasn't born, man. I sprouted full grown."

"What does that mean?"

"Youse figure it out. Youse the guy with the fancy education."

"Where do you live?"

"I don't live nowhere permanent-like."

"I need some kind of address."

"My old lady's got a place I flop at occasionally, but she's a bitching drag. And those sniveling brats of hers are always a pain. Man, I need a cigarette. And a drink."

"As I told you last time, there's no smoking or drinking allowed in here."

"Then what's I doing here?"

"What are your parents like, Roy?"

"I never had no parents."

"Everyone has parents, Roy. Did yours die?"

"Look, I tell youse. I ain't got none. Never did."

"Who raised you?"

"I raised me."

"Were there adults around?"

"I was around. I was the adult. See?"

"I'm not sure I do."

"Well then youse not so smart, are you, shrink?"

"Perhaps not, Roy. Why don't you smarten me up?"

"Waste of my time."

"What do you remember about your childhood?"

"Look, I ain't got no childhood and this is gettin' to be a real drag. I don't need no shrink. I need a cigarette and a drink."

"You also need someone to help you with your blackouts."

A suspicious sneer curled Roy's lips. *"I don't need no help with nothin'."*

"Roy, do you know what happens to you when you black out?"

Roy's eyes narrowed as he looked directly into the camera. *"Hey, that damn thing's on!"*

"Yes. It's a video camera."

"I know's what it is. Why youse got a video camera on me? What is this?"

"I want to film what we say to each other, Roy. Does that bother you?"

His gravelly voice deepened with new suspicion. *"What youse want me on film for?"*

"Just to record our talks. I'll show you the video later if you'd like."

Roy suddenly lunged forward, his eyes darting around the room like a wild animal looking for a way out of his cage. *"Who's watching me now?"*

"No one is—" Damian began, but Roy didn't give him time to finish. He leaped suddenly from the lounge chair and disappeared out of camera range.

The sound track was still picking up the conversation between the men in another part of the room.

"I'd like to talk to Lee now," Damian was saying in his calm, steady tone.

"So talk to him," Roy's angry, raspy tone answered. *"I'm gettin' outta here. Hey! Let go my arm!"*

Kay could hear what was obviously a scuffle. She was so caught up in the scene that she was now sitting on the edge of her seat.

Damian's voice on the sound track had risen and become commanding and insistent. *"Lee, wake up! Lee!"*

The scuffling sounds abruptly stopped. Several long seconds of absolute quiet passed. Kay found herself literally holding her breath.

"Why are you grasping my arm, Dr. Steele?" Lee's bland voice finally asked.

Kay's lungs deflated with a relieved sigh and she settled back on the couch.

"Lee, would you return to the chair, please?" Damian's taped voice said, amazingly calm and steady.

"Yes, of course. I didn't realize I had gotten up."

Lee came back into the camera's view and he sat down. Kay could immediately see the difference in him. The bland expression was back on his face, the sneering wrinkles gone, his shoulders unhunched, his hands open and relaxed. Even his eyes seemed to have grown larger and, she could swear, no longer seemed bloodshot. The change from Roy to Lee was as astonishing as it had been from Lee to Roy. Once again an icy chill shot between Kay's shoulder blades.

"What can you tell me about Roy Nye?" Damian asked when Lee had settled himself.

"Roy Nye?" Lee repeated in his typically cool, bland tone. *"I can't tell you anything, Dr. Steele. I don't know any Roy Nye."*

DAMIAN COULD TELL from Kay's rhythmic tapping of her foot and the tightness of her mouth that she was still reeling in response to the lightning-fast switches from Lee to Roy and back again during the first one-hour session. He knew she needed time to assimilate what she was seeing and try to understand it before seeing any more. He pressed the stop button on the remote and turned to face her.

"Ready to ask some questions?"

"Yes, but I don't know where to start."

He smiled. "That's a good beginning."

She flashed him a quick look. "And that's something only a psychologist could get away with saying."

His hand moved forward to finger a small honey-gold strand of hair that had escaped onto her neck. "And that's something only a lawyer could get upset about."

His finger captured the silky strand. Or the silky strand captured his finger. He wasn't sure which. She didn't seem to notice. Her mind was obviously still struggling with her impressions of the taped session.

"Roy's accent and syntax—everything about his speech seems so different from Lee's. He even seems less intelligent."

"In many ways, he was less intelligent."

A short silence ensued during which Kay seemed to be mulling over his words. "Did you ever find out when Roy was born?" she finally asked.

"I surmised it after a while."

"Surmised it?"

"The individual I treated didn't know when he was born."

"You mean Roy didn't know?"

"Neither personality remembered."

"So the few personal memories Lee had didn't include a date or place of birth?"

"That's right."

"What specifically does Lee remember from those early times?"

"Being in an attic. Playing with numbers. Sleeping. Watching things happen in the outside world through his window."

"But that was really just a mental attic, wasn't it?"

"Yes, but a totally real attic to Lee. That's where he lived from the moment of his birth."

"Didn't you tell me that it was the Roy personality who emerged in childhood to handle the abuse that was meted out by the man his mother lived with?"

"Yes."

"Well, then, why did Roy continue to deny a childhood and parents on that tape?"

"Because he was never a child."

"Well, now I'm even more confused."

"Remember Roy's comment that he had sprouted full grown?"

"Yes."

"Do you also remember your Greek mythology?"

"Are you referring to the myth about a god springing forth full grown from the head of Zeus?"

"Yes. Roy's phraseology was quite astute, considering his limited intellect and vocabulary."

"You've lost me, again. If there is a beginning to this, I wish you'd start at it."

Damian smiled. "All right. From the beginning. As a small child, this individual was being constantly terrorized and brutalized. His mother was too weak or maybe too indifferent to come to his aid. There was no one he could turn to. He could not physically escape, so he mentally escaped. He split into two new personalities, Lee and Roy."

"What happened to the child's original personality?"

"I'm not certain. I never found a trace of it during the time I treated Lee."

"What do you think might have happened to it?"

"I believe that like the rough diamond, LeRoy disappeared with the cleaving into the two finished parts of Lee and Roy."

"When did Lee and Roy appear?"

"From what I can gather, when the child was physically about two."

"Then Roy *was* there as a child."

"No. Roy came to life as an adult identity in the small child's mind."

"Now wait a minute. How is it possible for a child's mind to give birth to an adult identity?"

"As little as we understand about outer space, Kay, it is a lot compared to what we understand about the human mind. We don't know where personality originates or how or when it becomes fixed and unalterable. We don't even really know what it is. These incredible identities that multiples create can point us to some fascinating signposts on the mind's outskirts. But we still have an immense inner galaxy to explore."

"Well, before I go trekking into the unknown, I need some logic under my feet. Where was this Roy personality when Lee was being abused?"

"Lee wasn't being abused. Lee was tucked away in a mental attic, sleeping and watching the world pass by, but not affected by it or interacting with it, remember?"

Kay shook her head as though trying to get her disjointed thoughts to settle into place. "Right. I forgot. Lee grew up in a mental attic. So it was Roy who took the abuse, right?"

"No."

"No?"

"It's time for you to see the next tape. This is Roy and his first memories. It might help you to understand what I have to tell you."

ROY FLOATED UP to the ceiling of the shed, crossed his legs and lit a cigarette. He inhaled deeply and then blew out two perfect smoke rings. They wobbled through the air, expanding and dissipating until they broke apart and drifted away.

Finally, that damn, whiny kid had shut up. About time. His ears were still ringing from the kid's clamoring every night. He was getting really tired of that wimpy little brat.

The kid was just a skinny, runny-nosed, pain in the butt. He deserved everything he got. His old lady, too, for that matter. What a pair of losers. He didn't know why he wasted his time with them.

If she ever opened her yap again about his cigarette ashes burning holes in the carpet or starting fires in the bedding, he'd knock the rest of her teeth out.

He took another drag on his cigarette and entertained himself by blowing some more smoke rings. These spurted out with such momentum, they smashed into a spiderweb in the shed's corner.

He watched the spider come running out, all eight legs spinning. It spewed out a thin thread and began to rappel itself to the safety of the earthen floor.

Roy's tight lips drew down into a sneer. He held out the lit end of his cigarette to burn the spider's slim lifeline.

"You nonsmokers are really starting to piss me off."

As the spider fell, Roy began to laugh, a hollow, tuneless bellow that ricocheted off the ceiling until it totally filled the shed.

Chapter Six

"Damian, what was that all about?" Kay asked.

"Roy's earliest memories."

"But his descriptions sounded so bizarre, particularly that thing with the cigarette rings and the spider. Were they drug-induced or alcoholic hallucinations?"

"No."

"Then what in heaven's name were they?"

"Kay, from the very beginning of his existence, Roy floated on a mental ceiling, generally with a cigarette in one hand, sometimes a drink in the other."

"He was smoking and drinking? On a ceiling? At two years old?"

"I know it sounds strange. But, remember, all these things were happening in his head and perfectly real to him. Roy *knew* himself to be an adult. He dissociated himself from the child's body when it was subjected to abuse and lived a separate life from it."

"Floating on a ceiling. Good Lord. Who would believe this?"

"Maybe only a psychologist trained in multiple personalities, or other multiples who have experienced similarly strange states of altered awareness."

"I know you warned me I might not understand what I was seeing, but I never expected...this. There has to be some logic here somewhere. Damn, I'm a lawyer. Logic is what I live by."

"The human mind is not always logical, Kay. In my field, there aren't hard-and-fast rules to go on a lot of times."

"Then what do you go on?"

"At times simply on what I hope to be right. Multiples have performed what is tantamount to mental miracles to survive horrendous childhood abuse. What a psychologist does to treat these patients sometimes seems more like voodoo than science."

She shook her head. "Having to cope with such illogic and imprecision must drive you crazy."

"Crazy?" He smiled. "On the contrary. It's what keeps me sane."

She looked at him for a long moment with other questions in her eyes that had nothing to do with psychology or the case, and everything to do with being a woman thoroughly intrigued by the man she was with.

Damian had always known he could control himself around a woman. But looking into those blueberry eyes filled with so much candid and curious interest, inhaling the sweet scent of her skin and hair and feeling his body's immediate and urgent arousal, he wondered if he'd been kidding himself. His stomach muscles tightened involuntarily as a hot poker of desire stabbed through him.

He deliberately stopped playing with her silky honey-gold hair and leaned back. He harshly reminded himself that she was off limits, repeating just that several times in rapid succession.

Finally, she looked away. He breathed a sigh of both relief and profound regret.

"All right, answer me this, Damian. If Lee was in his mental attic and Roy was smoking and drinking up on his mental ceiling, who was conscious in the child's body as it was being abused?"

"No one."

"No one? How can that be possible?"

"Roy was the caretaker of the child's body when it was growing up. This arrangement worked because the abuse didn't bother him as he never accepted it as happening to him. He floated up on his mental ceiling and the child's small body went numb."

"Leaving no personality to have to endure the pain?"

"That's right. Although, as you may have surmised from his comments during the sessions, Roy was plagued by the echoes of the child's pain."

"You mean that crying he spoke of?"

"Yes."

"How could he hear crying from pain that wasn't being felt?"

"You're looking for neat, logical explanations again, Kay. I'm sorry, but I don't have any to offer you."

"Did Lee ever hear the crying?"

"No."

Kay sighed. "The personality of a child growing up in an attic shielded from emotion. Another personality born full grown floating on a ceiling and full of violent emotion. Memory echoes of a crying child who mercifully could no longer feel any pain. This gets more and more bizarre."

"And yet, Lee's case is relatively simple compared to those of other multiple personalities. There are MPD individuals who possess twenty, forty, eighty, even as high as one hundred different personality fragments or alters, as they're often called."

Kay shook her head as she raised her fingers to massage her temples. "Dear heavens, and I'm having trouble handling just two."

"If it makes you feel any better, so did I, Kay. So did I."

She gave him a small smile before she went on. "I can almost understand an unemotional Lee personality, protected from the awful reality of the abuse. But I can't understand this Roy personality. He seems so uncaring and heartless. The more I learn about him, the harder it is for me to understand how the mind of a poor abused child could have created a part so abhorrent—so inhuman."

Damian was uncomfortable with her pain. Too uncomfortable for his own good. He turned more fully toward her, took her hands down from her temples and held them gently.

"Probably one of the human mind's most illogical acts occurs when it finds itself embracing that which it most abhors."

She looked up at him, her eyes cloudy and confused. "That which it most abhors?"

"Kay, you see it all the time. The abused child grows into the adult abuser and repeats the repugnant pattern."

"But, Damian, that can't be true in this case. This child didn't grow up to be Roy. You said yourself that Roy sprang full grown from the mind of the child when he was only two."

"It happens sometimes to children forced to endure constant and unspeakable abuse and who are told by their abusers that they deserve what they get. A part of their mind begins to believe they must deserve it. It's that part that recreates the persecutor personality."

"The persecutor personality?"

"Best way I can explain it is by likening the process to that old adage, 'If you can't beat them, join them.'"

"Wait a minute. You can't mean—"

"Yes, Kay. Roy was a recreation of the child's real-life abuser."

"My God. The child's own abuser internalized in his mind. This is so damn...tragic."

His arm came to rest lightly across her shoulders. He understood how difficult this had been for her. Not just to accept mentally, but emotionally. He had wanted to spare her. She had insisted. Seeing the look on her face now, he wished he had gone with his instincts and refused.

Particularly since he knew she hadn't seen or heard anywhere near the worst yet.

He gave her shoulders a light shake, intent on breaking up the sadness in her face, finding he could not bear to see it anymore. "Look, Kay, I'm starving. And I have to warn you that we beasts get unruly if not fed frequently."

Kay's eyes dropped to her watch. "Eight o'clock already. I hadn't realized. Is there someplace around here where we can get something quick before resuming?"

"Only place I know of is right down the hall in the kitchen."

Her eyes looked up into his. "Are you offering to cook?"

"Offering to cook? No. Offering to slap together a couple of roast beef sandwiches, yes. Of course, I'd be happy to step aside if you'd care to razzle-dazzle me with your culinary skills."

A smile relaxed the tightness that had gathered around her mouth. "What culinary skills? To me, cooking *is* slapping together a roast beef sandwich."

Damian smiled back as he slipped his hand into hers and helped her to her feet. He continued to hold her hand for no other reason than that it felt so very good in his.

"What would you prefer, beer, wine, a cocktail? Dinner might be simple, but I'm not a half-bad bartender."

"I'd love a glass of milk if you have it. Nonfat or low fat, preferably."

"Milk?"

She smiled in response to the incredulity of his tone. "Yeah, you know, that white stuff full of bone-building calcium. We small-framed, Northern European types have to guard against getting osteoporosis."

"All right. A glass of milk for dinner and then afterward a nice liqueur—"

"Afraid not. Alcohol isn't good for bones or for keeping mentally alert. There's work to do, remember?"

"Then a coffee liqueur. The coffee will counteract the alcohol."

"No, coffee is bad for bones, too."

He curled her hand into the crook of his arm and let out a dramatic sigh. "Ms. Beauty, whatever do you do for fun when you're not snitching flowers from a beast's garden?"

"I'm snitching roast beef sandwiches from his kitchen. Come on. I'm suddenly quite hungry. And I'm warning you, we lawyers can get unruly if we're not fed frequently."

He chuckled as he led the way into a large cavern of a room that he used to call the pit as a kid, because the stone of its floor and walls had been blackened by the coal stove that used to be in the far corner. Despite the fact that it had been replaced long ago with an electric range and other modern appliances, the kitchen still seemed like a pit.

He switched on the overhead fluorescents, which he had had installed just the month before in hopes of eliminating some of the gloom.

"The light doesn't help much," Kay said, mirroring his own reaction.

"There's so much that has yet to be done to this old place just to make it livable."

"Have you ever thought about tearing down this dungeon and starting over again?"

"That, my dear Ms. Kellogg, is blasphemy. I grew up in this . . . ah . . . dungeon."

"Your parents lived with your grandparents?"

"No."

He purposely turned away from her questioning eyes and quickly went on. "You have to admit that for a boy with a fertile imagination, its endless dark corridors make excellent hiding places for evil sorcerers and fire-breathing dragons."

"Well, before any come slinking into this kitchen, point me in the direction of the raw materials and let's get started on those sandwiches."

Damian was waving toward the cupboard where the bread was kept, when he was interrupted by the ringing of the telephone. He answered with a relaxed hello.

He didn't stay relaxed for long.

"I knew you were home now. Just called to let you know," the breathy voice on the phone whispered.

"Who is this?" Damian demanded.

"You'll find out when it's time. But it's not time now. Besides, it pleases me for you to just worry for a while. It pleases me very, very much."

A dial tone blared in Damian's ear.

KAY KNEW something was wrong when his telephone conversation ended so abruptly after his demanding to know who was calling. She also suspected who was on the line.

"It was the person who left the earlier message on the answering machine. The one with that strange, breathless voice, wasn't it?" she asked.

"Yes."

"Have you been getting a lot of calls from that kook?"

"The phone has been ringing off the hook since Fedora Nye's first tearful interview last week. Most yell obscenities. But this one—this breathless one—is different. More disturbing."

"Damn, I'm sorry, Damian. I should have warned you that the crazies come crawling out of the woodwork when a case is high-profile."

"Not a problem. I anticipated it and let the answering machine accept the brunt of the abuse."

He lifted a loaf of bread out of the cupboard and pitched it toward her. She surprised herself by catching it.

He reached into the refrigerator for the roast beef, lettuce and jars of pickles, mustard and mayonnaise. He gathered them into his arms and started for the butcher-block table in the middle of the cavernous kitchen.

"As soon as I get in touch with all my patients and give them my private number, I'll have the listed line disconnected and get rid of the breathy-voiced caller."

Kay opened a couple of drawers until she found the silverware. "You don't feel uncomfortable giving your patients your private number and seeing them in your home?"

He opened the jars of condiments. "You mean because of all the crazies I treat?"

She lavished lettuce, mayonnaise, mustard and pickles on both slices of the bread.

"I don't mean to imply that all people who seek out a psychologist do so because they're dangerous, any more than all people who seek out a lawyer do so because they're criminals. But, I have to tell you, *I* wouldn't have wanted to be alone in the same room with the Roy character."

He smiled at the emphasis on her words as he laid thin pieces of roast beef on both of their prepared slices of bread. "I'm continuing to see only my most critical cases. The rest I've referred to colleagues."

"Still, isn't it dangerous? And don't you find the professional distance compromised?"

"I agree it's neither professional nor smart to conduct one's practice out of one's home. Truth is, this arrangement has been forced on me by some recent, unforeseen circumstances."

"You don't mean publicity from the trial?"

"No."

"What then?"

"I needed to vacate my previous offices somewhat quickly. I have yet to find suitable space in which to relocate."

"What forced you out of your previous offices?"

He paused before he answered, seeming to focus all his concentration on putting the final touches on his sandwich.

"An affair with the psychologist who shared them with me."

Kay heard a funny buzzing sound in her ears as she stared at Damian in the seconds following that unexpected admission. Several surprising reactions and questions popped into her mind. The one she ended up voicing surprised her most of all.

"I can't believe you'd do that, Damian."

His answer was even more of a surprise, particularly since it was delivered with a laugh and a candid look. "Hard for me to believe, too. Just goes to show you, I can be as big an idiot as the next guy. Even bigger."

She liked the good-humored sincerity in his laugh. For all Damian's ability, confidence and understanding of the human condition, he didn't place himself on an intellectual or emotional step above the rest of struggling humankind. Rather, he clearly saw himself as just a fellow struggler.

Kay was finding that she liked someone who viewed life—and himself—this way. She also liked looking at his rugged face when he said these things. She liked hearing the intelligence and simple sincerity in his deep voice. She liked far too much about this man. Far too much.

She pressed her sandwich together, cut it in half and reminded herself that she was a lawyer and Damian was her client. But she couldn't quite achieve the nonchalance she was trying for in her tone. "So how did this affair happen?"

Damian walked over to the refrigerator to retrieve the milk. He returned with two full glasses and a bowl of freshly washed blueberries, strawberries, raspberries and giant blackberries. They sat opposite each other on the bar stools around the butcher-block table. He didn't pick up his sandwich right away. Instead, he popped a bright wild strawberry into his mouth and looked directly at Kay.

"For the last three years, Dr. Priscilla Payton and I shared the administrative costs of office space and clerical staff. Our relationship was as professional colleagues and casual friends. We discussed cases and shared a few personal items over occasional lunches."

"Until?" Kay prodded.

"Until one afternoon when I walked into her adjoining office to find her crying. In the three years I had known her, I'd never seen Priscilla cry. I didn't think it possible. I was rather taken aback."

"What had made her cry?"

"She had her final divorce decree in her hands. Like her, her ex-husband was thirty-two. Only, unlike her, he was still in college. He had several degrees; he just didn't want to look for a job. She had gotten tired of supporting a perennial student. She had initiated the divorce. Still, the finality of it hit her hard."

"Is that what she said?"

"She wouldn't say anything at first, just sat there and cried. That was the same day that the insurance company's lawyer told me he was going to settle Mrs. Nye's suit out of court and, if I didn't like it, the insurance company was just going to wash their hands of me."

"So you were feeling pretty rotten, too."

"I'd certainly had better days. Anyway, I told Tim, our receptionist, to call and cancel whatever appointments Priscilla and I had and then to take the rest of the day off himself. Then I dragged Priscilla out to my car and drove us to the nearest bar."

"And had a few."

"And had quite a few. Black Russians. Doubles. I told her about the Nye case and the insurance company. After the first two black Russians, she stopped crying and told me about the divorce. After another two, we both started laughing, and I don't remember what we talked about. After six of those doubles, we were seeing double. There was no way I could drive. I saw her home in a taxi. I started to leave her place and she started to kiss me."

Kay tried not to sound disappointed. She tried to sound unaffected, unemotional and understanding. "So being a gentleman, you couldn't refuse—"

"So being a gentleman," he interrupted with that direct look of his, "I pulled away and told her that it was just the drink and the emotional letdown of the divorce, and that I wasn't staying."

"But she overcame your objections?"

"She told me the drink had nothing to do with it and the only letdown she was experiencing was a letdown of her previous inhibitions. She said she needed me to stay the night."

"So you stayed."

"So I stayed. The next morning, I woke up with a horrible headache that got progressively worse as Priscilla brought me eggs and bacon, served along with a plateful of love-and-marriage talk."

"Love and marriage?"

"Her assumption that my spending the night with her meant I loved her was in itself a very unwelcome surprise. But when she talked about our getting married, that really put me in shock. I had told her several times during our casual lunches over the years that I never intended to marry."

"You don't believe in marriage?"

"For some people, it's great. I'm just not one of those people."

"You've tried it?"

"You don't have to jump off a cliff to know the landing won't be pleasant."

So to him, marriage was like jumping off a cliff? No wonder he was still a bachelor at thirty-four.

"Anyway," he continued, "I told her I didn't love her and reiterated that I had no desire or intention of getting married."

"What did she say?"

"She laughed and told me I'd change my mind after we spent more time together."

"To which you replied?"

"I told her I had no intention of our spending any more personal time together. I apologized for allowing the drink to cloud my judgment. I totally accepted the blame for the inappropriateness of our sleeping together. I promised her it would never happen again. Then I left as fast as I could."

"I take it this incident is what later precipitated the severance of your shared offices?"

"And not a whole lot later. Only a few hours after my leaving her place, she stormed into my office and accused me of lying to her until I got what I wanted and then dumping her."

"She couldn't have really believed that?"

"I'm certain that during the time I left her place that morning and the time she appeared in my office, she'd convinced herself of it. She was livid. She screamed her accusations at the top of her voice. They could hear her all over the building. The more I tried to get her to lower her voice, the louder she yelled. My other multiple-personality patient, Bette Boson, was waiting in the reception area. She fled. Tim, our shared receptionist, fled. And still Priscilla raged. I finally fled. The next day, I began packing to move out."

"You never suspected Priscilla would respond that way? Even after knowing her for three years?"

He picked up his sandwich and looked at Kay over the top of it. "I would have given you any odds against it. Which only goes to prove that we're all mysteries just waiting to unfold. Who knows what any of us might be capable of given the right set of circumstances?"

His words echoed strangely in Kay's ears as she gazed into the sudden hard glint of his eyes. For a moment, she had a glimpse of something very dark and very deadly. She felt an inexplicable rise of the peach fuzz on her arms.

Then he winked at her as he licked off an excess gob of mustard escaping through the crack in the crusts. The quick glimpse of that dark side faded like a sudden summer rain.

He was just a ruggedly attractive and far-too-charming man biting into a roast beef sandwich.

She put as much professional control in her voice as she could at the moment. To her dismay, it wasn't a whole lot. "I could never accept such a philosophy."

"Philosophy?"

"The way you talk about everyone being a mystery in so nonchalant a tone. If I couldn't be sure of a person, particularly someone I was close to, it would drive me crazy. Are all you psychologists so irritatingly tolerant of uncertainty?"

He smiled that wonderful charming smile of his that made her stomach jump in several different directions all at the same time. "And you talk about psychologists with so much damnably delicious pique. Are all you lawyers so enticingly aroused without your logic?"

The heat in his words and in his eyes poured through Kay like hot honey. Every ligament around every bone in her body threatened to liquefy at once.

She took a big bite of her sandwich, both because she could think of no coherent retort and because she was afraid if she didn't put something in her mouth soon, she might be tempted to lean forward and kiss this entirely too charming beast with the dash of mustard on his chin.

LEE NYE OPENED his eyes to suddenly find himself throwing a baseball in a grassy park on a bright, sunny afternoon. He was surprised and just a bit disturbed. Nothing looked familiar. Not the rolling hills of grass. Not the full, green leaves of the alder trees. Not the boys yelling insults at one another on the nearby baseball diamond as one of them came up to bat.

How had he come to be here? Why had he come? What was going on?

A rangy-looking black-and-brown mutt shot forward after the thrown ball. Lee watched it in a sort of stunned fascination as it dashed purposefully across the grass and scooped the ball into its mouth. He envied it. It seemed to know precisely what it was doing here.

The rangy mutt tore back toward him at full speed, stopping just short of his shoes, dropping the drool-washed sphere and wagging its tail like a happy flag.

Lee bent down to pick up the baseball, although he wasn't quite sure why he would want to. That was when he noticed that he was wearing shorts and walking shoes. But how could he be? He was certain he hadn't put on shorts or walking shoes this morning.

"Hey, give us back our ball," a young voice yelled from behind him.

Lee slowly turned around to find himself confronted by an obviously irate eight-year-old with a catcher's mitt hanging from his hand on his less-than-patient, shoved-out hip. About fifteen feet away, another youngster with another catcher's mitt waited with an expression of similar displeasure on his young face.

"And give me back my dog," a girl of no more than six demanded as she stomped up and dropped next to the mangy mutt and put an arm around it possessively, as though Lee had been trying to steal it from her.

"I don't want your ball or your dog," he said calmly.

"Then why you got 'em?" the little girl challenged.

Lee dropped the ball. He turned from it and the dog and the children and walked quickly away. He headed up the slope toward what he could see of a parking lot. He hoped he'd find his car there. He hoped he'd figure out where he was.

"A big guy like that saying he wanted to play with us. We'd better tell Mom when we get home," one of the boys commented behind him. "There are laws against guys like that bugging kids. You know what he really wanted, don't you?"

The boy's voice descended into a conspiratorial mumble. *Guys like that? What he really wanted?* Lee knew he didn't want anything. What did that annoying child mean?

And what was he doing here in this park full of kids and dogs, his two least favorite things of all?

He glanced down at the calendar watch on his wrist and got an uncomfortable jolt. Sunday. One-thirty. The last thing he remembered was coming out of Ms. Kellogg's law office on Saturday afternoon around four.

And now it was one-thirty on Sunday? Could this be true?

It must be true. He was losing time again. Over the last few weeks, he'd begun to suspect as much. He would be doing something, and the next thing he knew, he'd be on the other side of the office or in another room of his apartment, doing something else. But it had seemed like only a few minutes here and there, and he'd told himself his mind had wandered.

But he knew his mind hadn't wandered today.

He hadn't been in his mind today. He hadn't been in his mind since yesterday.

Roy couldn't be back, could he?

No. Of course not. That was just as absurd as thinking that he was trying to steal some kid's baseball or some other kid's rangy mutt.

Wasn't it?

Perhaps he'd best call Dr. Steele and tell him about the lost time. Yes. It would be the sensible thing to do.

The decision suddenly rose into the attic in Lee's mind. Then both it and Lee once again disappeared from the sunny day.

A ROUGH, SQUARE HAND shot out quickly to snatch Dr. Van Pratt's article right out of Kay's hands.

"Damian, we have a million things to do this afternoon in preparation for your trial tomorrow," she protested. "I have neither the time nor inclination for this...kayaking thing."

She watched him completely ignore her protest as he slipped her light suit jacket off the clothes tree in the corner of her office and held it out to her.

"It's a beautiful Sunday afternoon in Seattle, and I refuse to spend it in your office as we've spent the last six days and nearly every night. I need a break."

She took her jacket from his outstretched hand but immediately hung it up again. "You go then. I'll stay here and—"

"And what? Waste another fifteen minutes reading a page you've already read?"

Damn, she wished he wasn't so observant. And persistent. She also wished he didn't smell so clean and look so tanned and healthy and appealing in that short-sleeved, mint-green T-shirt that emphasized rather than hid the impressive physique it hugged. No wonder it had taken her fifteen minutes to reread that last page. He was more than distracting. A lot more.

"I don't know anything about kayaking," she continued to protest. "I've never even seen a real one."

"You saw that model in my office, remember? It's shaped like a long, slim canoe, made for just one person. You'll love paddling it."

"If it's made for just one person, what do you need me along for?"

"Company. You don't want me to get lonely, do you?"

"I burn in the sun."

"We'll douse you in sunscreen."

"I can't swim," she admitted.

"How lucky then that we're not going swimming."

"I'm not all that fond of water—"

"Kayaking is great exercise."

"I use a treadmill every morning and a rowing machine three times a week. I don't need any more exercise."

"You need fresh air in your lungs."

He retrieved her suit jacket and put it back in her hands. Then he grabbed her shoulders lightly and spun her around toward the door. She reacted to his touch, once again, with that crazy warm streak zigzagging down the back of her thighs. She knew she couldn't blame the sensation on too-high heels anymore. She didn't even have heels on today.

His strong hands held her shoulders firmly. She twisted her neck to look up at him and tried to hold on to her reason. "Look, Damian, your financial well-being—not to mention your professional integrity—are both on the line here. Have you forgotten that?"

"No, I haven't forgotten."

His rugged face was smiling. Yet the knowing glint in his eyes told her he realized only too well what was at stake. And it told her something else, too. He was doing this as much for her as for himself. Her resistance began to crumble as she spoke after a nervous sigh.

"I have to warn you, I'm terrible at sports. I always have been. Only course in school I ever got a C in was physical education, and they gave you that grade even if all you did was show up."

"Don't worry, I grade on the curve."

"Who else is included in this curve?"

"All the other lawyers I've taken kayaking."

"You take all your lawyers kayaking?"

He exhaled in dramatic weariness. "Only the exasperating ones who can't swim and who I have a chance of drowning."

She was still resisting his push toward the door, though not too strongly anymore—just enough to show him she was not succumbing too easily.

"Are all you psychologists so pushy?"

"Are all you lawyers so stubborn?"

"I know I'm going to regret this."

"You're going to love it. Soon, when another beautiful summer day like today comes along, or even a snowy winter one, you'll automatically play truant, tie your kayak to the roof rack of your car and head out to Lake Union for a paddle."

"I'm sure I'd never neglect my work for—"

"Never be totally sure of anything, Kay. Life's more enjoyable when it can surprise you. And it can be even more fun when you end up surprising yourself."

"Is that sage advice from some psychological theory?"

"No, it's sage advice from my grandfather."

"My clothes—"

"We'll stop by your place so you can change."

"This is crazy. When I think of all the work—"

"So don't think about it. We're taking this afternoon off and we're going to have some sun, some exercise and some fun."

"But why kayaking? Why not some nice, safe sport like golf?"

"Life wasn't meant to be safe, Kay. Life was meant to be exciting."

"More sage advice from your grandfather?"

"No, last Friday night's fortune cookie."

She smiled in spite of herself. "Where do we get these kayaks? Can we rent them at the lake?"

"I always bring my own. I have two foldable ones downstairs."

"You brought them here? You planned this?"

"One must always be prepared for life."

"Psychological theory, grandfather or fortune cookie?"

"Boy Scout motto. Now stop stalling. We're going. And that's all there is to it."

She sighed in good-natured defeat. "I'm going to bill these hours to you."

He smiled far too charmingly. "I had no doubt you would."

"AT FIRST, it might feel a little tippy, like when you first tried to balance on a bicycle," Damian explained as he eased Kay's craft into the water.

"Tippy as in tip over?" Kay said, her tone clearly raised in some trepidation.

"Don't worry. I'm going to hold it steady at the back in order to give you a chance to get your balance."

"Oh, good. Training wheels."

Damian smiled. "Not for long, so concentrate on getting your balance quickly or else you'll find yourself learning to swim the hard way."

Once again, she sighed for dramatic emphasis. "No mistaking you for Sir Galahad, that's for sure."

"I thought you didn't want to be treated like a baby?"

"Do all you psychologists listen to everything people say so you can use it on them later?"

"Do all of you lawyers make such difficult students?"

"I haven't seen any teaching yet. When is it going to begin?"

Damian smiled. She could certainly hold her own in a verbal exchange. And despite all her comments to the contrary, he could tell she was excited and expectant. As he suspected, she needed this mental and physical break. They both did.

"Is this thing you call a spray deck supposed to circle my waist so snugly?"

"Yes, it'll help keep you dry, just like the paddling jacket."

"So what now, Professor?" she prodded.

The sun glistened through her honey-gold hair, and even the sparkle of the water paled next to the blueberry of her eyes. He knew what he'd like to do now. He'd like to forget all about being a gentleman. He took a deep breath. But what he would do was teach her how to use a kayak.

"Okay, you remember how I showed you to paddle?"

"Yes."

"Now, once you begin paddling, you'll be moving forward in a straight line. That's what a kayak is designed to do."

She tried two swipes with the paddle and her craft immediately began to wobble.

"You sure this kayak knows about this straight-line business?"

He laughed. "Don't worry, when I let go, your forward motion will help you to maintain your balance. Just like a bicycle, remember?"

"What if I don't maintain my balance? What if I start to tip over?"

"Slap the flat side of your paddle blade against the water's surface you're tipping toward and just push yourself back up."

"*Just* push myself back up. Oh, sure."

"Part of the fun is getting dunked once in a while."

"Fun? You obviously have a strange idea about what's fun."

"Don't you consider anything but work fun? Where do your dates take you?"

"I haven't had much time for dating recently."

"Because you let your work crowd out any social life."

"Not true. I manage to fit in a social life. I was even in love once a couple of years back."

"What happened?"

"He was an attorney. We went up against each other in a case. I won. He couldn't accept it. I finally realized he could never really accept me."

"That's a shame."

"Not really. He wasn't the marrying kind of man, anyway. Our relationship could never have led to the kind of commitment I'd want, the kind that includes marriage and children. No point in continuing down a dead-end road. Hey, I think I'm getting the hang of this."

She was, too. Despite all her protests and denials about physical capacity, her balance proved excellent and she did quite well. Soon Damian settled himself in his own kayak and paddled alongside. He kept them on a straight path across a shallow end of the lake, since her turning still needed some work and he wanted to build up her confidence first.

It was a lovely afternoon, one of those rare but perfect seventy-degree summer days in Seattle, when tourists got sucked into the illusion that the cool, clear, clean skies could be had all year long and made the mistake of contacting real-estate agents.

Perhaps because the perfect weather was so rare, this was Damian's favorite view of Lake Union, beneath a blinding sun, with the distant hum of speedboats, and dotted with canoes and kayaks and sleepy white sailboats.

Damian loved the feeling of freedom and solitude he got from gliding through the water in the one-person craft. It was alone with the rhythmic paddling that he felt most in touch with the world and with himself. It was alone with the breeze clearing out the clutter of life's trivia that he always felt most in control.

But he was glad he wasn't alone today. The surprise and pleasure that had erupted on Kay's face when she had kept her balance, the eagerness with which she now paddled beside him whisked away any need he had for solitude.

There was a flush to her cheeks that had never been there before. A very becoming flush. This was all new and exciting for her, and he was finding the pleasure she was deriving from it more than infectious.

"Do you do this every Sunday?" she asked.

"Every morning," he answered. "It's a perfect workout for mind and body."

Her voice raised to be heard over a powerboat coming too near. "You were out here this morning?"

"At dawn. It's always the best time."

"You go kayaking at dawn? Every morning? Even when it's raining? Snowing?"

He found himself having to raise his voice, too, as the annoyingly loud boat engine came closer. "Rain and snow aren't a problem. Although a head wind of more than twenty knots can prove troublesome. The kayak originated along some of the coldest coasts of the world precisely because it can be used in most any kind of weather."

"Well, I don't know about when it's raining, but beneath the sun it's certainly..."

Damian frowned in irritation as the now far-too-loud speedboat engine drowned out the rest of Kay's sentence. He stopped paddling to turn around, intending to wave off the idiot behind the wheel, who obviously wasn't watching where he was going.

But Damian's wave did not deter the driver of the speedboat. Quite the contrary. After seeing his wave, the driver deliberately accelerated the boat directly toward him and Kay.

Even if Damian could have shouted a warning loud enough to be heard over the deafening engine, he had no idea what the warning could be. There was no way to out-paddle or outmaneuver a speedboat—not one heading directly for them at full throttle.

Chapter Seven

Damian did the only thing he could think of. He shoved his kayak between Kay's and the speedboat.

The driver of the speedboat waited until the last second—the very last second—before swerving to avoid colliding with the small crafts in his path. Damian grabbed the sides of the cockpit as the force of the powerful wave generated by the boat's deep wake slammed into the side of his craft. It hit his kayak like a closed fist against a paper bag.

Damian's kayak flew into the air. The next second, Damian found himself head down in the water, the kayak floating above him.

He knew what he had to do and he wasted no time in doing it. He strengthened his grasp on the sides of the cockpit and somersaulted his weight forward. The pointed, dartlike kayak sliced a half circle through the water, flipped and landed right side up. Damian's eyes immediately searched the water.

The strong, undulating waves of the speedboat's wake still spewed milky-white crests over much of the surface. He blinked his eyes against the spray, looking for Kay. But she was nowhere to be seen.

"Kay!" he yelled, the sound echoing off the waves and pounding through his head.

There was no answer. He knew he had to find her quickly. He paddled frantically toward where he judged she had been when the brunt of the wake hit, every beat of his heart registering an eternity.

"Kay! Kay!" he continued to yell.

Finally, he saw her kayak. Floating bottom end up.

Like him, she'd been capsized. But unlike him, she of course didn't know how to somersault to right her craft. She was underwater, unable to release herself from the tight fit of the spray deck.

Damian whirled the paddle through the water, propelling his kayak forward, slicing through the waves, desperate to reach her in time. The instant he approached her capsized craft, he grabbed hold of the end and, with every ounce of his strength, he sharply twisted the hull. The kayak flipped over and splashed obediently back on its bottom.

Damian yanked the end toward him until the cockpit was alongside his.

She was hunched over. He grabbed her shoulders. His heart was stabbing him so hard, it felt as though it were puncturing holes in his rib cage.

"Kay? Kay? Are you all right?"

In answer, she pitched her head over the side of her craft and coughed up water.

She was alive. Alive!

He held her shoulders, feeling them shake and shiver. Her breath wheezed loudly through her lungs in what sounded like painful gasps.

He wrapped his arms around her, rested her head gently against his chest and rocked her as she fought to fill her lungs. The awkward position nearly capsized them both. But he didn't let her go. He couldn't let her go. His arms wouldn't allow him to let her go.

He began to curse the speedboat driver with every foul word and phrase he had ever heard. As his experience was extensive in this regard, it took some time to get them all out. He needed that time.

Finally, the anger that had grown out of his fear for her subsided, and he felt both their breaths coming more easily.

He released his death grip on her, but still held her to him. He made his voice deliberately low and threatening. "If I ever find that bastard, I'll..."

He knew the imagery his next words described bordered on inspired, even for him. When the spew of obscenities finally abated he took another deep breath.

"He won't get away with that stupid stunt, Kay. Imbeciles like that don't last long. If the authorities don't get him, some other irate kayaker or boater will track him down and shove a paddle up his—"

This time he stopped himself from completing the vulgar sentence and gave her shoulder a hard squeeze. "Sorry. I'm afraid I let my language get a little out of hand there."

She giggled, a wet breathless little laugh that surprised him completely.

"You call that a little out of hand? In the last few minutes, you've expanded my vocabulary considerably."

Her laughter told him more than anything that she was going to be okay. That she was *really* going to be okay. A tightness inside his chest he hadn't even realized was there began to loosen.

His husky voice answered her with a lighter tease, underlying a spurious seriousness. "That's because we psychologists frequently find ourselves in need of the proper technical terminology."

She giggled again. "Proper technical terminology? So that's what that was. Well, you certainly have an impressive command of that proper technical terminology. By the way, in case I haven't mentioned it, thanks for saving my life."

He held her close to him again and kissed the top of her drenched head and then both of her cheeks. He felt so relieved that she was all right and safe in his arms.

His voice was still a little too husky. "Saving your life was the least I could do after endangering it. For someone who doesn't swim, you held your breath...amazingly well."

"That's because we lawyers frequently find ourselves in over our heads."

He smiled, enjoying the playfulness of her retort.

"I hope this...ah...little mishap doesn't put you off kayaking."

Wet and bedraggled, but with a sparkle in her eyes and a lovely pink flush in her recently kissed cheeks, she heaved a deep sigh and stared up into his face.

"Little mishap, huh? Well, I'd say that depends."

"On what?"

"On whether I can expect to have as much *fun* the next time."

Damian laughed then and she laughed with him. He finally released her and they slowly paddled, side by side, back to shore.

But the tension refused to leave his body. He was on guard every stroke. And a nagging unease skipped along on the edges of his alertness. He didn't like the feeling. He couldn't even clearly focus on its cause.

All he knew was that it had something to do with the dark figure behind the wheel of that powerboat, speeding directly at them so deliberately, so deadly.

"KAY, I wish you wouldn't insist on our viewing more of those videotapes of Roy this evening. I can think of a lot more pleasant—"

"No you don't, Damian Steele. We've already wasted the afternoon. My Puritan upbringing will not stand for any more frivolity."

"Frivolity nothing. Kayaking is part play, and play is very serious business for the human psyche."

"And work is a very necessary business if we're going to win this case. Now, I'll just go upstairs to my condo and change out of these damp clothes, and then we'll head for your place."

"Invite me up. I won't bite. Unless it's necessary, of course."

Kay looked over at the lustful lift to his grin and sighed. How could a gal resist a guy like this?

"Okay. Come on up."

He found her contemporary condominium small and uncluttered, everything in its logical place. It was a quiet and secluded unit at the very back of the complex. The view from the windows off the white and cream-colored living room was a lovely one of Elliott Bay. He opened the sliding glass door and stepped out onto the balcony as she disappeared into a back room to change.

She had four different kinds of potted plants flourishing out there, each well tended and scrupulously healthy.

He stepped back into the living room and closed the sliding glass door behind him. He could have predicted everything about her place—except what was peeking out of the room divider on the opposite end of the living room.

She returned dressed in a pale silver pants and blouse set, which gave off a soft powdery look that enhanced her natural femininity. Her hair was still damp, once again drawn up in a silver barrette. She was, as always, lovely.

He kept wondering what that honey-gold hair would look like long and full and dry, cascading over bare shoulders.

As Kay finished buttoning the sleeve of her blouse, she looked up at him, her eyes trying to read the expression on his face. He turned away and pointed to the drums only partially hidden behind the room divider, allowing a smile to draw back his lips.

"Shouldn't those be a flute?"

She laughed. "That's what Mom and Dad would have preferred, no doubt about it. But I love the drums. They have so much energy to them. Just give me a minute to check my messages and we'll be off."

There was just one message. Kay pressed the button.

"It's AJ, Kay. I have more bad news concerning Croghan. Damn, why can't you wear a beeper? Buzz me back the moment you get in."

Kay picked up the receiver and punched in one of her speed-dial numbers.

"Busy," she said to Damian as she hung up the phone. "I wonder how this bad news compares to the last?"

"So why don't you wear a beeper?"

"Oh, I don't know. My one token rebellion to staid lawyering I suppose. Let's go. We'll have to stop by the office so I can pick up my car. I'll try her again there. You ready?"

His eyes went to his wristwatch. "It's nearly six. Why don't we forget those tapes for tonight and go out for an early dinner?"

"No, Damian. You're not going to stall again. Last night after dinner, you said you had phone calls to make to patients that you couldn't put off. This morning, you insisted we had to meet at my office to go over those articles by Dr. Van Pratt your librarian had sent over. This afternoon, it was kayaking. If I didn't know better, I would think that maybe you're just finding excuses to avoid showing me the rest of those tapes. I do know better, don't I?"

Damian came forward and rested his hands lightly on her shoulders. There was genuine concern in his voice that combined with the warmth of his hands to make her feel light-headed.

"Kay, your seeing those tapes will serve no possible good. It might even do you harm."

"Damian, the decision about what I'm prepared to see has to be my decision. I'm not a child, remember?"

For the first time, Kay heard a note of frustration in his deep voice as his hands cupped her shoulders more tightly. "Unfortunately, that is something I can't forget."

She looked up into his ruggedly handsome face and the hot glint that suddenly flashed in his eyes. The warmth of him seeped through her, setting off that crazy streak of sensation through the back of her thighs. She inhaled quickly, trying to catch her breath, trying to keep hold of her thoughts.

"Don't tie my hands while I'm trying to defend you. We've a rough road ahead. You have to let me go with my instincts."

"Your instincts?"

"Yes, my instincts. They tell me I must see those tapes. Aren't you ever prodded by your instincts to do something?"

His left hand slipped down to her waist and pulled her body to his so quickly, Kay had no time to resist. She sucked in a surprised breath and let out a small gasp at being suddenly held so closely against the long, lean, hard length of him.

The breath stalled in her lungs. Her heart began to beat very fast. His right hand swept up to the back of her head. He brought her face forward until they were just a kiss apart. His soft breath blew tantalizingly across her lips.

"Yes, Kay. I am prodded by my instincts to do something."

He kissed her then, with a mouth moving over hers in hot, incendiary sweeps, hungry with desire. A world of feeling flooded Kay, drowning out every coherent thought in her head. He was an iron strength and a burning heat, and he was pounding her will to pulp and igniting every one of her cells.

And she wanted it to go on forever.

Except a mere second later, he pulled away and held her from him.

He was breathing hard. His green eyes glinted as though lit from within by barely leashed lust and a lot more.

"But I am in control of my dangerous instincts, otherwise I would be carrying you to bed right now and forgetting all about my promise to be a gentleman. We have a ten-minute drive back to your office. And then another half-hour drive to my place and those tapes. You have exactly forty minutes in which to change your mind and control *your* dangerous instincts."

He withdrew his hands, stepped back, turned and marched toward the door. Kay stared at his retreating back. Her whole body was trembling. She couldn't seem to catch her breath.

She wondered if she would ever be able to catch it again.

DAMIAN DROVE FAST. Too fast. He knew Kay was having a hard time keeping up with him in her Camry. That knowledge did not make him slow down. And every mile, he debated with himself about whether he was doing the right thing by letting her look at those tapes.

On the one hand, he knew each person had the right to decide what to see and what not to see. But on the other hand, his feelings for Kay clearly demanded he protect her from seeing what was on those tapes. And in this battle of head against heart, Damian was unsure which would be the victor—if there was to be a victor. This was beginning to look like one of those no-win situations.

His head reminded him she was sharp. She was balanced. She wasn't easily spooked. But his heart had always somehow sensed the gentleness in her, the tender spot that could be reached and hurt. He had already seen it assaulted during the first two hours of those tapes.

He knew no armor of logic could protect her tender core when she came face-to-face with the other, far sharper spears of reality so shockingly depicted in his patient's later sessions. And, yet, Damian knew, too, that Kay had a potent need to be recognized as strong. How could he become like all those other men who had refused to accept that strength?

No-win, no-win, no-win, the words chanted in his head, causing it to ache.

As soon as he turned up his block, Damian immediately saw the two cars parked in front of his house. One was a police car with a uniformed officer leaning against the hood. In front of it was a long, white Lincoln.

He checked his rearview mirror. Kay was nowhere to be seen. He wasn't surprised. The way he'd been driving, she was probably still half a mile back. He pulled up behind the police car and got out. The uniformed officer walked over to him.

"Dr. Damian Steele?"

"Yes. I'm Steele. What's going on?"

A man was getting out of the driver's side of the long, white Lincoln. Damian didn't get a good look at him because he was too occupied with the white paper the officer was shoving at him. "This is a court order, Dr. Steele."

"For what?"

"For any and all records in your possession pertaining to the treatment of one of your patients, a LeRoy Nye. I will accompany you inside and you will gather these records so I may take them with me now, please."

Damian was immediately and thoroughly alarmed. "For what purpose? What are you going to do with these records?"

"Judge Ingle wants to take a look at them," Croghan spoke up from behind the officer. The attorney was smiling from ear to ear.

Damian realized that it was Croghan who had been sitting, waiting in the white Lincoln and who was obviously behind the confiscation of his records. He opened the court order and read it carefully, plodding through as much of the legalese as he could. His eyes riveted on the one part that was clear—far too clear.

"All paper and taped records, including voice and *video.*"

He refolded the paper, his unease growing. Was that typical legal language to cover all the bases, or did someone have inside knowledge of his videotaped sessions with Lee?

He turned as he heard Kay's car pulling up. She jumped out of the driver's seat and came running over to the three men. He handed her the court order in response to the question on her face. She read the document quickly, her back straightening perceptibly as the import of the court order made itself felt.

"So this is why AJ was trying to get in touch with me."

"Any way to fight this?" he asked.

Her eyes rose to his. Her expression remained composed, her voice even. Only the stiffness of her body language gave away her inner agitation. "No."

Damian held his own frustration in check as he turned toward the house and slowly walked up the sidewalk. He dug into his pocket for his key, opened the door and stepped inside. Kay was right behind him, the policeman behind her and Croghan bringing up the rear. Damian led the single-file procession directly to his study.

And all the while his mind raced. Somehow, he must find a way to block these tapes from being made public. Somehow.

He opened the door and flipped on the light.

The instant he did so, he stiffened at what he saw.

The primitive shield lay on the floor. The enormous wall to the file room stood ajar.

Damian charged forward, grabbed its edge and swung it wide, fearing what he would see and, even worse, what he would not see.

His worst fears were realized. Inside, all the shelves were empty.

"YOUR HONOR, this is nothing but a blatant attempt by the defense to suppress evidence!" Croghan yelled in Ingle's private chambers less than two hours later.

"It's obvious that Dr. Steele took those tapes himself because he knew they would be favorable to the plaintiff's case. He fabricated this whole robbery scenario in a transparent attempt to cover up!"

"That's rubbish," Kay responded, having to fight to keep her voice even. She turned away from Croghan and faced the judge.

"It's ludicrous for Mr. Croghan to suggest such a thing. Those videotapes would not have aided the plaintiff's case. On the contrary, they would have proved the defense's case beyond any doubt. Defense is far more disadvantaged now that the tapes have been stolen."

"Stolen? Who are you trying to kid, Counselor?" Croghan's booming voice blasted in Kay's ear. "I was there, remember? Dr. Steele opened his front door with his key. The lock showed no signs of being forced. No windows were found broken. How did this supposed thief break in?"

"So now you're a crime-scene investigator, is that it, Croghan?" Kay said, her volume soft but not her tone. "Funny, I didn't see you checking to see if any window had been forced. Nor did I see you dusting for prints."

"Still sticking with the theft story, huh? Okay, Kellogg, how do you explain that the videotapes of the LeRoy Nye sessions were the only things stolen?"

"How do you know that the videotapes of the LeRoy Nye sessions were the only things stolen? Dr. Steele hasn't even had a chance to check to see what was taken yet."

Ingle rapped his knuckles on his desk. Kay could tell he was clearly enjoying the verbal sparring but had apparently decided it was time to ring the bell for this round. Besides, even though the judge had requested this emergency meeting in his chambers following the policeman's report of the missing tapes, Kay surmised by his more formal wear that Ingle had been reluctantly pulled away from a previous engagement.

Although what kind of function would welcome a middle-aged man with a mohawk, golden rings hanging out of his nose and ears and wearing a silver tuxedo with a purple stripe and purple running shoes, she absolutely could not imagine.

"Okay you two," the judge said. "You got your respective jabs in. Now sit down and calm down. Until such time as we have the police report, we will proceed with this trial and leave the matter of sorting out the missing tapes to them."

"But I need those videotapes," Croghan complained.

"Give it a rest, Mr. Croghan." The judge turned to Damian. "Now, Dr. Steele, do you have any other records of your conversations with your patient?"

Kay's eyes swung to Damian's face. He appeared and sounded as calm and perfectly controlled as ever as he sat beside her.

"Just those written case notes that you have in your hands. They're from the first three months of sessions," he answered.

Ingle flipped through the large stack of pages, not looking too enthusiastic. "Is there anything about the Roy Nye personality in these notes?"

"The last several sheets deal with the session in which the Roy personality first appeared. Again, I want to stress that these records are protected by doctor-patient confidentiality and that this court has no right—"

"Yes, yes. As Ms. Kellogg has been declaring quite vehemently over the last thirty minutes. But as I understand it, Lee Nye, not Roy Nye, came to you as a patient, isn't that correct, Dr. Steele?"

"Technically yes, but—"

"Technically will do just fine for me, Doctor. And since Roy Nye was technically *not* your patient, it is only your interactions with him that I will consider reading or letting Mr. Croghan read."

"But without psychological training—"

"Yes, yes." Ingle waved away Damian's concerns with an impatient hand. "You and Ms. Kellogg have both made that abundantly clear several times now. But Mr. Croghan claims the psychological sessions will support his case, and before I can decide if this is true and give him a chance to see these notes, I must read them first. Too bad Roy only appears briefly in these. Are you certain you have no idea who may have stolen those tapes?"

"None, Your Honor."

A knock sounded on the door to the judge's chambers. Ingle yelled for whoever it was to come in. Kay thought that the judge had certainly shed his stodgy demeanor with amazing ease. Maybe this other side had been there all the time. Maybe he just had been looking for an excuse to let it out.

We're all just mysteries waiting to unfold. Why were Damian's words coming back to her now?

The door opened partially, the burly bailiff with the smudge of a mustache curving his head around its corner.

"I thought I heard raised voices a few minutes ago. Everything all right, Your Honor?"

"Fine, fine. We're finished here. You can escort this trio out and go back to whatever you were doing when we interrupted you this evening. I'd say this ends our prologue, ladies and gentlemen. Jury selection tomorrow morning. Then on to Tuesday morning and chapter one. I'm expecting great things from you two. Don't disappoint me."

"DAMIAN, were the tapes the only things taken from your place?" Kay asked as they walked to their cars, which were parked in a covered lot a few blocks down from the courthouse.

"I believe so."

His voice was calm. If he was angry over the incident, he certainly had that anger in control.

Kay switched her attention to his face, but it was shrouded in the dark night and the equally dark parking lot.

"So Croghan was right. Someone was only after those tapes. Who knew you had them?"

"Outside of Lee and the other doctors I mentioned them to, no one knew."

"Who knew about that secret file room?"

"Some of the patients I've seen in my home may have surmised it was there, although, to be honest, that seems unlikely since I never opened it in front of them."

"Did you ever see Lee in your home?"

"Yes."

"Who else?"

"Bette Boson, my other multi-personality case and a few other patients during crisis periods in their treatment."

"Of the people who knew about or could have known about the tapes and hidden file room, who would or could have stolen those tapes?"

"I don't know that any of them could or would. It doesn't make sense. I can't see how stealing those tapes would benefit anyone."

"Could anything on those tapes possibly help Croghan's case?"

"No. And if he knew what was on them, he certainly wouldn't have brought them to Ingle's attention or be pressing for them to be found."

"You mean because of how despicable the Roy personality reveals itself to be on those tapes?"

"Yes."

"So you think Croghan's just engaging in a fishing expedition?"

"He has to be. Those tapes can't do anyone but a psychologist studying MPD any good. In anyone else's hands, they can only do harm."

"I wish I could have seen them before that damn thief got to them."

"Sorry, but that's one wish I can't share."

She looked at his face as they passed beneath a dim light on the parking structure wall and could have sworn she saw a small light of satisfaction glinting in his eyes.

"You know, Damian, if I hadn't had you in my sights nearly the entire time, I could almost suspect you'd stolen those tapes yourself just to keep me from seeing them."

"Could you? My, my, how can you lawyers be so suspicious?"

"And how can you psychologists be so damn good at keeping secrets?"

The sudden charming smile that lit his lips was deliberately and thoroughly disreputable.

Momentarily lost in that captivating smile, Kay almost missed the significance of the racing engine nearby. When it finally got her attention, it was almost too late. The car was burning rubber and accelerating directly for them.

There was no time left for her to think, much less act.

Damian's strong arms grabbed her as he leaped out of the way. Kay actually felt the air from the fender as the car whizzed past them, out of the parking lot, its tires screeching, its engine whining.

She collapsed gratefully against Damian's solid, safe chest, feeling his strong heart beating as her own heart hammered relentlessly against her rib cage.

"Are you all right?" he asked, his voice husky.

"Yes. Thanks," she muttered a moment later when she could, still trying to keep her knees from buckling beneath her, both from the close call and the closeness with which he held her.

"You're welcome," he said, his voice still husky, his breath stirring against her hair. He didn't let her go.

She didn't know if it was reaction to the car almost hitting them or to how good his arms felt around her, but she had a hell of a hard time catching her breath for several more seconds.

Even when she could, she did not attempt to pull away. He felt so good. So damn good. Her voice, when it finally came again, was still a shaky sigh.

"First a speedboat and now a car. Whoever said Seattle was one of the safest big cities in America?"

"Real-estate agents. Kay, your heart is beating as fast as a frightened bird's. Are you really all right?"

"No, I'm not all right. Damian, I don't believe in coincidences. Two such close calls in the same day is way out of the law of averages. What's going on?"

His arms tightened around her. She felt him plant a brief, warm kiss on the top of her head.

"I don't know. I just don't know."

"We have to go to the police."

"And tell them what? Did you see who was driving that speedboat or that car? Can you even describe the boat or car?"

"No, I can't, but, damn it, there must be something we can do."

"Yes. There is something I can do. Consider yourself fired."

She pushed away from his chest to try to see his face in the dark parking lot. "Fired?"

"You bet, fired. You wouldn't be having these close calls if you weren't representing me in this cuckoo case."

"Cuckoo case? You, a psychologist, use a term like *cuckoo case?*"

"What, too technical for you?"

Kay pushed herself all the way out of his arms. "Oh, very funny. Damian, you can't fire me."

"I just did."

"No, you didn't. We have an agreement, remember? You gave me your word of honor that you'd only fire me for incompetency."

"That was agreed upon before we became the target of some serious kook."

"Do you think it's the same person who's been calling and leaving those breathy messages? Do you think he or she is getting violent?"

"I don't know what to think. But I know what to do. You're off this case, Kay."

She could feel the tension in his taut body like a steel beam that would not bend. The man may not know it, but he'd met his match. "No, I'm not off this case. I'm seeing it through. I'm not letting you fire me. I'm holding you to your word of honor."

"Kay, don't make this any more difficult than it is. I know once I explain, Adam will take over the case and—"

"Adam can't and won't take over this case. For one, he's up to his ears in a very complicated maritime law case of his own. For two, he'd never take back a case he'd given to me. We respect one another at Justice, Inc., too much to behave in such an underhanded way. You might as well face it, Damian, I'm your attorney through the end of this trial."

He exhaled a heavy, frustration-laden breath. "Damn it, Kay. Don't you understand you could get hurt if you continue representing me?"

"And don't you understand that you could lose your shirt if I don't? Damian, another lawyer couldn't get up to speed in time for your trial. Think about it. Maybe that's what all of this is about. Maybe the breathy messages and the close calls are just scare tactics so you will fire me and lose this lawsuit. Maybe that's how this kook is really trying to harm you."

"Maybe," he agreed reluctantly.

"Maybe, nothing. I'm convinced of it. I'm not letting you play into this crazy's hands by caving in to these terrorist acts. I refuse to let you take a professional and financial beating."

"I can't allow—"

"You don't have a say in the matter, Dr. Steele. I'm remaining as your attorney and that's that. Damn. Are all you psychologists so difficult to convince?"

He laughed suddenly and she sensed the previous tension in his body dissipating into the dark night. "Damn. Are all you attorneys so difficult to fire?"

Chapter Eight

"Dr. Steele, did you kill Roy Nye?" the reporter yelled as Kay and Damian shouldered their way through the throng of newspeople on Tuesday morning.

Kay smiled into the bright lights of the cameras as microphones were shoved into hers and Damian's faces. "Dr. Steele will be making no press statements for the duration of this case. Please direct your questions to me, ladies and gentlemen."

They edged ahead as best they could against the pushing bodies. Kay was not surprised that the reporters completely ignored what she'd said and continued to shove microphones in her client's face and bark questions at him.

"Dr. Steele, Mrs. Nye is asking for three million dollars in damages. Will you settle if she comes down to two million?"

"Dr. Steele has no reason to settle. He is in the right," Kay emphasized.

"What about one million?" another reporter asked.

Kay didn't waste her breath answering this time.

"Dr. Steele, how much is half of a dual-personality patient worth, would you say?"

"No comment," Damian answered.

"How many other personalities have you murdered?"

"No comment," Damian repeated.

"Mr. Croghan says your paper records on Roy Nye aren't sufficient for him to present a true picture of his client's husband. How do you feel about that?"

"No comment."

"Dr. Steele, is it true you destroyed Roy Nye's session videotapes so they couldn't help Mrs. Nye's case?"

Kay had warned Damian to always smile when he refused to answer questions, particularly when those questions got nasty, like that last one. She was delighted to see how well Damian complied, while surreptitiously shoving the obnoxious reporter out of their way.

Another group of reporters were hovering around Croghan and his client, like flies around fresh meat, as they also tried to advance toward the courtroom.

"Yes, we fully expect to win," Croghan was saying. "We have right on our side," he added as he deliberately bumped Kay, beaming his full set of large, shiny teeth at the cameras.

Kay kept her balance only because of Damian's sturdy, strong arm that immediately came out to encircle her.

She knew her reactions to this man were getting more and more out of line and illogical. But ever since Sunday, when he'd rescued her from drowning and from that speeding car and held her in his arms against his warm, strong chest and kissed her so thoroughly and thrillingly, Kay had been feeling anything but logical.

Now, as Damian slowly withdrew his arm from around her body, it was with a sense of deep regret that she reminded herself that she had best sharpen that professional line between them that had been fading far too fast.

"Show time, Ms. Kellogg," Croghan quipped. "I just can't wait to get in there and get going. I'm about to make history."

Kay smiled back at her adversary, quite aware of the camera lenses trained on them and the open microphones.

"You mean you're about to *become* history."

The corners of Croghan's lips rose toward his ears in a smile that reminded Kay of a python just before it swallowed its prey.

Kay started suddenly as she heard a commotion behind her. She whirled in time to see Fedora Nye crashing into Damian.

Damian grabbed the off-balance woman to steady her. When Fedora looked up and realized whose hands held her, she let out a sharp screech.

Damian released the woman immediately.

Croghan rushed forward and swept the end of his cape around his client's shoulders like the protective wing of a father bird.

"Mrs. Nye, are you all right?" he bellowed, staring accusingly at Damian the whole time as though Damian had struck her.

Kay deliberately stepped in front of the rolling cameras and curled her arm around Damian's. She leaned in close enough for a hurried whisper. "Let's get out of here."

He whispered his answer. "I'll dig a hole through these ghouls if I have to use my head as a battering ram."

"Dr. Steele," a reporter shouted. "Why did you just try to knock down Mrs. Nye?"

As the baiting questions continued to multiply like virulent bacteria, Damian pushed their way through the thick circle of reporters. His strong shoulder finally slammed through the courtroom doors, leading Kay thankfully away from the less-than-dignified members of Seattle's fourth estate, who were now being forcibly detained by two court officers, demanding they come to order before being let into the courtroom.

Kay breathed a sigh of relief as she flopped into her chair at the defendant's table. "I wouldn't be surprised if Croghan didn't push his own client into you," she said.

"Or convince her to pretend to be pushed in order to provoke the confrontation," Damian replied.

"He's really escalated this case into a media circus. You can be certain he leaked that information about the missing videotapes. In his previous life, you just know Croghan had to have slithered around on his belly.''

"So it would seem," Damian answered distractedly as he pulled a blue envelope out of his jacket pocket. He looked at it, an uncharacteristic frown puckering his forehead.

"Something wrong?" Kay asked.

Damian swung around in his chair and looked first at Croghan and Fedora Nye at the plaintiff's table and then turned back to look at the throng of newspeople jostling with other spectators for the best seats. Kay followed his eyes and saw them rest on a woman with a short cap of black hair.

"Damian? What is it?"

He turned back to Kay, the blue envelope still clutched in his hand, his eyes cold, green marble. "Did you see anyone slip this into my pocket?"

"No. What is it?"

He shook his head as he repocketed the envelope. "Nothing important." His smile expanded as hers failed to appear. He briefly rested his hand on hers. "Really. It's nothing."

"Who is that woman with the short, black hair?"

"Dr. Priscilla Payton."

"Oh."

The lift of his lips did not reach his eyes. "Probably here hoping to see me professionally crucified."

"Then she's going to be thoroughly disappointed," Kay said with a vehemence that surprised even herself.

This time his grin was genuine and absolutely devastating. Kay let out a deep internal sigh. No. She couldn't be falling for a client. And certainly not a guy who thought marriage akin to jumping off a cliff. Every ounce of logic she possessed rejected the possibility.

Kay resolutely turned away from Damian's smile.

Judge Ingle made his entrance. Kay rose and then sat down with the rest of the court.

From now on, she'd keep all these inappropriate feelings in check. From now on, she'd keep her mind strictly on business.

"Kay?"

His breath blew tantalizingly against her ear, sending that crazy, exciting quiver down the back of her legs. She swallowed hard. "Yes?"

"Are you ready?"

Kay's mind went blank. Suddenly, all she could think about was how wonderful it was to look into those deep green, mesmerizing eyes of his, to smell the spicy scent of his after-shave, to feel his closeness beside her.

"Kay, the judge just asked if you were ready. Are you all right?"

Kay's right earlobe suddenly itched fiercely. She rubbed it hard as she crossed her legs and crossed them again. And yet again.

"Ms. Kellogg?" Ingle inquired.

"Yes, Your Honor," Kay answered, rising to her feet. "Defense is . . . ah . . . ready."

"LADIES AND GENTLEMEN of the jury," Croghan began in his opening address. "I am representing Mrs. Fedora Nye, the little widowed lady sitting at this table here."

Kay watched Croghan as he purposely stood behind Fedora, drawing the jury's attention to the forlorn-appearing, brown-haired woman in the old, faded print dress that looked like something Croghan had probably picked up from a thrift shop.

They made an unlikely pair, this modest, mousy client and her flamboyant, flashy attorney. Croghan was decked out in his white suit, with his golden belt buckle and swinging watch chain periodically colliding and clanging through the courtroom like a muffled fire bell.

"This is a complicated case, an important case," Croghan broadcast at his louder-than-life volume. He left his client and headed toward the jury box. "It involves two separate and distinct personalities inhabiting the same body. One of these personalities was named Roy.

"It is Roy Nye who I want to tell you about, because he is the reason you are here. Roy was Fedora's husband, the father of her children. These two were young lovers, meeting first as teenagers. Roy and Fedora would have been celebrating their silver anniversary soon."

Croghan's forehead sliced into a scowl. "But that can never happen now, because Roy was taken from his wife and children. Tragically taken. Against his desire. Against his will. Not by illness. Not by injury. Not by an act of God. No, ladies and gentlemen. By an act of that man!"

Croghan swung suddenly toward Damian, his right arm straight out, his index finger pointing accusingly.

"Roy's life was in that man's hands. That man deliberately, maliciously, unconscionably, with malice aforethought, murdered Roy Nye!"

Croghan swung both hands onto the railing in front of the jury. He gripped it as though trying to control his anger, closed his eyes as though trying to collect himself. Every legal instinct Kay possessed told her it was an act. Still, there was no denying it was a very good act. After a moment, Croghan opened his eyes and drew in a deep, dramatic breath before continuing.

"The defense attorney is going to try to convince you that since Roy Nye's body is still walking around, no real death has occurred. She's going to say that since another personality exists inside Roy's body, we have no wrongful death here, no grounds for personal liability.

"Well, don't you believe her, ladies and gentlemen. Roy is dead. Everything that made him a distinct human being is gone, deliberately cut out of his life by Dr. Damian Steele with his bloody, psychological switchblade!"

Croghan paced in front of the jury, head down, fists by his sides, again posturing as though he were trying to hold in his anger and righteous indignation. Kay grudgingly admitted that, no doubt about it, her adversary was delivering a powerful performance. Finally, he turned back toward the men and women whose attention he had so adroitly captured.

"You are going to be deciding nothing less than the definition of human life in this trial. Yes, that is what this case is all about. It is up to you to say if a man is a mere stack of muscle and bone, or if he is his memories, his loves, his hopes and his dreams.

"And if you decide a man is more than mere flesh, then you must also decide that Roy Nye has been taken from his family by the wrong and willful act of that man, and you must compensate his grieving widow accordingly. It is up to you, ladies and gentlemen, to redress this grievous wrong. It is up to you to send a message to this psychologist and all others who dare to set themselves up as God!"

DAMIAN WATCHED as Croghan stalked back to the plaintiff's table. The courtroom was so quiet, he could hear Kay's fingers drumming on the table, a visible and audible vibration of the revving of her mental engine.

Damian's mind was racing, too. Croghan had made one hell of an opening statement. The jury looked as if it was ready to find for Mrs. Nye already. What could Kay possibly say in rebuttal?

She rose in one fluid movement, her back straight, her hands at her sides and a smile on her face. Damian was amazed at how confident her soft voice sounded and how well it carried throughout the courtroom, like a balm to the eardrums after Croghan's far-too-loud blast.

"Ladies and gentlemen, my name is Kay Kellogg. I represent Dr. Damian Steele, the defendant in this case. You've just been told by the plaintiff's attorney that you are going to be asked to determine the definition of human life in this trial. I find it ludicrous that Mr. Croghan would actually try to make you think such a thing."

Kay laughed, a gentle, amused sound that sang in the ears and quickly relieved the dramatic tension that had hung in the wake of Croghan's closing. Feet started to shuffle, chairs to squeak. Her soft laughter gradually drifted into the background noises of people regaining their comfort. Damian understood she had laughed precisely so they would regain their comfort.

She walked up to the jury and smiled, raising her right hand as though taking an oath. "Let me reassure you. You will not be asked to determine the definition of human life in this trial. When life exists and when it ceases to exist has already been determined and documented in both medicine and law.''

She dropped her hand and slowly and deliberately made eye contact with each one of the jurors.

''But you will be asked to try to understand about a man with two identities, two very distinct and separate personalities.''

She paused, let a small space of time go by.

''Mr. Croghan mentioned one of those personalities to you. I want to tell you about both of them. I'm going to start off with the personality Mr. Croghan failed to tell you about. His name is Lee Nye.

''Lee is a good, decent man who was troubled by terrible blackouts. He went to Dr. Steele for help. He was trying to make a life for himself, trying to hold down a job. But as Dr. Steele discovered, a dysfunctional personality fragment inside Lee's mind was interfering. That dysfunctional fragment was Roy.

''Now, I want you to try to visualize this. You're working at your job when suddenly you black out and wake up more than a day later. You're filthy dirty in a stinking alley, reeking of alcohol, with the pain of broken ribs from a recent barroom brawl shooting through your side and rats biting at your fingers.''

Kay shuddered as she paused to let her image sink into the minds of the jurors.

''Incredible to imagine what it would be like living through repeated episodes of such experiences, isn't it?''

Some of the heads in the jury box nodded.

''That's because a mind divided into more than one identity is not something we deal with every day. In order to visualize how this could take place, let's borrow a couple of familiar images from literature. Do you all remember the story of Dr. Jekyll and Mr. Hyde?''

Damian watched as most members of the jury nodded this time. She had their attention and clearly their interest.

''Then you'll also remember that when Dr. Jekyll was in control of the shared consciousness, reason and rationality ruled. But when Mr. Hyde took over the consciousness, immorality and inhumanity came to the fore.

"We have a remarkably similar situation here. Lee was the reasonable, rational side, like Dr. Jekyll. Roy was the immoral, inhuman side, like—"

"I object to that analogy being drawn, Your Honor!" Croghan bellowed, jumping to his feet.

"This is just Ms. Kellogg's opening statement, Mr. Croghan," Judge Ingle said. "And I've already instructed the jury that these are opinions, not facts. Besides, as I recall, you wielded a few unfavorable analogies against the defense in your opening statement. It's time for Ms. Kellogg to wow us with her verbal punches. Objection overruled."

Damian knew that Inglé had been following Kay's every word, taking copious notes, and like the rest of the courtroom, couldn't wait to hear what else she would say to counteract Croghan's opening statement. Croghan grumbled as he retook his chair.

"Thank you, Your Honor," Kay said, managing to flash the whole courtroom a brilliant smile as she turned back to the jury.

"Yes, Roy was the immoral, evil side of the man once known as LeRoy Nye. Those terrible blackouts where Roy took over and the horrible aftermaths were the reasons that drove Lee to Dr. Steele for help. And Dr. Steele did help him. Lee Nye is now free of those dreadful blackouts, because he is now free of Roy."

She strode up and down in front of the attentive men and women of the jury, her hands clasped behind her back, a thoughtful look on her face.

"Roy is gone. But he is not gone in the sense that you or I will someday die, because Roy was never alive in the sense that you or I are alive. He existed in the mind, like a malignant tumor exists."

"Your Honor, I object!"

"What again, Mr. Croghan?" Ingle asked. "Give us a break here. Overruled."

Damian got the impression that Croghan was deliberately attempting to break Kay's conversational stride by interrupting. Still, he didn't seem to be having much luck. She picked up just where she had left off.

"Yes, ladies and gentlemen, Roy invaded Lee Nye's mind much liked Mr. Hyde invaded Dr. Jekyll's, much like cancer invades the body."

She raised her hands, circled them around a large, invisible ball that she stared at with undisguised horror and disgust.

"You know what cancer is like. It grows out of control, clumps together into a malignant tumor and sucks the life out of healthy cells. If not eliminated from the body, it will eventually kill it. Mr. Hyde was the cancer in Dr. Jekyll's mind that finally killed him."

She dropped her hands to the railing of the jury box and leaned toward the jurors, her soft voice deadly calm and deadly serious.

"Roy was the malignant growth in Lee's mind, violent, uncontrolled. In order for Lee, the healthy part of the mind, to survive, Roy had to be eliminated."

She removed her hands from the railing and leaned back.

"Mr. Croghan calls that murder. The legal and medical professions do not agree. That's why no death certificate has been or ever will be prepared for Roy. That's why no police investigation has been or ever will be initiated. Since neither the law nor medicine recognizes a death here, it's ludicrous that Mr. Croghan demand you do."

Kay turned and strolled into the middle of the courtroom. All eyes followed her. She pivoted, swung around and faced the jury once more.

"So now you must be wondering what you will be asked to decide in this case? Well, it's simple, really. You're being asked to decide if Dr. Damian Steele acted responsibly when he extinguished the malignant psychological tumor inside Lee Nye's head so that Lee could become a healthy, productive member of society and not end up destroyed as Dr. Jekyll was destroyed."

Kay strode back to the defendant's table and stood beside Damian, resting her hand on his shoulder. "We're confident that the evidence will clearly support Dr. Steele's decisions and actions in respect to the care of his patient, Lee Nye. Very confident."

She looked down at Damian and smiled warmly, confidentially—giving the impression that she was talking only to him while at the same time her soft voice carried throughout the courtroom.

"Dr. Damian Steele literally gave Lee back his sanity. He's the kind of doctor we all desperately search for but so seldom find. He's competent, confident, committed, compassionate. Mr. Croghan says Dr. Steele played God when he helped Lee Nye. If that's playing God, then by heaven, it's a game we should all be playing."

Kay quietly circled behind Damian and took her chair. No doubt about it, K. O. Kellogg knew her stuff. Her opening statement had been as powerful and compelling as Croghan's.

Ingle rapped for order as the courtroom erupted in an appreciative mumble from many spectators who obviously agreed with Damian's silent assessment.

"Look, folks, I'm enjoying these performances, too," Ingle said. "But don't get too rambunctious or I'll have to give somebody else your seat. The bailiff tells me there's a slew of other folks outside who are just panting to get in. Am I making myself clear here?"

The room immediately drew quiet.

"Good," Ingle said. "Mr. Croghan, please call your first witness."

"Thank you, Your Honor. I call Mrs. Fedora Nye."

KAY WATCHED Fedora Nye rise timidly to her feet. Croghan gently took her elbow and escorted her to the witness box. She slogged beside him, clutching her small, black purse to her breast with both hands as though it were some kind of lifeline. She reluctantly relinquished her stranglehold on it when asked to raise her right hand to swear to tell the truth.

She lowered herself nervously to the edge of the witness chair. Her bowed shoulders and movements bespoke a weary woman in her late fifties. When she stated her name and address for the record, the judge had to ask her to pull the microphone closer to her mouth and speak up.

"Mrs. Nye," Croghan began. "Fedora," he corrected himself with a smile at his client. "When did you meet your husband, Roy?"

"In high school."

"Tell us about those days."

Her face lightened momentarily, losing a few of its lines and its years. "It was right after I was picked for the cheerleading squad. The gym coach said I learned the cheers faster than anyone. It took a while to convince my parents to let me wear the short skirt of the uniform, however. They were very strict."

"This was a private, religious high school they had sent you to, wasn't it?"

"Yes. They would have never let me go to a public school."

"They wanted you to have a strong religious center?"

"My family has always been a God-fearing one. And they knew that academics were not stressed nearly as strongly in public schools."

Kay's foot began to tap nervously. Fedora came across as both pathetic and sincere. What was even worse, Kay was beginning to think she might just legitimately be both.

"It was a shame our school's football team wasn't very good," Fedora went on. "Still, our cheering squad was voted one of the best in the state. Roy told me he only came to the games to see me. I was so thrilled. I had never had a boyfriend before. Roy was the only man I ever...was with."

"And you young lovers were subsequently married?"

Fedora sighed as a light from that youthful memory actually shone through her faded eyes. "Yes. It was a beautiful church wedding. Simply beautiful."

Fedora dug into her purse for a handkerchief and dabbed at the moist corners of her eyes.

"Fedora, was your marriage to Roy blessed with any children?"

"Our son, Larry, came first. And then, just eighteen months later, our daughter, Rosy, was born. They were beautiful babies. Everything a parent could desire."

Kay's foot picked up its pace. This woman sounded as though she believed every word she was saying. Could anyone really be this good an actress?

"And did your little family visit the park on Saturdays and go to church on Sundays?"

"Oh, yes. And the children attended a good religious school. They have been brought up properly."

"Fedora, during all these years that you and Roy raised your family, did your husband ever seem to be taken over by the personality of another man?"

Fedora shook her head adamantly. "No, never. Not, at least, until he started seeing that man."

Croghan leaped toward the bench. "Let the record reflect that Mrs. Nye is pointing at Dr. Steele."

Ingle nodded and Croghan reoriented both his position and his attention to Fedora.

"Now, tell us when you first had an inkling that something had happened to Roy?"

"It was four years ago, when a stranger in Roy's body stood before a judge and said his name was Lee. He said that the Roy personality that used to be inside him was gone and that he, Lee, wanted to divorce me."

"And that is the first time you heard of this Lee?"

"Yes."

"And what of your husband, Fedora? What of the father of your children, the man you had fallen in love with when you were a high-school cheerleader. The only man who has ever been in your life. What happened to Roy?"

"He's gone. Dead." Her voice cracked on the word. It took a few seconds before she could continue. "Otherwise, he would have come back to me. I know it."

"Fedora, you heard Dr. Steele's attorney speak about your husband, Roy. She said he never lived, so he can't be dead. What do you say to that?"

"I don't understand how she could say such a thing. Roy was my husband, the father of my children. How can a man be these things and not have been alive?"

Tears began to roll down Fedora's face.

"Fedora, I know this is difficult, but I only have a few more questions. Do you feel up to going on?"

She nodded mutely.

"You're very brave," Croghan said as he laid his hand on her arm.

"Fedora, does your religious belief recognize divorce?"

"No."

"Do you believe that once two people are married, they are husband and wife forever?"

"'What God has joined together, let no man put asunder,'" she quoted.

"When Lee divorced you, he left you penniless, didn't he?"

"My children and I received nothing. This person in Roy's body said he had never been a husband or father. He said that I wasn't his wife and my children weren't his children. He said this right to the judge."

"In the divorce court?"

"Yes. And it doesn't make any sense."

"What doesn't make any sense, Fedora?"

"This Lee said he had never been a husband or father. What right did Dr. Steele have to decide that Lee should live and Roy should die?"

Her voice broke on her last words, her chin came down and her chest began to heave as sobs wracked her body. She rocked and cradled her small black purse as though it were a baby she was holding to her breast.

Kay felt a little sick to her stomach.

Croghan stood in front of Fedora, making no attempt to comfort the distressed woman. Rather, he shook his head sadly as though he might be joining her in tears at any moment.

Judge Ingle took copious notes, appearing quite satisfied with the show. He let a very long dramatic minute pass before finally glancing at his watch and declaring, "We're going to take an early lunch to give your client time to compose herself, Mr. Croghan. Court is recessed until two o'clock."

He rapped the table and bounced toward the judge's chambers on his white tennis shoes.

"LET THE COURTROOM clear out, Damian. The bailiff agreed to help us exit through the jury room once it clears so we can avoid the press."

Her voice was soft, businesslike, as always. But Damian knew immediately she was not as always. He moved closer to her so that his voice wouldn't carry over the clatter and hum of the clearing courtroom.

"We have time," he said on a whisper. "I'd like to take you out to lunch at a real restaurant for a change. I'm tired of grabbing sandwiches and gobbling them down as we work. You have to be, too."

She gathered her papers and shoved them into her briefcase a little too vehemently. "Thanks, but I have to prepare to cross-examine Mrs. Nye this afternoon."

"I thought you told me yesterday that you were already prepared."

She closed the latches on her briefcase and swung it off the table. "That was before I heard her testimony."

"She got to you, didn't she, Kay?"

Her eyes rose to his—clear, cool, but never quite guarded enough to hide the warmhearted woman dwelling behind them. "What makes you say that?" she asked in her most crisp, professional tone.

He kept his voice low and gentle and looked directly into her eyes. "You drum your fingers when you're mentally excited. You tap your foot when you're anxious or distraught. You were tapping your foot all through her testimony."

She held her professional profile for several seconds more before her shoulders sagged. A rueful smile circled her lips. "Looks like I'm going to have to watch both my hands and my feet when I'm around you."

His palms cupped her shoulders lightly. "It's okay, Kay. I was tapping a mental foot, myself."

She exhaled a frustrated breath as a frown appeared between her eyebrows. "The thing is, I didn't expect . . ."

When her voice faded away, Damian guessed what she had been going to say. "To feel sorry for her?"

"Yes."

Damian glanced at the last of the spectators exiting through the courtroom doors. The jury had already followed the bailiff out. Damian turned his attention back to Kay, his voice less of a whisper now that they were alone.

"Fedora is a victim. There's an instinctive part in all caring people that yearns to help a hapless victim. You're obviously strongly tapped into that feeling."

"After her testimony, the jury will also be tapped into it, Damian—all through their long lunch, thanks to Croghan's infallible timing. He has to know Fedora very well. Every feeling he brought out in her on that stand came across as genuine. He played her like a violin virtuoso would a sad refrain."

"Will that change the way you cross-examine her?"

"It has to. And the longer the jury thinks about what they just heard and saw, the harder it will be to change their minds."

"Does that worry you?"

"It makes me a little . . . uncomfortable about the lengths I'm going to have to go to in order to counteract the effect."

He brought the rough edge of his thumb up to trace the smooth surface of her worried temple, then down to the gentle curve of her cheek.

This woman could make him forget many things, not the least of which was his promise to act like a gentleman and maintain a professional distance between them.

Ever since he had held her in his arms and kissed her Sunday, he had been aware of no distance between them—professional or otherwise. All he was aware of was the softness of her skin, the sweet fragrance of her hair, the full richness of her blueberry eyes, watching him so intently.

Until his sixth sense told him other eyes watched.

Damian stiffened. His gaze darted over Kay's shoulder to scan the room. When it reached the spectator area, he realized he was wrong in thinking they were alone in the courtroom.

"What is it, Damian?" Kay asked, twirling around to follow the direction of his stare.

The woman who had been watching them turned and headed out of the room. Her stride was sturdy and determined. She threw open the door and charged out.

"Damian, do you know her?"

"Yes." Damian dropped his hand. "She's Bette Boson, a former patient."

"The other multiple personality patient you were treating?"

"Yes. Only I think it might have been Bob, one of her male-personality alters, who just stalked out of the room."

"She has a male alter?"

"He's her protector. For the past few months, he's come out whenever she feels threatened."

"Something about her or his presence seems to have disturbed you."

"Just surprised me," Damian lied. He was disturbed. He did not like that look on Bob's face. Bette's protector was angry. But at whom or what? And why?

"Do you think there's anything wrong with your former patient's being here?" Kay asked.

"No, of course not. She's probably just curious." He hoped that was it. "Come on. I'm overruling your objections. We're going to that proper restaurant. A good meal will revitalize both your mind and your mood."

But when he tried to capture Kay's arm into the nook of his, she pulled away, her eyes riveted on his suit pocket, a look of absolute horror on her face.

"Damian, no!"

He was shocked at her response. "Kay, what on earth—"

The smoke filled his nostrils at the same second as he felt the first flash of pain against his palm.

Chapter Nine

Damian snatched off his suit coat, threw it to the floor and stamped out the flames leaping from his right-hand pocket. Fortunately, the coat's dense material quickly smothered the fire. The last trail of pale smoke dissipated and died.

The pain hit him then. When he looked down at his palm, he wasn't surprised to see the seared flesh. Unfortunately, Kay saw it, too. She stepped closer. Her voice filled with a sad anguish he had never heard before.

"Damian, you're hurt!"

The burly bailiff had just reentered the courtroom from the back door to the jury room. Hearing Kay's exclamation, he rushed over, his hand resting on the butt of his gun, prepared for trouble.

"What's wrong? What's going on here?" he called warily as he approached.

"Nothing," Damian said quickly. "Just a small accident." He swung down and grabbed his suit coat with his uninjured hand.

The smoke from the fire still hung in the air. The bailiff scowled. "There's no smoking in here."

"I'll remember that," Damian said, laying an unburned part of his coat over his injured hand.

But the bailiff had already gotten a look at Damian's palm. "That's a nasty burn. You better have it looked at."

Damian nodded. "My doctor is just a few blocks away. Is the jury room clear now for us to exit that way?"

"Yeah. I'll show you out."

Damian cupped Kay's elbow with his uninjured palm and urged her after the bailiff. But she held back a few paces. As soon as the bailiff was far enough ahead to be out of earshot, she leaned closer and whispered, "Damian, you don't smoke and you certainly weren't lighting a cigarette. How did your suit coat catch fire?"

"DR. STEELE, you should have reported these threats before this," the sallow-faced detective admonished as he hitched up his pants over a sagging middle. "First a speedboat and then a car try to hit you. You're lucky you only got a burn on your hand. This sicko could just as easily have decided to rig a bomb to that envelope he slipped into your pocket."

Delightful thought. Kay could have cheerfully kicked this detective for sharing it.

Damian responded patiently. "Detective Roth, if I reported every threat I've received since this case hit the news, you'd be up to your ears in paperwork. Besides, I don't know for certain that the driver of the speedboat and the driver of the car are the same person or if either incident is related to the phone calls and letters."

"You're telling me you really think these are all different sickos bent on terrorizing you?"

"No, I concede that would be rather improbable."

"Well, I'm glad to see we agree on something."

"Still, there was no way for me to know this letter writer would cross the line into violence."

"What do you mean, there was no way for you to know? You're a psychologist, aren't you? Figuring out sickos is what you do, isn't it?"

Damian responded even more politely. "No, Detective Roth, that's not what I do."

Kay could see that the more provoking this detective got, the more polite Damian became. He was a superbly disciplined man.

But Kay's admiration for how he was handling this difficult detective did not mitigate her anger at her client one iota. Damn it, Damian should have told her about the letters. And damn it, this detective should be remembering who the injured party was here.

Her eyes frequently strayed to Damian's bandaged palm. She tried not to relive that awful moment when she saw the smoke rising from his coat pocket and the flames catching hold. She knew if Damian's reflexes hadn't been so instantaneous in snatching off his coat and smothering the fire, his injury could have been far worse.

It was bad enough. She'd caught a good long look at the raw, seared flesh of his palm while the doctor bandaged it. She didn't know how Damian had sat so unflinchingly and patiently through the process.

"Look, Detective," Kay spoke up, finding she could keep quiet no longer. "Recriminations aren't going to be much help right now. Why can't we just concentrate on trying to find out who did this and stop them from committing any more terrorist acts?"

Detective Roth rubbed his receding hairline with undisguised irritation, sat down in his chair and picked up the report form he had partially filled in.

"I don't suppose you kept the tape of the telephone threats of that breathy voice or the threatening notes?" he asked Damian.

"Naturally I did."

The detective's gray-brown eyebrows rose. "You did?"

"Seemed to make sense to keep them until I could figure out who was sending them."

"And did you figure it out?"

"No."

"You know of no one who would do this to you?"

"No one."

"No previous patient who didn't like your treatment?"

"No."

"So where are the taped conversations and other notes?"

"At my home. I'll bring them to you."

"You said you think someone slipped this last envelope into your pocket when you and Ms. Kellogg were being jostled by reporters outside the courtroom."

"That's right."

"At around the same time you came face-to-face with the woman suing you."

"Yes."

"And you still cannot suggest a suspect?"

"If you're asking me do I think Fedora Nye did it, I don't know. She did bump into me, so the opportunity was there. But a lot of people I didn't see also bumped into me while Ms. Kellogg and I were making our way through that crowd."

"A lot of people aren't suing you for the loss of their husband."

"So, naturally, questioning Mrs. Nye will be foremost on your agenda."

"Naturally," Detective Roth replied with a sarcastic smirk. "Of course, it's just possible this is all the reckless, stupid act of some sicko who saw your picture on the news and has gone off the deep end."

"I don't think this is some sicko gone off the deep end, as you put it."

"Oh? Why not?"

"Because the content and structure of the first four letters and the telephone calls were all very concise and carefully worded. I believe the writer and caller is someone who is quite angry at me, but that anger is controlled and very unlikely to result in physical violence."

"You don't consider trying to hit you with a speedboat and then a car physically violent? Or passing you a letter sealed with flammable chemicals so that friction or body heat causes it to burst into flames?"

"Of course I do. It surprises me that the same person who composed the first four notes was behind the last incident or the close calls with the boat and car."

"Are we back to the theory that there is more than one person out to get you?"

"No. I'm certain the last envelope was exactly the same as the others, so I know the note writer is the same, at least."

Roth sneered. "Then you have to be wrong about the tendency to violence, don't you?"

"It tells me that there's an inconsistency here somewhere," Damian agreed reasonably, once again refusing to rise to the detective's conversational bait.

"Well, I may not have any fancy degree, but I can smell a sicko a mile off. I'm warning you, you'd better call me if you get any more of those blue envelopes."

"Your number will be the first to flash through my mind," Damian said politely as he rose from his chair.

"Where are you going?" Detective Roth demanded. "I'm not finished taking my report yet."

"Ms. Kellogg and I are due back in court in less than twenty-five minutes. I must find something between now and then to wear in place of my ruined suit coat, which you're now holding as evidence."

"Now, wait just a min—"

But Damian didn't wait. Not even for a second. He pivoted sharply and walked away. As Kay scurried to keep up with him, she stole a glance at his profile. It was calm and serene, just as it had been throughout the difficult interview with that difficult man.

Yes, Damian Steele was a superbly disciplined man. Even the dangerous part of him that Kay occasionally sensed below his surface calm seemed a servant to that splendid discipline.

Only once had she seen him lose control—Sunday afternoon on Lake Union, when he had held her so closely and cursed that speedboat operator so magnificently.

Kay moved closer to his side as they headed for the door. "There's no reason to rush. I'll go to Judge Ingle and obtain a continuance until tomorrow."

"If you tell the judge about the threatening notes and the fire, the press will get hold of the story. I think this letter writer wants that to happen."

"You think that's why this sicko is doing it?"

"Whoever slipped that envelope rigged to burst into flames in my pocket did so to see and hear about the result. The person is probably eagerly waiting for news this very moment."

"And you don't want him to get it?"

"Or her. No."

"Because you think if the sicko doesn't receive satisfaction, he'll stop?"

"Possibly."

"But what if not receiving satisfaction just goads this person into doing something else? Something even rasher, perhaps?"

"That's also a possibility."

"He could decide to send a letter bomb next. What if—"

"Don't worry. I was caught off guard this time. I'll be prepared if there's a next time."

"Damian, since you obviously had this all figured out, why didn't you explain it to Detective Roth?"

"Roth wasn't interested in anything I had to say."

Kay couldn't argue. She knew he was right. "You realize you'll never be able to buy a new coat before court resumes."

"Then I'll roll up my scorched sleeve, keep my bandaged hand under the table and appear with no coat. You said the jury's mulling over Fedora's testimony all through the lunch hour would be harmful, and I agree. Letting it stand overnight would be worse. The longer a point of view is held, the harder it is to extinguish. Whatever you can do to challenge the woman's testimony needs to be done this afternoon."

He was right, of course. Again. It was getting to be an irritating habit. Still, Kay hesitated. "We never got a chance for lunch. Aren't you hungry?"

"I can wait. But you're the one who has to be thinking on her feet. There's a grill down the street. We could get something quick to go."

A grill? Seared flesh? After seeing his injury? No way. "I've rather lost my appetite," Kay admitted aloud. "Besides, I think we'd make better use of our dwindling time by taking a trip to the lost and found at the courthouse."

"The lost and found?" Damian repeated, obviously surprised.

"Yes. You wouldn't believe the selection of coats, jackets and sweaters that people have left around the building. Just tell them you lost a sweater and suit coat and they'll bring out the bunch. You're bound to find something that fits and that works with your suit slacks. I'll help you pick it out."

A charming smile raised the corners of his mouth. "Well, well. I am truly shocked. The ethical Ms. Kellogg not only suggesting a theft, but offering to aid and abet. And as we're walking through a police station, too."

That smile of his was too damn infectious. Kay had difficulty sprinkling the proper amount of starch on her tone.

"You're not stealing the clothing. You're borrowing it. Have whatever you select cleaned before you return it, and your conscience should be clear."

"Should it?"

"Are you one of those sneaky psychologists who always answers a question with a question?"

"Are you one of those sneaky lawyers who never answers a question?"

His ruggedly charming grin perfectly matched the deep, green glint in his eyes. No one could have guessed what he'd just been through. He possessed real strength—the kind that wouldn't let adversity break his stride. Damn, but this guy could be absolutely irresistible. And for once, Kay didn't even try to resist. She beamed back at him.

"I like your smile," he said as he curled her hand into the crook of his arm. "Very much."

And she liked being this close to him, feeling the strong muscles of his forearm beneath her hand, inhaling the exciting male scent of him. She liked it way too much.

And then there it was again. That strange, warm sensation, streaking down the back of her thighs.

Stop signs and red warning lights flashed in her mind. This was not the way an attorney felt about or behaved with a client. Particularly not her and particularly not with this client.

She should move away. She didn't.

What was happening to her? Why were all the inescapable conclusions of her infallible logic no longer able to push her away from this man and let her reestablish her professional distance?

We are all just mysteries, waiting to unfold, his words repeated in her mind. She was beginning to think he was right about that, too. Too damn right.

Trouble lay ahead. Plenty of it. With the trial. With this kook who had targeted Damian. With these illogical, crazy, exciting feelings she had for this man. No matter what direction she looked in, Kay Kellogg saw herself in a lot of trouble.

"MRS. NYE, are you feeling better?" Kay asked of the obviously nervous woman in the witness box.

Damian watched a look of surprise steal over Fedora's face. He suspected that Croghan had told his client to be prepared for an adversarial attack from Kay. The solicitous inquiry left the woman clearly off balance—which Damian suspected was just what Kay had intended.

"I'm . . . better," Fedora said, obviously uncertain she should be admitting it.

Kay smiled at her. "You had a nice lunch?"

Fedora's death grip on her purse relaxed a little. "Yes. Mr. Croghan took me to a restaurant. I'm not used to being waited on, so it was a nice change."

"You're not used to being waited on?" Kay repeated politely.

"I'm a waitress. I'm usually the one waiting on people."

"Oh, I see. How long have you been a waitress?"

Fedora leaned back in her chair. Kay's soft tone, clear attentiveness and encouraging smiles were working to extinguish the woman's initial nervousness. Her answers were coming faster and far more easily now.

"Twenty-two years."

"Twenty-two years," Kay repeated, letting the awe creep into her tone. "That's a long time. Ever have any problems with your legs from being on your feet all day?"

"Oh, no. I have strong muscles."

"Developed during the time when you were a cheerleader in high school, no doubt," Kay said, still with that encouraging tone and smile.

Fedora actually smiled back, seeming to be happy to be reminded of that time. "I certainly exercised them a lot then."

"How old were you?"

"The year I was a cheerleader?"

"Yes."

"Sixteen."

"And how old are you now, Mrs. Nye?"

The question seemed to surprise Fedora. "Thirty-eight."

Kay paused and let her eyebrows rise. She wasn't the only one. Damian saw similar surprised looks on several members of the jury, who had obviously been judging by appearance and thought Fedora Nye much older.

"So, it's been twenty-two years since you were a cheerleader in high school," Kay continued. "Right around the same time you started waitressing?"

"Yes."

"Mr. Croghan said you and Roy would have been celebrating your silver wedding anniversary soon if Roy were still around and if you two were still married. When did you marry Roy, Mrs. Nye?"

Fedora answered a bit more hesitantly. "Twenty-two years ago."

"So you were married to Roy when you were only sixteen?"

Fedora shifted a bit uneasily in her chair. She didn't look quite as relaxed. "Yes."

"Did Roy attend the private school where you were a cheerleader and where he came to watch you when the team played?"

"No."

"What school did he attend?"

"He didn't attend school. He was older."

"How much older?"

"Twenty-one."

Kay paused again to raise an eyebrow.

"Did your parents know you were seeing this man who was so much older?"

Her voice lost some of its volume. "No. They didn't allow me to date at all."

"But they allowed you to marry at sixteen?"

Fedora's chin sank to her chest. Her voice got even smaller. "I . . . had to."

Kay's voice remained soft, understanding. "Because Roy got you pregnant?"

"Yes."

"Because if Roy hadn't married you, your father was going to have him prosecuted for statutory rape?"

"Your Honor, I object!" Croghan bellowed. "This is totally irrelevant!"

"On the contrary. It is totally relevant," Kay said. "These incidents explain the character of the personality known as Roy."

"Roy is not on trial here!" Croghan protested.

"But he is!" Kay answered. "Your Honor, the plaintiff's attorney has painted the Roy personality as a loving husband and father. Defense is fully entitled to test this characterization to see just how well it holds up."

"Right you are," Ingle said, his eyes bright in anticipation. "Objection overruled. Go for it, Ms. Kellogg."

Kay's voice remained soft as she turned back to Fedora. "Mrs. Nye, is it true that your father had Roy arrested for statutory rape?"

"Yes."

"Is it true that if Roy hadn't married you, your father was going to have him prosecuted on that charge?"

"But he didn't. Roy married me. And he never divorced me, not through all those years."

"Let's talk about those years, Mrs. Nye. You testified this morning that Lee divorced you four years ago, is that correct?"

"Yes."

"So, in fact, you and Roy were married for eighteen years, a full seven years short of that silver anniversary Mr. Croghan alluded to earlier, is that correct?"

"Yes."

"You said you started waitressing twenty-two years ago, is that right?"

"Yes."

"So you began working right after you married?"

"Yes."

"You went to work even though you were pregnant and only sixteen?"

"I had to. My father could only give us a little money to get started with."

"Wasn't Roy working?"

"Roy had . . . difficulty finding work."

"Difficulty," Kay repeated. "Mrs. Nye, in the eighteen years that you and Roy were married, what jobs did Roy hold?"

"I . . . don't know."

"You don't know? Are you saying he never held a job?"

"I don't know."

"Mrs. Nye, would it be true to say that you know of no job that Roy might have held during those eighteen years because he was seldom living with you?"

"He . . . left a lot. And he didn't always come back right away."

"Right away? Isn't it true that Roy often only spent a few weeks with you before he would take off for one, two, even three years at a stretch?"

"Y-yes."

"And when he did return, isn't it also true he did not contribute to the support of either you or your two children, but, rather, you supported him on the money you made waitressing?"

"I . . ."

Kay still spoke softly, gently. "Mrs. Nye, please tell us if that is true."

"Yes."

"These Saturday afternoons in the park and the Sunday mornings in church that you described earlier, did Roy ever attend any of those events with you and the children?"

"I . . . no."

"Did Roy ever express any desire that his children be sent to religious school or taken to church or, in fact, did he ever show any interest in them at all?"

"No."

"So you alone saw to the children's needs and welfare?"

"Yes."

"Did Roy get drunk often?"

Fedora's fingers dug into her purse. "He liked his whiskey. And beer. He got . . . upset if I didn't keep enough on hand."

"He got upset," Kay repeated. "Did he physically abuse you?"

"I . . . He used to get very . . . upset sometimes."

"Upset," Kay repeated before returning to the defense table to retrieve a file. "Your Honor, may I approach the witness?"

"Yes, Ms. Kellogg," Ingle said.

Kay stepped up and handed Mrs. Nye a page from the file. Her voice was still soft, her manner gentle.

"Mrs. Nye, you have in your hand a police report on Roy dated twelve years ago. Would you read for the court what charge he was booked on?"

"Assault with a deadly weapon."

"Whom did he assault?"

Her voice was tiny, barely audible. "Me."

"There is a description of your injuries beneath the charge. Would you read them, please?"

"A fractured jaw, a fractured wrist, severe bruises and abrasions over shoulders, back and legs."

A small murmur rippled through the courtroom. Kay waited until it died down.

"What was the instrument that Roy used on you to cause these injuries?"

"My son's baseball bat."

This time, the murmur that ran through the courtroom was louder and longer. Shoes shuffled. Benches squeaked. Damian knew that Kay had again paused to let the horrific images sink in.

The harshness of Kay's next words were once more mitigated by their soft delivery. "Was this the only time that Roy became *upset* and inflicted such severe injuries on you, Mrs. Nye?"

"I . . . don't remember."

"Perhaps this will help to refresh your memory," Kay said as she handed the witness another piece of paper from the file she held, still keeping her voice and manner gentle.

"This is a copy of an arrest report for Roy dated ten years ago. Please read the list of your injuries this time."

"A concussion, a broken hip, severe bruises and contusions."

"And how did you receive these injuries, Mrs. Nye?"

"Roy shoved me down the stairs."

"Were you the one who called the police on these occasions?"

"No."

"Who did?"

"Neighbors hearing the noise, I think. I'm not sure."

"Are you not sure because you were knocked out from these beatings and woke up in the hospital?"

"Yes."

"Was Roy ever tried and convicted for these assaults on you?"

"No."

"Why not?"

"I . . . wouldn't testify against him."

"Why not?"

"A wife cannot dishonor her sacred vows to love, honor and obey her husband."

"Do you think your adherence to those vows might have been the real reason that Roy never divorced you?"

"I don't know what you mean."

"I mean, Mrs. Nye, that you were the perfect wife for Roy. You served and supported him on the rare occasions when he chose to come home to you. You endured his drunkenness and violent abuse. Why would he have wanted to divorce you?"

Fedora dropped her chin again, as she clutched her purse to her breast.

"I object! Argumentative!" Croghan bellowed.

"Sustained," Ingle answered.

Kay stepped a little closer to Fedora, her voice as soft and gentle as always. "Mrs. Nye, you didn't contest the divorce when Lee brought suit four years ago, did you?"

"No."

"Were you glad Roy was gone?"

Her head rose, her face clear and childlike. "How could you think such a thing? That would be a sin against God."

Damian had heard these kinds of statements before from battered women. That didn't make Fedora's statements any easier to listen to.

"You testified this morning that you received no financial support as a result of that divorce. Isn't it true that you didn't receive anything because Lee didn't have anything?"

"He was only a mail clerk at some marketing firm making minimum wage."

"So the fact that Lee said that he didn't consider himself to be your husband or the father of your children had nothing to do with the judge's decision not to award spousal and child support, did it?"

"No."

"You didn't get anything because there wasn't anything to get, isn't that correct?"

"Yes."

"But Lee's financial status has changed significantly during the last four years, hasn't it, Mrs. Nye?"

"I . . . believe so."

"You believe so? Mrs. Nye, isn't it true that last year you filed suit to reopen your divorce settlement?"

"I . . . yes."

"And in that suit, didn't you state that evidence uncovered by a private investigator showed Lee to now be worth in excess of five million dollars and that you were claiming half his current assets plus half his future earnings in alimony?"

"Your Honor, I object!" Croghan shouted as he jumped to his feet. "Neither that suit nor any other suit has a bearing on this case!"

"Nice try, Mr. Croghan," Ingle said with a smile. "Overruled. Answer the question, Mrs. Nye."

"Mr. Croghan hired the private investigator," Mrs. Nye said.

"Mr. Croghan?" Kay repeated. "Your attorney in this suit?"

"Yes."

"So Mr. Croghan represented you in this reopening of your divorce settlement last year?"

"Yes."

"Mrs. Nye, was it Mr. Croghan who approached you and convinced you that you should go after Lee Nye's money?"

"I object, Your Honor!" Croghan yelled as he jumped to his feet once again. "What Ms. Kellogg is suggesting is ludicrous! Besides which, all communications between my client and me are privileged communications."

"That they are. Sustained," Ingle said. "Careful, Ms. Kellogg. No soliciting of privileged communications."

"Yes, Your Honor. Mrs. Nye, do you believe Lee to be your husband?"

"No. Roy was my husband."

"Then why did you try to get alimony out of Lee?"

"Mr. Croghan said I was entitled to it."

"Did you think you were entitled to it?"

She shifted in her seat uneasily. "I've worked all these years, fed and clothed and taken care of myself and the children, and even Roy when he came around."

Damian could tell that Fedora was trying to convince herself as she once more fidgeted in her chair before going on. "It didn't seem wrong to want a little something for myself. And it is Roy's body that made that money, after all. Those are his hands that built up that company he now owns."

"You mean that Lee now owns."

"Yes. I . . . it's confusing, this dual-personality thing. I don't really understand it that well. Roy's gone, I know that.

But Mr. Croghan says that since Lee was inside Roy all those years, I was married to Lee, too."

"Mrs. Nye, what happened to that suit you filed against Lee Nye?"

"It was dismissed."

"Why?"

"The judge said that the moneys were earned after the divorce and were therefore not community property."

"So, after failing to latch on to Lee's newly made wealth, Mr. Croghan got a bit more creative and decided to use you to drum up this ridiculous suit against Dr. Steele?"

"I object!" Croghan yelled, jumping up and down and pounding on the table.

"Sustained," Ingle ruled. "Try to keep them above the belt, Ms. Kellogg. And Mr. Croghan, no more pounding," he admonished without any real enthusiasm. Kay could tell he was obviously enjoying the fight too much to give anything but lip service to its rules.

"Yes, Your Honor," Kay said with a respectful head bow in his direction. She then turned toward the witness stand and smiled.

"Mrs. Nye, I believe I now understand the... ah...pressures that have been placed upon you to bring this suit."

"Your Honor!" Croghan shouted.

"I have no further questions for this witness," Kay said before he could get his objection out. She twirled around and strolled confidently back to the defense table.

Her face was glowing, her eyes alight with victory—as well they should be.

Damian understood now that Kay's enviable litigation record was attributable not only to her infallible legal logic, but also to the way she used her diminutive stature and soft voice to disarm.

She'd broken down Fedora's testimony without once attacking her and alienating the sympathetic jury. And with her last deft thrust, she had clearly implied that Fedora was but a pitiful pawn in the manipulative hands of her greedy attorney.

She was quite a lawyer. And quite a woman. And his promise to be a gentleman was getting to be more of a struggle than he had ever imagined.

"You're excused, Mrs. Nye," Ingle said. "Your next witness, Mr. Croghan."

"I call Carla Greene to the stand."

Damian watched Kay stiffen, all signs of her fresh victory visibly draining from her face. They exchanged quick glances. The name obviously meant nothing to either of them.

Damian snatched the proposed witness list Croghan had supplied. Kay slipped into the chair beside him. Together they started down the list as the bailiff left the courtroom to summon the witness.

Carla Greene was listed on the bottom of the second page. So Croghan had supplied the name of the witness as he was required to do. There were no grounds upon which to raise an objection.

Who was Carla Greene? And what would she testify to?

Both Damian and Kay anxiously turned toward the back of the courtroom, waiting for the mystery witness to appear.

Chapter Ten

"Mrs. Greene, please state your credentials for this court," Croghan said.

The sturdy-looking, no-nonsense, middle-aged woman with the short gray hair and large silver glasses leaned back comfortably in the witness chair. Her crisp, clear voice carried to the far reaches of the courtroom.

"I have an undergraduate degree in psychology and a master's degree in clinical sociology. For the past twenty years, I've been employed by the county as a social worker, the last ten years as a substance-abuse specialist."

"Mrs. Greene, did you ever have occasion to interview and evaluate a man named Roy Nye?"

"Yes."

"Would you explain those circumstances?"

"Mr. Nye was arrested and brought in because his violent behavior had resulted in a barroom brawl in which several patrons were injured. The bartender told officers that the man had been visibly shaking when he walked into the bar, drank two beers in rapid succession and then just erupted into an uncontrollable rage. I interviewed Roy Nye in order to assess the nature of his substance abuse."

"By substance abuse, you mean alcohol?"

"Yes."

"And what were your findings based on your twenty years of experience in these types of cases?"

"That Roy Nye was both physiologically addicted and allergic to alcohol."

"Describe to this court what you mean by physiologically addicted."

"He had to drink. It was a craving too strong for his body to resist. If he didn't drink, he went through extremely painful withdrawal symptoms."

"And now describe for this court what you mean by his being allergic to alcohol."

"Even though he had to drink, his body was allergic to alcohol. The manifestation of that allergic reaction was violence. When alcohol was in his system, he would lash out uncontrollably. He didn't know what he was doing. It was purely his body's allergic reaction to the alcohol."

"So is it your expert opinion that because of Roy Nye's addiction and allergic reaction to alcohol that he was not accountable for his actions?"

Mrs. Greene nodded her head of short gray hair in decided emphasis. "I am certain of it. Roy Nye did not know what he was doing when he was drunk. He totally lost control."

"Did Roy Nye deserve to die because of his problem?"

"Absolutely not! Roy Nye deserved to be understood and helped."

"Could Roy Nye have been helped, Mrs. Greene?"

"If Roy had been properly diagnosed and admitted to a hospital for treatment, he could have been detoxed, educated about his problem, overcome it and be leading a normal life today."

"Thank you, Mrs. Greene, for your expert testimony. I have no further questions."

Croghan positively beamed as he sent Kay a triumphant grin. "Your witness, Ms. Kellogg."

Damian knew that Mrs. Greene's testimony had been damaging. But without preparation, what could Kay possibly do to counteract it?

KAY STOOD UP and slowly approached Mrs. Greene. It was always difficult to take on a witness unprepared. And

Croghan knew what he was doing when he'd put this one on the stand.

Everything Kay had done to point out Roy Nye's drunken abusiveness in her cross-examination of Fedora Nye meant nothing under this woman's claim that he was being controlled by his allergic addiction to alcohol. She knew that the jury mustn't be allowed to think of Roy as a victim.

She would have to begin her cross-examination with a few old standbys and hope to hit pay dirt.

"Mrs. Greene, are you being paid by the plaintiff to appear in court today?"

"No," she answered with a satisfied smirk. "No one could ever buy my testimony."

She had been ready for that question. Too ready. Croghan must have coached her. Kay quickly moved on. "Do you often testify on the cases you've handled?"

"Only three times in my career and only in family court. This is my first time as a superior-court witness."

Hard for Kay to imagine. The woman's assurance made her come across like a veteran. She was precise in her answers, solid in her opinions and sure of herself.

Too sure of herself, perhaps? Yes, maybe that's where Kay could find her edge.

"Mrs. Greene, you said you've been a caseworker for how long now?"

"Twenty years as of last February fourth."

"And when did you see Roy Nye and make your evaluation regarding his condition?"

"Several years ago."

Ah. The woman's first imprecise answer. This was a path to follow. Kay stepped perceptibly closer and leaned the top portion of her body forward as though straining to hear.

"How many years ago was it exactly, Mrs. Greene?"

A hesitation, brief, but telling. "Fourteen."

"Fourteen years ago?" Kay repeated, deliberately letting her voice rise in surprise as she rocked back on her heels.

"Yes."

"How can you remember a case from so long ago?"

"I have an excellent memory for all my cases."

"Do you have any notes or official records from your evaluation of Roy Nye?"

"They were thrown out long ago. Our records weren't on computer then and there was no place to store all that paperwork. But it doesn't matter. I remember the incident clearly."

"Even though it was fourteen years ago?"

"Yes."

"Mrs. Greene, when you saw Roy Nye and made your evaluation of him fourteen years ago, you had only been a caseworker for six years, not twenty, isn't that correct?"

Her lips began to tighten. "Yes."

"And you weren't a specialist in substance abuse at that time, is that correct?"

"I frequently evaluated such cases."

"But you were not a substance-abuse specialist at the time you evaluated Roy Nye, were you?"

"No."

"How many times did you see Roy Nye before coming to your conclusions about his problems?"

"Once."

"*Once?*"

A flash of defiance crossed Mrs. Greene's face. "Once was all I needed."

"And how long did your evaluation take?"

"Thirty minutes."

"*Only* thirty minutes?"

Mrs. Greene's chin raised defiantly. "When you know what you're doing, you only need thirty minutes."

"Was Roy Nye under the influence of alcohol when you saw him this one time for thirty minutes?"

"Yes."

"Was he legally intoxicated?"

"He showed all the signs. And he shouldn't have. That's what made his condition so obvious. The bartender reported that he had only served him two beers, yet Roy Nye manifested all the symptoms of extreme alcohol intoxication."

"And those symptoms were . . . ?"

"Diminished physical coordination. Slurred speech. Uncontrolled physical violence that required his being restrained."

"You consider uncontrolled physical violence a manifestation of alcohol intoxication?"

Mrs. Greene's tone took on the derisory air of a master addressing an apprentice. "In Roy Nye's case, it was the manifestation of his allergic response to the alcohol. He'd only had two beers, remember."

"You mean, Mrs. Greene, that he'd only had two beers *that you know of.*"

"I'm sure he'd only had two beers."

"How can you be so sure? Was a blood-alcohol test done on him?"

"No, but the bartender said—"

"That he had only served him two beers, yes, I heard. But how do you know that the bartender was telling the truth? A man he'd served liquor to had just ended up violently assaulting other customers. That bartender may have been trying to protect himself against liability by saying he'd only served Roy two beers. Or Roy may have had several dozen drinks somewhere else before he walked into that bar. Isn't that true, Mrs. Greene?"

"I don't believe—"

"I didn't ask you what you believe. I asked you if Roy Nye could have had a lot more than two beers to drink when you saw him intoxicated? Yes or no, Mrs. Greene?"

The answer hissed through her teeth. "Yes."

"So you interpreted Roy's drunken behavior to be alcohol addiction and allergy to alcohol based on seeing him once for thirty minutes in a drunken state in which you thought he'd only had two beers?"

"I saw him, Ms. Kellogg," Mrs. Greene said defiantly. "You didn't."

"Mrs. Greene, please answer the question. Did you interpret Roy Nye's drunken behavior to be alcohol addiction and allergy to alcohol based on seeing him only once in a drunken state in which you thought he'd only had two beers?''

Mrs. Greene's lips folded until they were as thin as playing cards. She dealt her answer through them. ''Yes. But in my twenty years of experience, I've acquired the judgment—''

''But you only had six years of experience when you diagnosed Roy Nye. And that was fourteen years ago. For thirty minutes. Mrs. Greene, isn't it true that you could be wrong about Roy Nye's being addicted to and allergic to alcohol?''

Mrs. Greene folded her arms across her chest. ''I stand by my evaluation.''

''You said earlier that if Roy Nye had been properly diagnosed and admitted to a hospital to be treated, he could have overcome his addiction and be leading a normal life today, is that correct?''

''Yes.''

''Then why didn't you see to Roy's admission to a hospital and the administration of this proper treatment?''

''We were...are...not authorized to make such arrangements.''

''Not authorized? Mrs. Greene, do you have a medical degree?''

''No.''

''Is the reason you are not authorized to make such arrangements because alcohol addiction and allergy to alcohol are diagnoses that only proper medical personnel, using proper medical tests, can accurately assess?''

''I have never needed any such medical tests. All I've ever needed—''

''Is thirty minutes in a room with a drunken, violent man and too many self-serving assumptions,'' Kay interrupted.

''Your Honor, I object!'' Croghan yelled. ''Argumentative!''

''Withdrawn,'' Kay said, pivoting away from Mrs. Greene and heading back to the defense table. ''I have no further questions for this *expert* witness.''

DAMIAN SIGNALED across the restaurant to Kay so she could join him and Jerry Tummel at their table in the corner. She nodded and started forward.

Jerry gave a low whistle beside Damian.

"Very nice. Just the kind that makes you want to get out the old sword and slay a dragon or two."

Damian chuckled. "Believe me, Jerry, this one is pretty good at slaying her own dragons."

"Yeah. I caught the early news before coming over. The broadcast mentioned how well she's sliced up Croghan's witnesses so far. You sleeping with her yet?"

"Get your mind out of your pants, Jerry."

"So she turned you down, eh? Well, good for her. About time you met a lady with some class."

Damian snickered. "Too bad I can't find a friend with any."

Kay walked up just then, not giving Jerry time for a retort. Both men rose and Damian made the introductions before holding out a chair for Kay. When they were all seated again, the waiter walked over with a glass of milk and set it before her.

She looked over at Damian, tipped the glass in salute, took a drink and smiled. Damian felt the returning smile draw back his lips. He also felt Jerry's curious eyes swinging back and forth between Kay and him.

Jerry leaned across the table toward Kay.

"I caught some coverage of the case on television just before I left. Did you hear that their four newscasters are split down the middle on who's ahead after the first day in court?"

"I'm more concerned with what the jury thinks after the last day in court."

Jerry tipped his drink in her direction. "Well, lovely lady, if I were sitting in the jury box, you'd get my vote if for no other reason than you are such a lovely lady."

Damian noted Kay's returning smile was pleasant but offered no invitation. "I know you're very busy, Dr. Tummel, and I appreciate—"

"Call me Jerry. Please."

"Okay, Jerry. I just wanted you to know that I appreciate your willingness to testify."

"Well, old Damian here and I have been buddies since we were kids. He's gotten me out of more scrapes than I'd like to admit. About time I returned the favor."

"You were childhood chums? And both of you ended up as psychologists. That's...unusual, isn't it?"

Jerry laughed. "Not when you meet in a psychologist's office."

"You met in a psychologist's office?" Kay repeated, clearly inviting a further explanation.

"Yeah, we were both only about five, too. Pretty bad to be screwed up so early."

"You really needed a psychologist at five years old?"

Jerry grinned at her. "My uncle was the psychologist. My mother still claims she only sent me to him so he could take me out to lunch for my birthday."

"Wasn't it your birthday?"

"Oh, sure. That week. But what about the next fifty-two weeks when she kept insisting on dropping me off in front of his building instead of the movie theater?"

Damian could tell Kay didn't know whether Jerry was just being a tease or whether there was an underlying seriousness to his words. She seemed even more confused when Jerry punctuated his comments with the sneezy bark that passed as his laugh.

"I suppose it was your uncle's being a psychologist that got you thinking about becoming one?" she ventured after a moment, clearly still fishing.

Jerry shook his head. "Doesn't work that way, Kay. Nobody decides to become a psychologist. You just decide you're a screwed-up kid who needs to take some courses to try to get yourself unscrewed. The courses don't help a whole lot. But eventually you get old enough and rack up enough of them to qualify for a degree. So you grab the degree, give up trying to unscrew yourself and spend your adult life honestly telling other screwups that you know how they feel."

Jerry let out a few more short, sneezy barks before dipping his nose into his martini. Damian clapped him on the shoulder.

"Jerry's not really drunk, Kay. Or too deranged. It's just that four of his five ex-wives called him today to ask for more alimony. It always brings out his more cynical side."

"You have *five* ex-wives?" Kay said. "But you don't look any older than—"

"Thirty-four," Jerry interrupted with a slightly lustful look her way. "And presently single. In presentable condition. Five-ten. One seventy-five. Work out at the gym three times a week. And already in love with you, lady lawyer. From the moment you started walking toward the table tonight, I said to myself, 'Ah, number six.'"

Kay smiled. "Sorry, but six has never been a lucky number for me."

Jerry exhaled dramatically. He lifted his drink in salute. "Probably just as well. My first five wives all said I'm hell to live with. Stay away from psychologists, Kay. We're all screwed up. Damian's afraid to get married and I'm afraid to stay single."

"Damian's *afraid* to get married?" Kay repeated.

Damian punched his friend in the arm. "Careful, Jerry, or Kay and I will both get up and leave you with the check for the drinks."

Jerry sank his head theatrically to his chest as he winked at Kay. "He always knows he can get me to cower with such vicious financial threats."

"Stop flirting with my lawyer and let's see some evidence of all that time you spent with your uncle," Damian said.

Jerry made a great show of straightening his tie and slicking back his hair, then took a pipe out of his pocket and stuck it unlit into his mouth.

"I am now my professional self," he announced in an overly dramatic tone. "Let's get down to business."

Kay smiled at the antics before asking her first serious question. "Jerry, opposing counsel is putting Upton Van Pratt on the stand. You know who he is?"

"Who doesn't? Van Pratt is probably the most respected name in psychological circles, one of the major contributors to cognitive therapy. I took a course from him nearly fifteen years ago and he was already a legend then."

"Do you know how he treats multiple personality disorder?"

"I have no idea. The guy must be close to seventy now. Fifteen, twenty years ago, in his heyday, MPD virtually went undiagnosed. He may have written something on the subject since."

Damian interrupted. "No. We've checked all the journals. We can't find anything."

"Well, can't help you then. One thing I can tell you, although I'm not sure how much help it will be."

"What?" Kay asked.

"Van Pratt started out as a maverick speed demon in the way he overturned many psychological concepts. But like so many others, he became a middle-of-the-roader in his later years. He's also become extremely intolerant of fast- or slow-lane travelers."

"Ideas too old or new, you mean?"

"You're quick, Kay."

"Which would he consider Damian's handling of the Lee Nye case to be?"

"I would suspect he'd see it as speeding down the fast lane."

"It's hard for me to accept that a man of Van Pratt's standing is willing to testify in this trial, Jerry," Damian interjected. "You know him better than I. Can you suggest what might be making him do it?"

"You didn't hear? Van Pratt is in financial difficulty. Word is, he had his money in silver and took a beating. To get back on his feet, he's been hiring himself out to attorneys as their 'professional' witness on all sorts of cases dealing with psychological matters."

Kay leaned her forearms on the table. "Do you mean that Dr. Van Pratt is one of those psychologists who sells his testimony?"

"No. He certainly isn't one of that despicable bunch. And I don't mean to imply he's doing anything unethical. I may not always agree with his middle-of-the-road stands, but Upton Van Pratt is a man of integrity. He's simply let it be known that if any attorney wishes to have him consult on a case, he will render his expert opinion for a fee. If that expert opinion turns out to be something the attorney would like Van Pratt to repeat under oath in court, he will do so for an additional fee."

"So you're saying his opinion will be an honest one and he won't try to twist the facts for the sake of either fee."

"Yes, that's exactly what I'm saying."

Damian could see that as far as Kay was concerned, that wasn't good news. He realized that it would have been far easier for her to discredit someone on the stand who was there only for money than someone who would not compromise his principles.

Watching the momentary shadow cross her face almost had Damian missing the next exchange between her and Jerry.

"...to testify on Thursday?" Kay asked.

"Morning or afternoon?"

"My best guess is afternoon."

"I'll arrange my schedule to make myself available then."

"Thank you, Jerry," Kay said. "I sincerely appreciate your cooperation."

"Not a problem. Damian did his patient a major favor by extinguishing the Roy personality, believe me. I doubt if I could have pulled it off. There aren't many psychologists around who would have even thought of it, much less succeeded in doing it."

"You've never extinguished a personality?"

"I would have sworn it couldn't be done until I saw Damian's videotapes."

"You've seen all the videotapes?"

"All eighty-five hours' worth. Being a witness to those tapes is the reason I can be so certain in my support of Damian's decision in this case. I know you can't appreciate the unique situation a psychologist finds himself in when he attempts to treat a multiple-personality patient. The time and emotional investment is enormous.''

''Emotional investment?''

''The alters involved in the MPD patient's system can present a confusing array of exceptionally diverse personalities with varying levels of awareness of one another. When your patient switches to a totally different personality right in front of you, it can be like—''

''An icy chill between the shoulder blades?'' Kay finished.

Jerry stared at her. ''Yes. Exactly. I'm surprised you—''

''Before they were stolen from my place last Sunday,'' Damian interrupted, ''I showed Kay some of LeRoy Nye's videotapes.''

Jerry's voice rose perceptibly as he leaned toward Damian. ''You what? Are you out of your mind? How could you let her—''

''What's wrong with my seeing them, Jerry?'' Kay asked. ''I've gone through the first two-hour sessions, and with Damian's help, I'm gaining an understanding of the multiple-personality phenomenon.''

Jerry pushed his martini away, shoved his pipe prop back into his pocket and sat back. ''Look, Kay, I don't care why Damian did it, he shouldn't have. I sure as hell wouldn't let anyone but a psychologist trained in MPD see LeRoy Nye's tapes.''

''I'm a lawyer. I'm bound to secrecy by strict attorney-client privilege.''

''It isn't disclosure I'm concerned about.''

''What is it, Jerry?''

He leaned forward across the table. Gone was the glib clown. His tone was straight and very, very serious. ''You're not a psychologist who specializes in this stuff, Kay. You're not screwed up like us. And trust me. You don't want to be. If Damian ever gets back those tapes, don't let him show you any more of them. I'm warning you.''

KAY STOPPED ABRUPTLY beside her car in the parking lot of the restaurant where they had left Dr. Jerry Tummel nursing his third martini. She turned to Damian.

"What's going on here? What is on those tapes that Jerry was so adamant I not see?"

"Jerry only said what he did to get a rise out of you, Kay."

"Nice try, Damian. Jerry was in a comfortable, flirty mood until you mentioned my seeing those tapes. After that, he got exceptionally stiff and very uncomfortable. His reaction reminded me of that afternoon at my condo when you warned me against watching the rest of those tapes. There's something you haven't told me about this case, isn't there?"

"Like what?"

He was being deliberately evasive and she knew it. Kay leaned against the driver's-side door of her car and looked up at the man who could seem so open and yet still be so closed.

"It's something about Lee. Or Roy. Something that's on the rest of those tapes."

That impatient hand swept through his hair. The disciplined mind quickly returned it to his side. "Kay, you know as well as I that the police have no leads as to who stole those tapes. Since your chances of ever seeing them are probably nil, why don't you just forget them?"

"I don't really have to see the tapes, do I? You know what Jerry was talking about. You could tell me what's concerning you both so much."

"Kay, there is a lot that came out in my sessions with the Lee and Roy personalities. There are diametrically opposed...interpretations that can be drawn from certain parts of the uncovered material. Just because Jerry has one viewpoint—"

Kay leaned away from the comforting support of her car. "Wait a minute. Are you saying that Jerry and you don't agree on the full interpretation of this MPD case?"

"We agreed on the diagnosis and the treatment and that is what ultimately matters."

"Is it? What happens if I put Jerry on the stand and Croghan asks him if he agreed with all your interpretations on this case? What then?"

"Is Croghan likely to do that?"

"Of course he's likely to do that. Damian, he's not going to miss a trick. Damn. We're in more trouble than I thought. Did Dr. Pat Fetter also disagree with your interpretation of some of the material that came out on those tapes?"

"No. Pat and I were in full agreement."

"That cinches it. We must have her testify. Did you call her office again today?"

Damian nodded. "They've sent off a telegram to be delivered to the retreat. I'll just have to wait for her to get it and respond."

"We can't wait," Kay declared. "We've wasted enough time. We need her testimony. Now more so than ever. I'm calling AJ. She'll track down the elusive Dr. Pat Fetter."

"I will, will I?" AJ's voice asked from out of the shadows.

Kay jumped as AJ slid into view like one of those shadows. "What are you doing here?" she asked the investigator in surprise.

"Tracking you down," AJ answered simply.

"How did you ever find me?"

"Trade secret. You've forced me into using professional methods to keep track of you since you refuse to wear that beeper."

"Is this urgent?"

"Yes. The other partners are waiting for you back at the office."

"Waiting for me? Why?"

"Adam thought you'd best all see it together."

"See what together?" Kay asked.

AJ looked to Damian's face and back to Kay's before answering.

"You haven't heard? Croghan and Mrs. Nye are being interviewed live via satellite by Larry Kind. Your adversary has promised to announce a new development in your case. A big one. Something to do with a guy named Vince Boson. Ring a bell with you, Dr. Steele?"

Chapter Eleven

"Dr. Damian Steele is a violent man, particularly when it comes to multiple-personality patients," Croghan said as his split-screen image flashed on the screen. *"His callous disregard for the life of Roy Nye is only one aspect of his propensity for violence. Eight months ago, Dr. Steele severely beat Mr. Vince Boson, beside me here, and all because Vince was trying to protect one of his wife's multiple personalities."*

"What's the story?" Larry Kind asked the man.

Kay's eyes were glued to the television screen in the firm's conference room, where she and all the partners sat around the table to watch the show. AJ occupied a chair at the far back, near the door, in that quiet restlessness that was so much a part of her.

Vince Boson moved into camera range. To Kay, he looked like a mountain of a man with a fleshy, disagreeable face.

"All I was doing was trying to get my wife out of his office. She was okay before she started seeing him. But then she started changing, getting these weird moods and acting crazy like. She said this Dr. Steele told her she had a destructive personality inside her and he was working to extinguish it. Bunch of stupid bunk."

"So you didn't believe your wife needed this treatment?" Larry Kind asked him.

"'Course not. Bette was a good wife until she became his patient. Then all of a sudden she started refusing to meet her

wifely...uh...duties. Said Steele told her not to. I told her to stop seeing that damn shrink, but he must have hypnotized her or something because she went back. That's when I knew I had to get her away from him in order to try to save our marriage.''

''*And when you went to Dr. Steele's office to get your wife, that's when the trouble started?''* Larry Kind asked.

''*Yeah. Steele came at me. I mean, I didn't touch the guy, I swear. He just exploded into this uncontrollable rage. I tried to defend myself, but he was like a crazy man. My injuries were so bad that they had to rush me by ambulance to the emergency room at a nearby hospital.''*

''*The police have confirmed the unprovoked beating of Mr. Boson by Dr. Steele,''* Croghan cut in. ''*Who knows how many other patients and their spouses this man has injured? Who knows how many other personalities have been murdered by him! And Kay Kellogg from the Seattle law firm of Justice Inc. described him to the jury as a committed and compassionate doctor!''*

''*In case you've just tuned in,''* Larry Kind said, ''*we have with us live via satellite Mrs. Fedora Nye and her attorney, Rodney Croghan. Mrs. Fedora Nye is suing psychologist Dr. Damian Steele in Seattle's King County Superior Court this week for extinguishing her husband's half of a dual-personality patient. We also have with us Mr. Vince Boson, a victim of an alleged physical attack earlier this year by Dr. Steele, who was apparently trying to eliminate a personality from Mr. Boson's wife, also diagnosed with multiple personality disorder. Now we're ready to go to our phone calls. Virginia Beach, Virginia, hello.''*

''*Mrs. Nye, was your husband a Christian?''* a woman's voice asked.

Mrs. Nye's split screen image appeared on the TV.

''*Y-yes.''*

''*Then you must give him a Christian burial. Otherwise, his soul will never find its eternal rest.''*

''*I never thought of that,''* Fedora admitted.

"Excellent suggestion," Croghan said as his image popped up on screen. *"Roy's soul must be laid to rest. I will help Mrs. Nye arrange for a proper ceremony."*

"I'll just bet he will," Kay said, crossing her arms over her chest angrily. "Just think of all the additional publicity that will generate for him."

"Myrtle Beach, South Carolina, hello," Larry Kind's voice said.

"My question is for the lawyer," a man's voice said. *"My cousin is one of these multiple personality people. She says her psychiatrist claims it's not possible to kill off any personality. Do you think that maybe Roy is still alive somewhere inside this Lee guy?"*

"How I only wish that were true," Croghan lamented, shaking his head sadly. *"If we could but return this woman's husband to her, I would be overjoyed. But, sadly, every visage of Roy has been erased, blotted out as though he never existed."*

"Let's take a break from our callers and let me ask you a question, Mr. Croghan," Larry Kind said.

Croghan's face positively beamed. Kay could see that publicity certainly agreed with him.

"Ask anything you wish, Larry."

"What exactly do you hope to prove with this trial?"

"To prove, Larry?" Croghan's TV image looked and sounded shocked at the question. *"I'm not out to prove anything. I just want to remind people that it is only God who has the right to give life, and only God who has the right to take it away. And I want Dr. Damian Steele to know that he is not God!"*

The camera switched back to Larry Kind. *"In our next segment on tonight's show, we'll be meeting with the authors of three new autobiographical books on multiple personality who present the who, what and why. Don't go away."*

Adam moved over to the TV set in the corner and switched it off.

"I knew I had heard the name Damian Steele before,"
Octavia Osborne said from her position at the conference
table. "And now I know why."

"This show has jogged your memory?" Adam said.

"Yes. I was at the police station eight months ago, waiting for a client to be released on bail, when this guy, Vince
Boson, was filing his complaint against Dr. Steele. Boson
must have just come from the emergency room because he
was covered in bandages, everywhere, even his ears."

"His ears?" Marc Truesdale echoed.

"Yes. The bandages were shooting up and out like this,"
Octavia said with appropriate hand gestures. "Boson's
enormous, at least six-six. He looked like a gigantic white
rabbit. I remember thinking that if he was the loser, I really
wanted to get a look at the winner of that fight. When I
asked about Steele, the policeman who took Boson's complaint got this grin on his face and told me Steele was six
inches shorter, didn't have a scratch on him and had done
this damage to Boson with just his bare fists."

"What else did the detective say?" Adam asked.

"That's all."

"Croghan's mentioning the firm and Kay on a national
program means we'll soon be deluged with calls," Marc
said. "We'll have to release a statement, so we'd best get
prepared. I think that Adam, as senior partner, should answer the inquiries. What are your thoughts, Kay?"

Kay nodded at Marc's suggestion. "Yes, I think Adam
should say something direct and simple, like Justice Inc.
believes in Dr. Steele's complete innocence, and we are
confident that a trial of the facts by the jury, and not of in-
nuendo by the press, will vindicate him of all these ridiculous charges."

"*Are* we confident of that?" AJ asked from her position
at the back of the room.

"Of course," Kay answered without hesitation.

Adam turned to address his sister. "What's the full story
on this Vince Boson business?"

"I sent an investigator over to talk with the police. His
preliminary report is pretty sketchy. He was still looking for

the original officer who took the complaint eight months ago."

"Was Dr. Steele arrested after Boson's complaint?" Marc asked.

AJ shook her head. "We know he was taken down for questioning. Right now, that's all we know. We'll have to wait for my investigator to get back with the rest of the story."

Kay stood up and headed for the door. "You might, but I don't. I'm going to call Damian and ask him right now."

"You really believe it'll be that easy, Kay?" AJ asked.

"Why shouldn't it be?"

"He didn't tell you about Vince Boson, did he?" AJ said. "So?"

"What makes you think he'll come clean with you now?"

AJ's continuing questions were beginning to annoy Kay. "I just know."

"You just know?" AJ repeated. "How can you *just know?*"

Kay couldn't keep the irritation out of her voice. "You're questioning my judgment, AJ?"

"When it isn't surrounded by your normal, solid, lead-proof logic, yes, I'm questioning your judgment. And you should be, too. Where is that celebrated logic, Kay? You're not allowing yourself to get personally involved with this client, are you?"

Kay's back stiffened along with her words. "Of course not." She turned and headed out of the room.

"Are you sure?" AJ's words challenged behind her.

Kay yanked open the conference-room door. She swung back to AJ. "I'm sure," she said, her words escaping through clenched teeth.

But she was lying. And she knew it. That's why her teeth were clenched. And she hated reading the truth of those lies in AJ's cool, reflecting eyes.

"KAY, well this is a surprise. What are you doing here?" Damian asked the moment he returned to find her on his front doorstep.

"Where have you been?" she demanded over the roar of a jet plane passing overhead. "I called for thirty minutes straight before driving over here."

Damian shifted the bag in his arms so he could reach his key. Seattle's normal heavy overcast had rolled back in, casting her face in shadow, subduing what would have otherwise been the bright summer night. Still, he didn't need to see her features to read her state of mind.

Walking away from her and AJ in that parking lot without answering the investigator's question about knowing Vince Boson had been rude. But he had needed some time to think. And he had wanted to see what Vince Boson would say on camera before he offered any explanations of his own.

"Would you like to come in?" he asked as he put his key in the lock.

"I would like to know where you've been," she demanded in a voice that was as far from soft as the sound of a sledgehammer.

He swung open the door and switched on the porch light. He began to realize that she wasn't just upset. She was furious. And what was even more surprising was that she was showing it, from the hands on her hips to the fire in her eyes.

Faced with all that fabulous fury, Damian's own pulse began to race.

"After I watched the 'Larry Kind Show,' I discovered the cupboard was bare, so I went out for groceries."

Her tone rose into the realm of incredulity. "You watch your reputation being torn to shreds on a national program, and you respond by going out for groceries?"

He leaned inside once again to switch on the entry light and infused his tone with all the feigned innocence he could muster. "You think I should have had pizza delivered?"

"Pizza? Delivered? Have you gone stark-raving mad?"

Damian's stomach muscles tightened. He'd once wondered what she would be like stripped of that cool, logical, legal persona. And here she was giving him a glimpse, and then some.

The lady was nothing less than a keg of dynamite at the end of a lit and rapidly burning fuse. Her kinetic energy charge pulsed through him like a raw current of building need. He wanted her so badly, he ached.

For several seconds, she just stared at him with her mouth open. Finally, it seemed to dawn on her that because she'd been in the throes of all that fury, she had missed his not giving any serious answers to her questions.

Her hands slid off her hips. Her shoulders slumped. She groaned and put her head in her hands.

"No wonder people are popping up out of the woodwork ready to sue you and run you down in speedboats and cars and set your clothes on fire. Who can blame them?"

He laughed at the sudden and complete release of her fury and wrapped his free hand beneath her elbow. "Come on. You'll feel better after you've had something to eat."

He guided her inside and then released her elbow as he turned to close the door. But he never made it.

A sonic boom exploded overhead and something very large and very heavy hit him from behind shoving him into a very large pit of blackness.

"DAMIAN!" Kay yelled.

She dropped to her knees beside his fallen body and tried to lift the iron armor that now lay across his shoulder and chest. But it weighed the proverbial ton and she couldn't budge it.

It had seemed so firmly anchored to the wall by that heavy chain. Had the chain rusted? Is that why the armor had come crashing down on Damian?

He lay so quiet. So deathly quiet. Her heart twisted painfully in her chest.

"Damian? Can you hear me?"

The only answer was the squeaking door behind her as it swayed in a small night breeze.

She slammed the door shut with an impatient foot and looked around for something, for anything, she could use to pry the heavy armor off him.

The entry light was dim. All she could see was the mess of broken eggs and spilled milk and other spilled groceries.

She could do nothing by herself. She had to get to a phone and call 911.

But the instant she shot to her feet, she heard him groan. She dropped back to her knees and laid her hand gently on his forehead.

"Damian?"

He blinked as though trying to bring her into focus.

"Kay," he finally said.

"Damian, are you all right?"

"Yeah, I think so. What the hell happened?"

"The armor fell on you."

"You're kidding. It was chained to the wall."

"Not anymore. You're pinned beneath it. Don't move. I'm going to go call for help."

But as she attempted to get up again, his large hand shot out to halt her. "It's all right, Kay. It's not that heavy."

She sat back on her heels. "Not that heavy?" she repeated incredulously.

Then she watched as he sat up and lifted the heavy iron armor off him as though it were only paper. He rose to his feet in one powerful, fluid movement and reached down to help her up.

Her nerves were raw from her recent fright. She felt shaky. She braced herself by grasping his forearms. "Dear heavens," she heard somebody say, with a voice that sounded suspiciously like hers. "You're solid muscle."

He chuckled as he brought her to her feet. That enchanting psychologist's smile drew back his lips. "And all along, I imagined the way to your heart was through an interesting legal case. If I had known it was brute strength that would get me there, I would have rigged that armor to fall on me sooner."

He was entirely too charming and exciting and close, and that warm sensation wasn't just streaking down Kay's thighs anymore. It was rushing through her back and her neck and her belly and her breasts.

In the aftermath of the last few minutes of her roller-coaster emotions, she knew she was on the verge of forfeiting all reason and doing something totally illogical. Quickly, she jerked back, before the driving desires of her body could take control.

But she stepped in some spilled egg white, lost her footing and he caught her against him to keep her from falling. Her body rejoiced to be so close to his again, to feel those steel hands wrapped so solidly around her shoulders. That delicious, warm sensation rushed inside her feminine core, shimmering like a scorching liquid heat.

And then it was all just too late. Her eyes were lost in the green heat of his. Her arms were circling his iron-strong waist. Her lips were saying his name.

And he was saying hers with a groan that sounded like a curse as his mouth claimed hers.

His kiss was deep and hot and urgent. She melted into it, feeling the fire of his need fanning the flames of her own mounting desire. His strong heart challenged hers to a newer, faster pace. His large hands burned her flesh as he tore off her blouse and bra and threw them to the floor. He lifted her totally off her feet and wrapped her legs around his waist. Then he leaned her back as his wet, rough tongue sought and found the pink points of her nipples.

Kay moaned as she arched her back and shook as the sharp thrills from those wet kisses shot through her. She had never allowed herself to imagine what it would be like to make love to this man. She hadn't dared. She realized now that it was just as well. She could never have imagined this.

For he was no man tonight. He was a beast, with his growls and groans that ripped through her body as his hands ripped off the rest of her clothing. Even his smell was different, an aroma of smoky musk permeating its clean male spice.

An incredibly exciting, sexy smell that spilled hot juices throughout her body.

His throaty growls vibrated in her bones, their timbre matched to the most primitive beat of her blood, bringing it to a boiling point, blocking out all reason and logic.

If they hadn't, she might have come to her senses and remembered all the reasons that this must not happen. But his body—not his words—was speaking to her now in the language of life's most driving physical need and blocking out all her common sense.

His mouth blazed hot kisses over her naked flesh. She closed her eyes and gave herself up totally to the bolts of heat rocketing through her as his fingers laid claim to her moist, eager flesh. The world whirled around a center of wanton pleasure—her pleasure—and she reveled in it as she would never have imagined she could, opening herself more and more to his incendiary touch.

She felt him thrusting against her. She knew he wanted to be inside her and she wanted him there. She opened farther and accepted him.

A shock wave whipped through her as she felt the full size of him, followed by a jolt of pleasure so intense that it was near pain. She cried out as she thrust against him in a violent and glorious release.

Up until that second, that precise second, she hadn't thought that he was exerting any control at all. But it was she who hadn't been exerting any control.

Because at the precise second of her release, she could feel his control shatter. He grabbed her hips and plunged eagerly, madly inside her, bestial growls ripping through his throat. He was raw hunger now, tearing want, fierce in his final taking of her body.

He was claiming her as she had never been claimed, totally, unequivocally. His savage, unleashed need thrilled her to her very bone. This was passion as she had never known passion. This was desire so basic, so elemental, so mindless, so all-encompassing that it left no room for anything else.

And she wanted nothing else.

She rocked her hips to match each one of his deep, desperate thrusts. Once again she found herself caught up in the undeniable madness of those ancient mating beats embedded in a million years of memories vibrating through her cells. She joined their rhythmic percussion, in perfect tune with their timing. The pleasure began to gather again within her, spiral up, collect in the wet, hot folds of her femininity that danced so frantically against him.

She cried out again as it caught her in wave after wave of exquisite pleasure. And this time her cry was his name.

And then, with a tortured roar that sounded as though it was torn from the very core of his being, he erupted inside her with a final pounding plunge.

SHE WAS SPRAWLED over him, naked, the fingers of one hand thrumming a happy little beat against his scalp, as the top of her head nuzzled against his throat and she hummed "Climb Every Mountain" with no tune-carrying aptitude whatsoever.

Damian smiled in pure pleasure. For a very proper, serious and logical lawyer, Kay Kellogg continued to drum wonderful, delightful surprises into his life. Not the least of which was her total lack of inhibition both during their lovemaking and now in this peaceful aftermath that pleasured him in a way that rivaled even their physical joining.

Her humming beat drifted through his ears and his body. He knew he'd never be able to describe the sweetness of that sound or the warmth it brought to his heart.

"Isn't that stone floor cold on your back?" she asked solicitously.

"Maybe a little," he admitted as he let his fingers walk the vertebrae down her small, exquisite spine.

Her head rose. Blueberry eyes gently touched his face. "Do you want me to get up?"

Her skin was as pale as moonlight, her lips cherry ripe from the recent onslaught of his kisses. He could feel every soft, warm, feminine ounce of her.

"Never," he replied.

She rested her head again beneath his chin with a small satisfied sigh. "Well, what can I say except that that was certainly precedent-setting, Dr. Steele."

He chuckled. "Precedent-setting, Ms. Kellogg? I've heard a lot of reactions in my time, but that phraseology is definitely a first."

"I see you haven't made love with a lawyer before."

He chuckled once more as his hands drifted through the silk of her hair down to the satin of her bare bottom. "If I had known what I was missing, you can be sure I would have hired you a lot sooner."

She stiffened. "Damn. I wish you hadn't said that."

Her reaction instantly alarmed him. "Kay, I was only kidding."

She propped her elbow on his chest and rested her chin in the palm of her hand as she looked at him. "I know. But it just reminded me of the unprofessionalism of what I've just done."

He smiled. "You mean you've never made love on a stone floor in a beast's dungeon before?"

"I've gone against my word to you. And against the ethics of my profession."

His fingers brushed a strand of hair from her cheek. He wished he could brush the melancholy from her eyes. "This is my fault. I forced this. I'm sorry."

"No, Damian, this isn't Priscilla Payton you're talking to. You didn't force anything. I take full blame for my actions."

"Why take any blame at all? I'm not sorry we made love, Kay. Matter of fact, I'm planning on our doing it again very soon and as often as possible from now on."

He ran his hand to the back of her thighs and in a move so quick she couldn't see it coming, he rolled forward and sprang to his feet, cradling her in his arms.

His heart rejoiced at the small smile that returned to her lips. He planted a warm kiss there. "Only next time, I plan to have a nice, soft bed beneath us, so I can spend some time on top, too."

"Lusty beast," she commented with no complaint as she wrapped her arms securely around his neck. She drew back a finger and licked it. "Hmm. Chocolate icing from a smashed cupcake, I think. You also probably have dried egg yolk and milk all over your back. Aren't you going to take time to clean up the spilled groceries?"

He kissed her hair as he proceeded down the hall to the bedroom. "First things first."

She sighed. "We really should talk. That's what I came over here for, after all."

"I don't care why you came. I've wanted you here naked in my arms like this since the moment I met you. I don't want to talk. I want to make love to you until neither of us can talk."

He kicked open the bedroom door, switched on the dim ornate chandelier, and felt her body stiffen at the sight of the gigantic four-poster bed topped with enormous brass lion heads and covered with a black velvet comforter over black satin sheets.

"Typical lusty beast's lair, I see," she commented dryly.

He laid her on the top of the bed and stood over her, suddenly caught by the magic of seeing her long, honey-gold hair falling free and loose over her milk-white shoulders clear down to her waist. She was more lovely than his imagination could ever have envisioned. Much more.

He dropped to his knees beside the bed and bent to gently kiss those beautiful bare shoulders. This time he was going to take his time. The beast had been sated. Now he would show her how the civilized psychologist could and should please his lady.

She sighed and moved away, quickly wrapping the comforter around her. "No, Damian. Please. Heaven knows I want to make love to you until neither of us can move, but we must talk business, first. We're in serious trouble."

He exhaled in regret as he dropped onto the bed beside her and laid a leg in claim over hers.

He propped his head up with his hand and tried to remind himself that he was a sane psychologist. "All right, Ms. Lawyer. We'll talk business. See how well behaved the beast can be?"

"Can he? Then what happened with Vince Boson?"

Damian could hear the logical lady lawyer assuming control over the wild and warm lover of only moments before.

"I suppose I should have told you about Vince Boson," he admitted. "But I really didn't think it would become an issue."

"Wouldn't become an issue? Like the fact that Lee was a bit *unusual* wouldn't become an issue? Damian, I distinctly remember asking you if you'd ever been involved with the police, arrested or sued. You told me you hadn't."

"I didn't lie, Kay."

"Are we playing word games here? Did you or did you not attack Vince Boson?"

"I did."

"Did he attack you first?"

"He didn't attack me at all. He barged into my private session with his wife. He yanked her out of her chair, dislocating her shoulder. She screamed in pain as he dragged her to the door, yelling at me that he'd kill me and then her if I tried to interfere."

"Oh. And you ignored his threats and came to her rescue?"

Logical lady lawyer notwithstanding, he could hear the trust boldly evident in her tone. He could have predicted it would be there just by the way she had shown so much trust in him when they'd made love. A woman only opened herself like that with a man because she trusted him. It was that trust that would now make her believe whatever he told her.

For the first time, Damian saw with precision what he had only glimpsed before—that vulnerable, soft core of deep caring within the hard casing of her logic and intellect.

And he was seeing it so clearly now, he realized, because that deep caring was for him. And that deep caring was love.

Chills danced all over his skin as that knowledge sunk deep inside him. He knew a brief instant of intense joy that immediately ricocheted into alarm. He moved away from her. Lay on his back. Closed his eyes.

This is what he had feared from the first moment he saw her. This was what had made him try to walk away from her. This was what had also made him unable to. Like a brainless lemming, he'd kept marching right toward the cliff. And now here he stood, poised on its edge, the sharp rocks and boiling sea below.

Should he honor her trust? Or betray it? Which would be kinder?

As KAY WATCHED Damian draw away from her she had the eerie feeling that he was engaged in some internal battle and both sides were losing. He kept his eyes closed, as though he could no longer look at her. When he finally spoke, it was in that calm, controlled tone that she had come to know so well.

"I couldn't stop myself from beating Vince Boson."

"I understand. You were protecting Bette when you fought him."

Damian's eyes opened. He rolled to his side and leaned his jaw on his hand. The previous sexual heat of his eyes that had so deliciously baked her body and brains had disappeared like the trailing smoke of an extinguished candle. The cold green glint was back.

"I wouldn't call it much of a fight. After I dislocated *his* shoulder, I just beat the living hell out of him. He'd been doing it to her for years."

There was no anger in Damian's tone. Kay almost wished there was. His calm recitation of the facts was unnerving.

"One of Bette's personalities was a masochist, which split out when Bette was just a tiny little thing. Her masochist alter accepted the pain of abuse as pleasure in order to protect the child's mind from going insane. Vince Boson is a sadist who delighted in this personality part of his wife and didn't want me to extinguish it."

"If it had been in my power," Kay said with conviction, "I would have beaten him up, too. So what happened afterward?"

"Tim Haley, my receptionist, called an ambulance for both Bette and Vince. Bette corroborated my story to the police. Her medical records convinced them of the severity of the domestic abuse she'd been enduring for a decade. They decided my *fight* with Boson was self-defense and dropped the charges against me."

"And you continued treating Bette."

"The incident proved a breakthrough for her. She saw the abuse for the first time as a reenactment of her childhood horrors. She filed for divorce from Boson."

"So your fight with her husband gave her the courage to break out of an abusive marriage?"

"I'd been seeing Bette for five months. She'd been denying the severity and extent of her husband's abuse until then, just as vehemently as she'd been denying her parents' abuse of her as a child, which resulted in her becoming a multiple personality. The day she watched me beat up her husband, another personality called Bob made itself known. He's her protector. With Bob's help, Bette has made amazing progress ever since."

"So a lot of good came out of that confrontation Vince Boson forced on you with his threats."

"I didn't beat him because of his threats, Kay. I beat him because finally, after all these years, I got my opportunity to get the bastard."

Kay was certain she must have misunderstood. After all these years? But he just said he'd been treating Bette for only five months. What was she missing here?

"Damian, are you saying you were looking for an opportunity to beat Boson?"

"Beating him was only the start. If Priscilla and Tim hadn't pulled me off, I would have killed him. Any man who raises his hand to a woman or child should be pounded into a bloody pulp."

Damian's tranquil tone had remained absolutely even. One could easily have thought he'd been agreeing it was a hot summer instead of coolly admitting to being able to kill a man.

Until one saw the hard glint in his eyes, sharpened razor-fine from the grains of revenge refined over time.

That glint told Kay, more than anything else could, that Damian was deadly serious about everything he had just said. He wouldn't just have been able to kill that man. He had actually wanted to.

But why? Why would such a seemingly balanced psychologist have such a hatred for—

The answer flashed into her mind at the same instant it made the peach fuzz stand straight up on her arms. Her back snapped into a stiff board.

"You weren't just beating Vince Boson, were you? You were beating someone else—someone you've wanted to beat for a very long time. Who, Damian?"

He didn't say anything. It was the most chilling answer he could have given.

"Damian?"

His eyes were closed tight. She touched him on the shoulder lightly with her hand.

"Damian. I need to know."

After what seemed like a very long time, he began to speak, in that same far-too-calm voice. "My father beat my mother in uncontrollable rages. I would try to stop him. He'd just push me aside."

"How old were you?"

"Two. Three. Four. It had been going on since I was born. Then one night when I was five, I awoke to her screams and came running into the living room to find my father standing over her still body. He was kicking her, yelling at her to get up."

He paused. His jaw tightened. He swallowed hard, said nothing for a moment. Kay understood he was seeing it all again, reliving it all . . . with the eyes of a five-year-old boy. She could hardly bear the images his words evoked. She had no idea how he could. She waited.

His voice was barely a whisper now, a harsh, unhappy whisper. "When my father finally realized he'd killed my mother that night, he got out his gun and blew his brains out."

Kay sucked in a shocked breath. She would have sworn the images couldn't get worse. She'd been wrong. "Dear sweet heavens. You didn't . . . see that, too?"

His eyes came open then, glinting green and hard. Their look gave Kay a new chill.

"My grandfather told me about it later. A shame, really. I had so looked forward to beating him to death one day."

And he meant it, too. Kay could see the truth behind that hard green glint, hear it in the awful raw reality of his voice.

She shrunk back uncontrollably. "Dear God."

He smiled with no mirth whatsoever. "Yes, you would be smart to keep your distance. That uncontrollable rage runs through me, too. Even as a five-year-old child, I would explode. That's why my grandparents sent me to a psychologist. Nearly a lifetime of therapy and it still hovers, just below the surface. You see, Kay, just like LeRoy, I ended up embracing what I most abhorred. I ended up becoming my father."

She leaned forward again, horribly alarmed at the words. "How can you say that? You're nothing like that! Damian, you are a superbly disciplined man!"

"That's surface, Kay. The violence is there, waiting, believe me. It's why I'll never marry."

"But you're so gentle and protective. You'd never abuse a wife or child."

"Abuse comes in many forms, Kay. I see it every day in my practice. People swearing they'd never do to their children what was done to them. And then doing it. Violence is passed on to children by example more than anything else. It was passed on to me. I will not pass it on to another."

She shook her head. "No, I won't believe it. You are not subject to uncontrollable rages."

"If Priscilla and Tim hadn't pulled me off Vince Boson, I would have killed him."

"But you didn't. And you can't convince me you didn't only because Priscilla and Tim pulled you off him. I've seen how strong you are, Damian. If you had really been in an uncontrollable rage, no one could have pulled you off him. You *let* Priscilla and Tim stop you."

The hard, dark glint in his eyes softened. He reached out his hand to run his fingers through her hair.

"You're trying to convince yourself."

"I'm already convinced. I'm trying to convince you. Damn! How can you be so understanding of others and so blind when it comes to understanding yourself?"

The shrill sound of the telephone ringing added emphasis to her words. Damian leaned toward the instrument sitting on the nightstand and picked up the receiver.

A familiar, breathy voice responded to his hello.

"I purposely aimed for the old armor. Just wanted to let you know, next time it could be you."

Chapter Twelve

Kay read the newspaper headline that sat on the judge's desk in his private chambers: Shrink in Dual-Personality Court Case Dodges Shotgun.

Ever since Damian had received that telephone call the night before, her stomach had felt like a microwave turned on high with a ton of popcorn kernels exploding inside. She'd been a fool not to take those threats and close calls more seriously.

Ingle tapped impatient fingers on the early-morning edition of his newspaper and looked hard at her.

"Ms. Kellogg, I was awakened this morning by a Detective Roth, who not only told me that your client was shot at last evening, but that he's been getting threatening notes and telephone calls, speedboats and cars missing him by inches and even a letter bomb that exploded in my courtroom yesterday. And now, here it all is in gory detail splashed over the front page. Why wasn't I told about any of this?"

Kay spared a quick sidelong glance at Croghan's face. He was stroking his dark beard in pure pleasure at the judge's reprimand.

She spoke up quickly. "There was no letter bomb, Your Honor. An envelope, slipped into Dr. Steele's pocket, caught fire. I didn't mention it, or these other things, precisely because I didn't want the press sensationalizing the incident."

"Well, they are sensationalizing it, Ms. Kellogg, despite your failure to inform this court. And may I remind you, *I* am not the press."

"No, Your Honor, of course not. But you are a very busy judge, and it did not seem appropriate to bother you about the same kind of crank calls and letters that always start when a trial like this is so highly publicized."

"And what about that envelope that caught fire in my courtroom? Did you not think to *bother* me about that, either?"

"It ignited yesterday after court and in the presence of no one but Dr. Steele and myself. Furthermore, it was passed surreptitiously to Dr. Steele *before* he entered your courtroom."

Kay paused to glance at Mrs. Nye, looking so impossibly innocent as she sat next to her attorney. Was this woman such a consummate actress that she was fooling them all? "As a matter of fact, Dr. Steele found it in his pocket right after Mrs. Nye bumped into him in the hallway outside."

"I object!" Croghan yelled, flying to his feet.

"I'm the only one who can object in here, Mr. Croghan," Ingle said, waving the lawyer back to his seat. "Now, Ms. Kellogg, Detective Roth tells me a slug from a shotgun dropped an old suit of armor at Dr. Steele's home last evening, and could have just as easily dropped him. I trust you are no longer dismissing these incidents as cranks?"

"Of course not. But until last night's shooting and telephone threat, I thought that the perpetrator was just trying to intimidate Dr. Steele. That's why I was trying to keep the incidents out of the press."

"If you didn't inform the press of these matters, who did?"

"The reporters must have interviewed Detective Roth."

"To be expected, I suppose. All right, this is the way it's going to be. The bailiff will pass all spectators through a metal detector this morning to insure no weapons get inside the courtroom. And from now on, if either Dr. Steele or you receive any more threatening notes or calls, or if either of you even gets a hangnail, I want to be informed. Do you understand me?''

"Yes, Your Honor," Kay replied, hearing the former stodgy, by-the-book judge's voice returning momentarily beneath that ridiculous mohawk haircut.

Judge Ingle turned away from Kay and Damian.

"Mr. Croghan, when do you plan to complete the plaintiff's case?"

"This afternoon, Your Honor."

"Good. Be prepared to start your defense tomorrow morning, Ms. Kellogg. All right, ladies and gentlemen. Round three coming up. Get to your corners and come out fighting."

"LARRY NYE, what can you tell the court about your father?" Croghan asked as he paced in front of his first witness for the day. Roy Nye's son was in his early twenties, his hair slicked back into a long ponytail. He wore an ill-fitting dark suit and tie, the latter with which he fiddled constantly as though it were cutting off the circulation in his neck.

If Damian had to guess, he'd bet it was the first suit Larry Nye had ever worn. He saw more resemblance to Roy than Lee Nye in the young man's mannerisms and expression, which did not bode well for the man's future.

"My old man was okay when he wasn't drinking. He was a good father. But he got kinda crazy when he had a few. He was allergic to booze."

"So, you loved your father despite his drinking problem, Larry?"

"Yeah, of course. He couldn't help it if drinking changed him."

"Drinking changed him," Croghan repeated, obviously for emphasis. "Can you describe how drinking changed your father, Larry?"

"Well, he'd yell and cuss and beat up on us some. But he didn't mean it."

"It was the drink that made him do this?"

"Yeah."

"When he was sober, he was a good father to you?"

"I had no complaints."

"Do you miss your father, Larry?"

"'Course I miss him. He was my old man, wasn't he? Okay, so he weren't no choirboy. That don't give no psychologist a right to snuff him. He had a right to his life. Do only perfect people get to live? My old lady's got nobody now. It's not right."

"Thank you, Larry. That's all I have."

KAY WALKED UP to Larry Nye and watched the man's eyes follow her. He looked her up and down, and his upper lip curled as he casually leaned back and draped his short, stocky frame over the witness chair.

She read the contempt on his face as easily as if it had been painted on a six-foot billboard.

Just a female. Good for one thing, was what he was thinking. She was sure of it.

Larry Nye resembled Roy far too much.

She smiled at him to see if it would disconcert him enough to remove that sneer. The sneer remained fearlessly in place.

"Larry, what do you do for a living?"

"Construction work."

"Which means?"

"Digging ditches."

"Are you currently employed?"

"No."

"What is your source of income?"

"The old lady helps me out."

"Are you speaking of your mother, Fedora Nye?"

"Yeah. She's a nice old broad."

"So your *nice old broad of a mother* is supporting you?"

"Yeah."

"Are you expecting to get some settlement money if your mother's suit against Dr. Steele is successful?"

"Your Honor, I object!" Croghan cut in. "What the witness is or isn't expecting has no bearing on this matter."

"It goes to motive for the witness's testimony, Your Honor," Kay retaliated.

"I'll allow it," Ingle said. "You may answer the question, Mr. Nye."

"So what if she gives me half? You got a beef with that?"

"I ask the questions here, Mr. Nye," Kay informed him as she looked him deliberately in the eye. "How old are you?"

The sneer had begun to get a little frayed around the edges. "Twenty-two."

"Do you still live with your mother?"

"Yeah. I don't mind hanging around the old lady. She does the cooking, laundry. Like I said, she's a nice old broad."

"Yes, like you've said. You've also said your father was okay to you when he wasn't drunk, is that right?"

"Yeah."

"Did you do father-and-son things together?"

"Yeah. Sure."

"What type of father-and-son things did you do?"

"This and that."

"Can you be more specific?"

He repositioned himself in his chair, again. His head went back, his eyes wandered to the ceiling as though bored. "It was a while back. I don't remember."

"How old were you when you last saw your father?"

"Sixteen."

"You don't remember what you did with your father from the time you were small until the time you were sixteen?"

"He wasn't home that much."

"Did you and your father ever go to see a ball game together?"

"I don't remember."

"You *don't ever remember* going to see a ball game with your father?" she asked incredulously.

Larry's head came forward. "I wasn't home when he was."

"Why? Were you trying to avoid him?"

Larry straightened, a frown beginning to replace the previously enduring sneer on his face. "'Course not."

"Then why were you gone so much?"

"I had stuff to do."

He was strenuously resisting giving her straight answers. Kay could see it and she knew the jury could see it, too. "Mr. Nye, how many times was your father sober when he was home?"

"You expecting me to give you some number, or something?"

"How about an approximation. Half the time? A fourth of the time?"

"Yeah, a fourth of the time."

"And he was a good father to you when he was sober at least a fourth of the time when he was home?"

"I said I had no complaints, didn't I?"

Kay turned and walked toward the defense table. She retrieved a folder off the top of her papers. "May I approach the witness?" she asked the bench.

"You may," Ingle replied, an expectant gleam in his eyes as he saw the folder.

Kay slowly walked up to the witness stand. She handed the folder to Larry Nye. "This is from a police file on your father. Open the folder, please. Tell the court the title of the document inside."

The last of Larry's sneer faded. His voice turned sullen. "Summary of Juvenile Interview," he read.

"Who were the parties to this interview?"

"Me and a social worker."

"How old were you when this interview took place?"

"Thirteen."

"And why were you being interviewed?"

"Cops picked me up after I'd run away from home."

"Why had you run away?"

"Because my old man had beaten me. What's the big deal? I told you, when he got drunk he went crazy."

"Mr. Nye, please read for the court the paragraph I have highlighted in the body of that interview, the paragraph taken down verbatim by the social worker as your explanation for why you ran away from home."

He read in clearly reluctant, halting, jerky spurts.

"It was Saturday morning. I was in the kitchen. He'd just gotten out of bed in his usual foul, nasty mood. My old lady had taken my sister to some school thing. He was mad she wasn't there to wait on him. He started beating me with an iron skillet. I got out of there. I'm not going back. Not while that S.O.B. is alive."

Kay let the quiet after Larry Nye's reading extend for several seconds throughout the courtroom, giving its occupants full opportunity for his words to sink in.

"Mr. Nye, was your father drunk when he beat you with that iron skillet that morning?"

Larry's hand curled into a fist, twisting the file folder in his hand. "Yeah, he was drunk."

"After he had just awakened? He wasn't just in his usual foul, nasty mood as you told the social worker?"

"No, he was drunk, I tell you. Bastard was always drunk."

"I thought you said earlier that he was sober at least a fourth of the time?"

"So I got it wrong."

"Did you 'get it wrong' when you said he was sober at least a fourth of the time, or are you 'getting it wrong' now when you said he was drunk that morning?"

Larry leaned forward in the witness chair, his shoulders hunched, his mouth sneering. "You think you're going to get me to say he was sober when he beat on me, don't you? Well, he was drunk, see? Bastard hit us when he was drunk. Dr. Steele could have cured him. But instead, he killed him. Dr. Steele has got to pay."

Kay put a sad note in her soft voice that traveled into every ear in the courtroom. "I'm afraid a lot of people have already paid for your father's abuse, Mr. Nye. Far too many. And the price has been far too high. No one should have to pay anymore."

"Objection," Croghan yelled. "Counsel is speech making."

"Sustained," the judge said.

"I have no further questions," Kay said.

She turned from the man who resembled Roy Nye far too closely for comfort and walked slowly back to the defense table.

As soon as she sat down, Damian leaned over to her. "I hope I never have to be on the wrong end of a witness stand from you, lady lawyer."

She smiled, for a moment forgetting the danger that stalked him, the violence that haunted him, remembering only the warmth of his tone and his touch.

"Who do you think Croghan will call next?" Damian asked.

"Rosy Nye, the daughter."

"I call Dr. Upton Van Pratt," Croghan said, immediately proving Kay wrong.

Kay frowned. Why not the daughter?

DAMIAN SENSED Kay's attention being totally taken by the distinguished-looking, white-haired man with the very straight carriage and clear, light blue eyes, who approached the witness stand and raised his hand to be sworn in. He gave his name and address in a clear, crisp tone.

Dr. Upton Van Pratt sat comfortably in the witness chair, appearing neither nervous nor cocky. To Damian, it was obvious that this man had psychological training and many trial appearances beneath his belt.

For the next five minutes, Croghan had Van Pratt reciting a litany of his very impressive professional credits. The man had accomplished some pretty outstanding things in his thirty-five years as a psychologist; he'd held every important position possible for a clinician to hold and authored five books on cognitive therapy.

"Dr. Van Pratt," Croghan said, "is there a recognized and accepted treatment for multiple personality disorder in current psychological and psychiatric literature?"

"The field's official diagnostic manual terms the condition dissociative identity disorder, Mr. Croghan."

"Yes, Dr. Van Pratt. But because the jury knows it as multiple personality disorder or MPD, would you mind using those terms, please?"

"All right. The treatment goal for an MPD patient is integration."

"What do you mean by integration?"

"For the separated parts of the individual's personality to become one again."

"And how does integration take place?"

"First and foremost, a therapist must identify all alters present in the individual."

"What do you mean by alters?"

"Alters are the disparate personality pieces that exist within the individual. They are the separate selves."

"Why does a multiple-personality patient have these multiple personalities, separate selves or alters as you call them?"

"The patient has created each one of his alter personalities as a result of childhood abuse. Each represents a specific reaction to that abuse. Each alter is a split-out aspect, a caricature of one part of the whole personality that once existed in the mind."

"Are some alters more important than others?"

"No. All are equally important."

"So, no alter personality should be exalted over another?"

"That's correct. A therapist must treat all alters fairly and empathically. Each has its function in the final integrated human being."

"Each has its function?" Croghan repeated, obviously for emphasis.

"Yes."

"Is it common for an alter personality to be addicted to, even allergic to, alcohol?"

"Yes. Quite often, one or more alters are addicted to drugs and/or alcohol."

"Can they become abusive to others while intoxicated?"

"When an alter abuses others, it is often as a consequence of his own severe childhood abuse. They are victims, too, in need of help and must be treated as such."

"Is an alter with an alcohol problem and prone to abusing others of less value than an alter without those problems?"

"Absolutely not."

"But this alter would be harder to treat, wouldn't he?"

"Alters that are more disturbed than others will naturally need more attention and work, just like any whole personality patient with such problems."

"Dr. Van Pratt, would his special problems keep you from treating this more disturbed alter?"

"On the contrary. A good therapist would consider a more difficult alter an opportunity to hone his psychoanalytic skills and welcome the challenge the alter presented."

"So you would consider such an alter a challenge, not a dysfunctional personality fragment?"

"There is no such thing as a dysfunctional personality fragment in an MPD individual. All alter personalities have a reason for being, are equally important and must be treated accordingly."

"Would there ever be an occasion when you would consider trying to extinguish an alter from an MPD patient?"

"Never."

"Would it be wrong for a therapist to attempt this?"

"I would consider it extremely ill advised and potentially very damaging. A patient needs each part of his psyche to become who he was meant to be."

"So, attempting to extinguish an alter is always a wrong treatment decision for a multiple-personality patient?"

"Always."

"Can you give us an example of how a competent therapist would treat an MPD patient?"

"A therapist would help each alter understand that it was created in response to abuse and, since that abuse no longer exists, there is no further purpose to its separate existence. The alters can then agree to join and become whole."

"Become whole? Is that what you meant by your earlier term—integration?"

"Yes. The dissociated memories and personality fragments of the MPD individual all meld and become one, and the individual goes on to live a normal, healthy, integrated life.''

"Dr. Van Pratt, is this integration process for the treatment of multiple personalities just your opinion?"

"No, integration is the only recognized and documented treatment for multiple personality disorder in psychological journals and textbooks today.''

"I want this to be perfectly clear. Did you just say that the integration of *all* alter personalities is the *only* recognized and documented treatment for multiple personality disorder?''

"Yes, Mr. Croghan. The only one.''

"Thank you, Dr. Van Pratt. I have no further questions.''

Kay got slowly to her feet. No doubt about it. This man's testimony had been absolutely devastating. With every calm and confident word out of his mouth, he had condemned Damian's treatment decision regarding his patient, LeRoy Nye.

Van Pratt sat totally at ease in the witness chair. He was a man of impeccable credentials and impeccable presence, clearly honest and sincere, with no emotional investment in the outcome of this trial.

He was, literally, a defense attorney's nightmare.

Kay stood before him, knowing she was facing not just the most important witness of this trial, but also one of the most difficult witnesses of her career. Still, she was determined to use every scrap of legal shrapnel in her arsenal.

"Dr. Van Pratt, is the plaintiff paying you for your appearance here in court today?"

"Yes."

"Would you have testified without being paid?"

"No, my time is valuable."

"Are you presently a practicing psychologist?"

"I no longer see patients."

"How often have you testified in court over the last six months?"

"Possibly a dozen times."

"A *dozen* times in only six months?"

"Yes."

"And were you paid each time?"

"Yes."

"Very well paid?"

"Yes."

"Well, no wonder you no longer need to see patients. Being paid for your testimony is proving a lucrative profession for you, isn't it, Doctor?"

"Your Honor, I object!" Croghan shouted in his industrial-strength voice. "Dr. Van Pratt has every right to be compensated for his time. Ms. Kellogg is casting improper aspersions on the character of this most eminent psychologist!"

"It's rather a close call on this," Ingle admitted. "Let's just say you've made your point, Ms. Kellogg, and now let's move along, shall we?"

Kay smiled at him. "Yes, Your Honor."

She turned back to Van Pratt.

"Doctor, have you ever treated a patient with MPD?"

"Not personally."

"Have you ever consulted on a case of MPD?"

"No."

"Would it be true to say then that the opinions you have expressed in this court today concerning multiple personality disorder are not arrived at through personal experience?"

"I've read all the textbooks and case journals."

"But you've never been personally involved in a case of MPD, have you?"

"No."

Kay walked back to her desk and picked up another folder. "May I approach the witness, Your Honor?"

"By all means, Ms. Kellogg," Ingle said eagerly. He always got that eager gleam in his eye when she brought out another folder.

Kay opened and handed the folder to Dr. Van Pratt.

"Dr. Van Pratt, do you recognize this document?"

"It's an article I wrote for the *American Psychological Journal* ten years ago."

"Would you read aloud the third paragraph of the article you authored, please? It's the part I've highlighted in yellow."

Van Pratt took a moment to clear his throat. *"It is always a mistake for a psychologist to diagnose or suggest treatment for a patient whom he has not seen and for any case in which he is not privy to all the empirical data."*

"Thank you, Dr. Van Pratt. Did you write those words?"

"Yes."

"Are they a true and accurate reflection of your thoughts and opinions?"

"Yes."

"Do you still agree that no psychologist should diagnose or suggest treatment for a patient whom he has not seen and for any case in which he is not privy to all the empirical data?"

"Yes."

"Now, please tell this court, did you ever see Dr. Damian Steele's patient LeRoy Nye?"

"No."

"Did Dr. Steele or any other doctor consult with you about the particulars of Mr. Nye's case?"

"No."

"Do you have *any* personal, empirical data about the case?"

"No."

"Then how can you sit in this courtroom and presume to prescribe the proper treatment for Dr. Steele's patient?"

"I'm not prescribing the proper treatment for Dr. Steele's patient."

"Well, forgive me, Doctor, but I thought that's exactly what you were doing."

"Ms. Kellogg, I believe if you examine my testimony, you will find that not once have I referred to Dr. Steele's patient. As an expert in the field of psychology, I answered questions only about the treatment of multiple personality disorder."

"You may be an expert in the field of psychology, sir, but you have no personal experience in the treatment of multiple personality disorder, isn't that correct?"

"That's correct."

"So, all you were really doing was quoting out of a textbook, wasn't it?"

"I am fully informed on all the mainstream beliefs gathered by other psychologists—"

"Gathered by *other* psychologists. But nothing gathered by yourself. No empirical data of your own. Isn't that true?"

"Yes."

"You've never seen a multiple-personality patient, true?"

"True."

"So you've never met an MPD alter that was so vicious and abusive that it was ruining any chance for an individual suffering from the disorder to make a decent life for himself, have you?"

"I don't believe that such an alter exists."

"But you never met Roy Nye, did you, Dr. Van Pratt?"

"No."

"Do you believe a psychologist should diagnose or suggest treatment for a patient whom he has not seen?"

"No."

"So you cannot personally attest that Roy Nye was not such a vicious and abusive alter, can you?"

"No."

"And you cannot say whether Dr. Steele did the right thing in extinguishing him, can you?"

"He couldn't have extinguished him."

Kay stared at the witness, clearly uncertain if she had heard him right. "Excuse me, Dr. Van Pratt, did you just say Dr. Steele *couldn't* have extinguished Roy Nye?"

"That's what I said."

"Would you please explain that very startling statement?"

"No psychologist can extinguish an alter of a multiple-personality patient. The patient has created those alters. Only the patient can extinguish them."

"Let me get this clear. Are you saying it is your opinion—your expert psychological opinion—that Roy Nye still exists?"

"Yes."

"Well, Dr. Van Pratt, if Roy Nye still exists, we have no basis at all for this trial, do we? Thank you. I have no further questions."

Kay headed for the defense table with mixed feelings about the cross-examination of the eminent Dr. Upton Van Pratt. On the one hand, she knew that his firmly expressed beliefs based on the official psychological treatment of multiple personality disorder would hold potent sway in the jury's mind. On the other hand, she had just gotten Van Pratt to repudiate the basic cause of action of the plaintiff.

Sloppy of Croghan not to have explored that possibility with his witness. Her competent adversary had made his first mistake. And it was a serious one.

"Your Honor," Croghan said, "I call Roy Nye to the stand."

"What?" Kay said, twisting around, certain she couldn't have heard right.

Croghan was looking directly at her, a smile snaking within his dark beard. He latched his thumbs into his belt buckle and rolled back on his heels. "Ms. Kellogg just enthusiastically encouraged this court to believe that Roy Nye was still alive. She should have no objections to my calling him to the stand to make sure."

And that was when Kay knew Croghan had not made a mistake. He'd set her up.

Kay had not even seen the trap. And now here she was, securely caught in the steel jaws of its legal teeth.

Chapter Thirteen

"Your Honor, Mr. Croghan cannot call Roy Nye to the stand since Roy no longer exists," Kay said quickly.

"The defense attorney can't have it both ways, Your Honor," Croghan countered. "In one breath she encourages the jury to believe Roy is alive. Now she says he's gone. I call the body that once housed Roy Nye to take the stand, so the jury can see for themselves if Roy still exists."

Ingle turned to Kay. "Do you have a problem with Lee Nye's coming before this court and jury and telling us that Roy Nye is no longer a part of him, Ms. Kellogg?"

Damian knew Kay had a problem with it. She didn't want the bland Lee Nye to take the stand and have Croghan expose him as an emotional vegetable. Damian also knew that exposing Lee that way was in all probability Croghan's real reason for calling him.

"Your Honor, it would be improper for Mr. Croghan to call either Lee or Roy, as neither are on his list of witnesses."

"But they are, your Honor," Croghan once again countered. "On page three. Halfway down. L. Nye and R. Nye."

"But that's clearly misleading," Kay protested. "The initials L and R could easily have been mistaken to mean Larry Nye, the plaintiff's son, and Rosy Nye, the plaintiff's daughter."

"If you were unclear as to who Mr. Croghan meant, Ms. Kellogg, it was your duty to ask for clarification at the time you received the witness list. Objection overruled. Lee Nye will take the stand.''

It was hard for even Damian to listen to the first ten minutes of Croghan's examination. Croghan ruthlessly exposed Lee's lack of emotions. Every bland robotic answer out of his former patient brought new frowns to the jurors' faces. The way Kay's foot was tapping, Damian also knew that she, too, was adding up the damage being done and finding it far too high.

Finally, Croghan got to the supposed point for his bringing Lee Nye to the stand.

''Mr. Nye, when you were being treated by Dr. Steele, he found another personality inside you named Roy, didn't he?''

''Yes.''

''But even before you came to see Dr. Steele, you suspected something was amiss when you suffered periodic amnesia, didn't you?''

''Yes.''

''And you subsequently learned that those periods of lost time were when Roy had control over your body, isn't that true?''

''Yes.''

''And now you no longer experience those lost periods of time because Dr. Steele extinguished Roy, isn't that true?''

''No.''

Croghan was obviously surprised at Lee's answer, because he just stood there staring at him. He wasn't the only one. Damian found himself also staring.

''Mr. Nye, I don't think you understood my question,'' Croghan tried again. ''Let me rephrase it. Is Roy Nye, the dual-personality who once shared your body, still alive?''

''Yes.''

''What? But you can't be saying that Roy Nye is still inside your mind!'' Croghan protested.

''He has to be, Mr. Croghan,'' Lee Nye responded in his bland, emotionless voice.

''Your Honor, I object!'' Croghan blasted at the bench.

"You're objecting to the testimony of your own witness, Mr. Croghan?" Ingle asked.

Croghan's hands clenched as the blood suffused his face. "This witness is lying! I demand an investigation! I demand formal charges be laid against Dr. Steele and the law firm of Justice Inc.! I demand—"

"You *demand* nothing in my courtroom, Mr. Croghan. Ladies and gentlemen of the jury, you are instructed to ignore Mr. Croghan's outburst. As we are drawing close to the lunch hour, you are dismissed until two. Remember my admonition not to discuss this case or allow yourselves to be exposed to any media coverage concerning it." Ingle rapped his gavel. "In my chambers. Both counsel. Now."

"Your Honor, in view of Lee Nye's testimony, I move that this suit be dismissed," Kay said as soon as they got into chambers.

"No, Your Honor!" Croghan yelled. "We saw no evidence of the Roy Nye personality. It's clear Lee Nye is lying!"

Fedora Nye was tugging at Croghan's white suit sleeve. Some emotion Kay couldn't quite read flashed through the woman's eyes. "But what if Roy comes back? What if—"

Croghan grabbed her hand with his and stared hard into her face. "Roy is gone, Fedora. This is all just a trick. You understand that, don't you?"

She nodded mutely and sank back into her chair.

"Mr. Croghan," Ingle said, "you're bandying about some pretty serious charges."

Croghan faced Ingle once more. "They can be proved. Have a court-appointed psychologist hypnotize Lee Nye and see if Roy still exists."

"Yes, that would appear to be the next logical step."

"No, Your Honor," Damian spoke up. "I'm against any psychologist not trained in MPD hypnotizing—"

"Of course he is!" Croghan interrupted. "Dr. Steele is afraid of the truth!"

"He is not!" Kay countered. "Damian is only trying to protect his patient."

"All right. All right," Ingle said, his hands held up in a halt mode. "We'll get this matter cleared up once and for all. Tomorrow morning, a court-appointed psychologist will interview Lee Nye, under hypnosis if necessary."

"In front of the jury."

"No, Mr. Croghan. I'm dismissing the jury pending the investigation of this matter. The psychologist and Lee Nye will be in my chambers at ten o'clock tomorrow morning for this off-the-record session. Now, out of here. All of you."

As they exited the judge's chambers, Kay heard Croghan ask the bailiff to let him and Fedora exit through the jury room along with her and Damian.

"Appears our flamboyant adversary has suddenly become camera shy," she whispered to Damian. "You must have mixed emotions about the outcome of that session tomorrow morning. Shall we discuss them over lunch?"

"Later. I have to leave now."

Kay's eyes shot to his face. "Leave?"

"There's something I have to attend to." He smiled at her. "I promise a full-course, proper candlelit dinner. I'll pick you up at six-thirty. Okay?"

Kay nodded as Damian gave her forehead a quick kiss. She watched him all but run to the courthouse's back staircase and disappear behind the door. Where was he going in such a rush?

"Ms. Kellogg? What do you think of this morning's revelations?"

She turned to find herself face-to-face with an enterprising TV news reporter who had obviously begun checking the side halls when the principals to this case stopped exiting from the front of the courtroom. As the lights from the camera flashed in her eyes, Kay found that for once she didn't have to fake the smile that lifted her lips.

"Whichever way the jury chooses to look at the evidence that came to light this morning, they have to see that Mrs. Nye clearly has no case against Dr. Damian Steele. That's all I have time for now. So, if you'll excuse me—"

But as Kay turned and began to walk away, the persistent reporter followed.

"Ms. Kellogg, is Roy Nye alive? Did Dr. Steele fail to extinguish him, after all?"

Kay didn't turn around to respond to the question because she knew if she did, she would just be inviting more questions.

And also because she didn't have the faintest idea what answer she could give.

"WE'RE EATING in a hotel room, Damian?"

He closed and locked the door to the presidential suite and took her purse and wrap.

"Our faces are too well known to chance a restaurant. I doubt there's anyone in Seattle who hasn't heard of this case and isn't turning to their TV each night for the latest developments."

He brought her to him and just held her there, luxuriating in the feel of her warm, soft body and the sweet scent of her skin and hair.

"I want to have dinner with you in peace, Kay." He raised his wrist to check his watch. "And between now and when it's delivered, I intend to satisfy another appetite."

He swept her off her feet and carried her into the bedroom. She wrapped her arms around his neck in a happy sigh.

He laid her on the bed and undressed her slowly, gently, leaving a trail of soft warm kisses on every inch of her exposed flesh. Once again he was in awe of the way she fed her body to him with such openness and trust.

Her scent and taste were so sweet and so incredibly sexy that he nearly lost all his careful conscious control. Only his need to make this night special for her kept his desire in check as he ran his tongue and mouth over her scintillatingly hot flesh.

She pressed against him, a long suffocated cry breaking through her lips as she shot to her first peak. He smiled.

Never had the feel of a woman brought him so much pleasure. Never had he wanted to pleasure a woman so much.

She reached for him, but he held her back. He wanted more for her. He wanted everything for her with a hunger that grew more insatiable every second. Mercilessly, he licked and stroked and plundered her soft, steamy flesh. She moaned in frantic waves, yelling his name like a curse only to end up whimpering it softly like a benediction as wave after wave of a new climax shook her.

His eyes raked over her beautiful body as it lay relaxed and limp on the rumpled sheets. Sane psychologist be damned, his mind yelled in triumph. He was the ravishing beast and she the ravished!

Or so he thought for a second more before two surprisingly limber white legs suddenly shot around his thighs, captured them and dragged him to her. She sheathed him inside her in a bold, brazen move, contracting around him, planting searing kisses across his chest, knocking the breath right out of his body.

He gripped her hips, all reason and resistance shattered as he sunk deeper into her heated flesh, with each thrust happily, willingly becoming prisoner to her sumptuous heat.

He felt her shudders and his own tearing through their joined flesh simultaneously, and he knew her wholehearted entry into their lovemaking would always undo him.

She made him feel so damn powerful. And so damn weak.

He should end this. He wasn't the kind of a man who could give this woman the commitment of marriage and children that she wanted—deserved. The only decent thing he could do was to stop this. Now.

But he couldn't stop it. He wanted her too badly. He wasn't decent. He was selfish and greedy.

He was the beast, with beauty captured in his arms. And he wasn't going to let her go.

KAY SNUGGLED her back and bottom spoonlike against his chest and belly in spectacular contentment. And with absolutely no reason for that contentment.

Damian Steele was still her client. He was still that man so haunted by the brutality of his father toward his mother that he had ruled out marriage and family—the very things she wanted—from his life.

So what was she doing cradled in his arms so completely contented and happy? It was totally illogical.

We're just all mysteries waiting to unfold.

How true. How damn true.

He snuggled up to her, his breath warm and tantalizing against her ear. She sighed from the pure pleasure of feeling him so close.

"I have some good news," she said.

He nibbled on her ear. "Hmm."

"AJ found Dr. Pat Fetter."

"Hmm."

"AJ's the best, no doubt about it. She says Dr. Fetter agreed to come back Friday to testify. Depending on what happens tomorrow morning, of course, we may not need her. I left a message for Jerry Tummel to let him know I'll contact him if he doesn't have to show."

"Hmm."

"Could Roy really be back, do you think?"

"Hmm."

He laid a delicious string of kisses across the back of her neck. She sighed. "Damian, are you listening to me?" she asked a bit breathless and getting more so by the second.

His hands had circled to her breasts and had begun to work their magic once again. "Why, you say something?"

She sighed in ecstasy, finding it was impossible to be mad at the man who could do this to her body. "Are all you psychologists so damn sexy?"

"Are all you lawyers so damn talkative?" he responded before claiming her lips with his in a warm, wet kiss.

A knock sounded on the suite door.

Reluctantly, Damian let her go. "That'll be the food," he said as he slipped off the bed. He stepped into the bathroom and came back with two robes, a monogram of the hotel name on their breast pockets. He tossed one to her and put the other on, cinching it around his lean waist.

"The main course will be consumed in his-and-her terry cloth tonight. For dessert, however, dress is definitely optional."

He blew her a quick kiss before leaving the room to answer the door. Kay got off the bed and slipped into her robe, a happy little smile playing about her mouth. A whole night. Together.

"Dr. Damian Steele?" an official-sounding voice asked from the next room. Kay immediately stiffened.

"Yes. What is this?"

"Dr. Steele, please come with us. You're wanted for questioning."

Kay cinched her robe and rushed into the next room.

"Questioning for what?" Damian was asking.

Kay halted in growing alarm as she spied the two uniformed police officers standing just inside the suite. They flashed her a quick look before answering, "In connection with the disappearance of Lee Nye. Please get dressed. You, too, Ms. Kellogg."

"WHAT EVIDENCE do they have against me?" Damian asked as Kay and Adam sat across from him, prisoner barrier between them, in the holding cell interview room the next morning.

Adam's face was stoic, as always, his light reflective eyes giving no hint as to what his thoughts might be. "Lee Nye's neighbor saw you leaving his apartment moments after hearing a commotion."

"What kind of commotion?"

"She claims she was in the tub when an angry raised voice coming from Lee's apartment, followed by a suspicious thud, alarmed her. She slipped into a robe and came out into the hall. That's when she says she saw you leave. She knocked on Lee's door and got no response. She went back to her apartment and called 911."

"But they didn't find Lee inside his apartment?"

"No. But they did find blood on the carpet and a heavy, bloodied brass bookend, wiped free of fingerprints, on the floorboard in the back seat of your Jaguar."

"Of course it was planted," Kay spoke up quickly.

Damian sent her a brief smile before turning his attention back to Adam. "What else?"

"The blood on the bookend has been matched to the blood on the carpet. Lee's cleaning lady has identified the brass bookend as belonging to Lee. She claims it was in his apartment yesterday morning when she cleaned it."

"But no one knows the whereabouts of Lee Nye?" Damian asked.

Kay nodded. "The police know about the judge's order to have Lee Nye hypnotized this morning. They also know you were against it. They think you went to his apartment and got into an argument about it, then struck him with that bookend, wiped the apartment of your fingerprints, carried Lee's body out to your car and then dumped it somewhere."

Damian exhaled a heavy breath. "So I take it the inside of Lee's apartment was wiped clean of fingerprints?"

"Yes."

Kay moved to the edge of her chair. Her eyes and voice were soft, questioning. "Damian, did you go to Lee's apartment yesterday?"

Damian looked into those soft, questioning blueberry eyes.

"Yes, I went to Lee's apartment, but when I didn't get an answer to my knock, I left. I never was inside, so that neighbor couldn't have seen me coming out."

Kay nodded. "I knew it had to be something like that. Since the neighbor heard noises and then saw you walking away from the door, she just assumed you had come out of the apartment."

Damian smiled at her. She had certainly come to his defense quickly. For a hard-nosed attorney, the lady's faith in his innocence shone like a beacon.

"Why did you go to Lee's apartment?" Adam asked.

Damian turned his attention to the man with the pale, mirror eyes, knowing that intellect—never emotion—would guide the man's decision in this matter. "To talk to Lee and find out why he believes Roy is back," Damian answered.

"But he didn't answer the door, so you haven't seen him since his appearance in court yesterday?"

"That's right."

"What about the bloodied bookend?" Adam asked. "Any idea how it got into the back of your car?"

"None. I locked my car when I left it on the street in front of Lee's apartment. Only time I don't bother locking it is when it's parked at the house."

"So someone could have tossed the bookend in the back seat when you returned to your home yesterday afternoon?"

"Yes."

"Anything else you can tell us?" Adam asked.

"No. What are the chances of my getting out of here?"

"The police have some incriminating circumstantial evidence, but they don't have a body. They're detaining you on an investigative hold. If they don't find Lee's body by the time this goes before a judge tonight, I may be able to get you released."

"Tonight?"

"That's the soonest I can get you out of here, Damian. Investigative hold is twenty-four hours. I'll go get the wheels in motion right now. Hang tight. Coming, Kay?"

"I'll join you in a minute."

She waited until Adam had exited the room before turning to Damian.

"Adam is the best criminal lawyer in the state."

Damian wished this damn prisoner barrier weren't between them. He so wanted to touch her hand, her face, to try to wipe the sadness from her eyes. "Yes, I know."

She sighed. "I forgot. One of these days, you're going to have to tell me how you two met."

"Maybe one of these days. I see we made the front page of the newspaper this morning. The description of our being found together in 'intimate attire' in a hotel room must be causing you considerable difficulty. I'm sorry."

"Oh, don't worry about me. I'll weather whatever bad publicity comes my way."

She was trying to sound lighthearted and unconcerned. She wasn't fooling him. "What will happen to the civil trial?" he asked.

"Judge Ingle has formally adjourned it until next week, pending the outcome of the investigation into Lee's disappearance."

"And if Lee isn't found? Or worse yet, found dead?"

"I don't know, Damian. I just don't know."

The sadness in her eyes was suddenly too much for Damian to bear. He looked away, raked his hands through the sides of his hair. "This makes no sense. Who could have attacked Lee? And why?"

"Damian, could Roy really be back?"

Damian exhaled heavily as he dropped his hands and sat back in his chair. "I would have bet against it. But there are a lot of things that have happened to me lately that I would have bet against and lost. Yes, it's possible Roy is back."

Damian noticed then that her fingers were drumming on the table in front of her. Very rapidly. He leaned forward. "What is it, Kay?"

"I've been thinking about Lee. We both know it isn't in him to lie. Yet he got on that witness stand yesterday and said Roy was back. So that means Roy has to be, doesn't it?"

"And if he is?"

"Remember when you told me about the tug-of-war between Roy and Lee, the fight for control?"

"What are you getting at, Kay?"

"I'm not sure. Maybe I'm just thinking crazy, but you tried the door to Lee's apartment. It was locked. No one could get in. I keep thinking, what if there wasn't another *somebody* in there with Lee? What if it was Roy he was arguing with? What if it was Roy with whom Lee had the fight?"

"That's a very thought-provoking question, Kay. Have I been too arrogant in my assumption that I really did extinguish Roy?"

"So Roy could have tried to kill Lee with a blow to their shared body?"

"Yes, Kay. Many alters frequently inflict harm on the body, not fully realizing that the body of another alter is also theirs."

"Then this theory is possible?"

"More than possible. You realize what this could mean?"

"That we can prove your innocence and get you out of here."

He smiled at her, wishing again he could touch her hand or her cheek. "It also means that it might have been Roy all along who's been causing this trouble as he's been coming back to life."

"Trouble? You mean the intimidation against you?"

"It all makes sense. If Roy was angry at my attempt to extinguish him, he might have been seeking revenge. First through the notes. The threatening calls. Then the envelope that caught fire. The speedboat. The car. The gunshot. Even his dropping the bloodied brass bookend in the back seat of my car to implicate me in Lee's disappearance."

She shot to her feet. "I have to go talk to Adam and the police and explain about Lee and Roy."

"Kay, please be careful," Damian called after her fast-retreating back. "If it is Roy, he could be very danger—"

But Kay wasn't listening to Damian's warning. She was already out the door.

ADAM TURNED TO Kay as they exited the jail. "So you and Damian think it really could be Roy Nye behind this?"

"I know it sounds strange, but from what I've learned about multiple personalities, it makes sense, Adam. Let's go talk to the detectives on the case and explain."

"No, Kay. You're out of this."

"But, Adam, you didn't see those videotapes of Roy. I did. I have a much better chance of making those detectives understand what Roy's like and of convincing them that Damian is innocent."

"Kay, the detectives on this case aren't about to believe anything a lawyer found in a robe with her client in a hotel room is going to say about the innocence of that client. Don't you see? Your presence can only do him harm now."

Adam turned his back on her then as he strode away in the clearest and sharpest reprimand Kay had ever felt from her senior partner.

The hardest part of that reprimand was knowing she deserved it. She had betrayed one of her profession's strictest rules. And because of it, she had not only ceased to be useful to her client, she had become a liability to him.

Kay's feet dragged as she trudged over to Pine Street to catch the monorail back to the office. The sun was peaking through soft white, pillowy clouds. The monorail glided above Seattle silently, swiftly, like a lovely, breeze-borne sea gull.

Normally, she loved the sight of the busy city below. But not today. Today she saw nothing but Damian behind prison bars. Today the quiet ride was shattered as Adam's words pounded loudly through her brain: *You can only do him harm now.*

She exited the monorail and walked the last few blocks to the Justice Inc. offices opposite the Space Needle. She immediately sought the solitude of her private office and sank into her chair, burying her head in her arms.

She had committed the cardinal sin. She had gotten personally involved with a client. And not just personally involved, she'd fallen in love with Damian. Deeply, foolishly, fatally in love with him.

How could this have happened to her—the epitome of the logical lawyer? Had she gone insane? Did she need a psychologist?

She laughed mirthlessly at the irony of her question. Of course she needed a psychologist. She needed Damian.

Her intercom beeped. She pressed down the button. "Please," she said to her secretary, "no calls."

"I'm sorry, Kay, but a Dr. Payton is flipping over the phone lines. She says she has to talk to you. She says it's a matter of life and death."

Kay's back stiffened. "I'll take it," she said quickly, picking up the receiver. "Yes, Dr. Payton, this is Kay Kellogg."

"Ms. Kellogg, I must see you. Right away. There's something urgent you must know."

"Why can't you just tell me over the phone?"

"No. I didn't realize how far... This has to be in person."

"All right. Do you know where our offices are located?"

"I can't come there. You have to come here."

"Dr. Payton, I'm not—"

"You want him out of jail, don't you? I'm telling you, you have to come here!"

The woman sounded panicked. "Where are you?" Kay asked.

"My house. Get out a pen and paper and I'll give you directions. You'd better hurry. I don't know how much time I have."

"How much time you have? What do you mean by—"

"For God's sake, stop asking questions and just write!"

WITHIN TWENTY MINUTES, Kay was cruising the upper-middle-class neighborhood of Sand Point, just west of Lake Washington, following the last of Priscilla Payton's telephone directions.

She spied the address and parked in front of a nicely kept colonial peaking out over the top of a thick shrubbery barrier. She got out of her car and walked up the left side of the circular driveway. As she approached the front door, she noticed it was slightly ajar.

Had Dr. Payton left it open for her?

"Dr. Payton?" she called out. "It's Kay Kellogg. We spoke on the phone?"

No one answered.

Kay wasn't one to step into someone's house without a clear invitation, despite the fact that she'd just been summoned by an urgent telephone call. But as she turned around to leave, she heard a noise from inside.

"Dr. Payton?" she called.

Again there was no answer. The little hairs began to stand up on the back of Kay's neck. Then she heard a voice, faint and indistinct, coming from inside.

"In here."

Kay stepped through the open doorway, cautiously following the direction of the voice. She found herself in an empty living room, boldly decorated in red-and-black checks.

"Dr. Payton?" she called again.

"In here," the voice repeated, still muffled, still indistinct, seeming to come from down a hall.

"I'll wait in the living room for you," Kay said. This walking through someone's house on the trail of an eerie voice was beginning to give her a very unsettling feeling.

"I've fallen. Please, help me," the muffled voice cried.

Kay hurried down the hallway where the voice seemed to be coming from, chastising herself for her earlier hesitation. She should have realized it right away. The woman was clearly in trouble.

"Where are you?" she called out.

"In here," the faint voice replied.

Kay turned toward an open bedroom door. She rushed inside only to stop in her tracks. Dr. Priscilla Payton was in trouble, all right. She lay on the carpet, her eyes open and glassy in death, slashes of fresh crimson blood splashed across her chest.

The danger immediately closed in on her. Kay turned to flee. But it was too late. A hand grabbed her arm and yanked her forward, a cruel hand with a cruel grip that threw her viciously to the carpet. She landed on her back, so hard that the breath was knocked from her lungs.

A wave of white dizziness swept through Kay. It took a moment for her head to stop spinning and her vision to clear. When it did, she wished it hadn't. She could see the blood still dripping from the knife that had killed Priscilla Payton—the knife that Priscilla's murderer now held over her.

Chapter Fourteen

"Croghan!" Kay cried, fear tearing his name from her throat.

Croghan's lips drew back into a sneer. "So Priscilla didn't tell you about me over the phone? Now that's a relief. What did she tell you?"

A drop of blood from the knife splashed onto Kay's cheek. She opened her mouth to speak, but only a pitiful squeak came out. She closed her eyes, fighting off a wave of nausea and numbing terror.

A sharp kick registered in her ribs. She cried out uncontrollably as pain shot through her.

Her eyes flew open again to see Croghan's cruel sneer.

"That get your attention? Good. Now, if you don't want to end up like Priscilla, you'd better tell me what I want to know."

Kay fought down the nausea and the fear whirling inside her and searched her mind for the words that could stave off the knife poised so purposely over her.

Trial attorneys learned to think fast under pressure. Still, this was pressure the like which Kay had never known. For it wasn't just the outcome of a trial in the balance. It was her life.

"Well?" Croghan prodded.

"Priscilla asked me to come over to talk about the tapes."

"You're lying. I burned Roy's videotapes. You think I was going to let you introduce them into court after what Priscilla told me was on them?"

Kay quickly absorbed Croghan's offered facts. So he was the one who had stolen the videotapes? Yes, it was beginning to make sense. He'd just put on an act about wanting those tapes. The man defending the memory of Roy Nye could not have permitted the jury an opportunity to see the tapes that revealed the Roy personality for what it was.

"I wasn't talking about Roy's videotapes," Kay quickly improvised. "I was talking about the tapes Priscilla made that revealed you were the mastermind behind all this terror against Dr. Steele."

Croghan's eyes darted around the room wildly.

"She made tapes? That bitch! And it was her idea to begin with!"

"Her idea?" Kay echoed, a persistent voice inside her telling her to keep this man talking, keep his mind away from using the knife in his hand.

"She came to me when I was ready to go to trial against Steele. She told me she knew Steele well and could help me make trouble for him. She made the calls to Steele and wrote the first letters. She was the one who told me about the secret videotape room and how to get into Steele's house by climbing the wall and coming in through the garden."

"But you were the one who expanded on the idea," Kay guessed. "You were the one in the speedboat and the car and behind the letter fire. You were the one trying to escalate the terror campaign so it would make the news and generate more publicity for the case. Priscilla didn't want publicity."

"No, all she wanted was to play on Steele's guilty conscience. But she didn't tell me to stop when she learned about the speedboat, car, letter fire, even just missing him with the shotgun. No, she laughed about them. It was only when I got him arrested that she got all scared and started talking wild."

"Because she knew you'd murdered Lee Nye."

"She acted as though I had a choice. Hell, I even offered to cut Lee in. But he kept saying that Roy had come back and that he would have to admit it. So I smashed in his stupid face. Damn zombie brought it on himself."

"And then Dr. Steele conveniently showed up."

"He must have heard me moving around the apartment wiping off my fingerprints. He called out after ringing the doorbell. I waited until he left and the nosy biddy from next door went back to her apartment before I carried Nye's body to my car along with the bookend. I dumped Nye's body in a ravine off the highway and then went to Steele's place and dropped the bloodied bookend in his car. It all went like clockwork."

"Until Priscilla got alarmed about the murder."

Croghan grasped Kay's arm and yanked her to her feet. He brought the knife to her chin. "Where are her videotapes?"

Kay felt the sharp end of the blade against her throat. She was afraid to swallow, almost afraid to speak. But she knew she had to. And she had to say just the right thing.

"Priscilla sent the first tape to me in the mail. I won't be getting it for at least another day."

Would that lie keep her alive until tomorrow?

"Then why did she want you to come over?"

"She insisted on giving me what she called 'the part-two details' in person."

"Is that all there is, part one and two?"

"No, part three is also on a tape that she said she was going to mail to me tomorrow if I kept my half of the bargain and didn't go to the police until after she left."

"Left?"

"She was planning to leave the country. She didn't want to be arrested as an accessory to murder."

Were these lies sounding plausible?

Croghan's eyes flew around the room. "I see no signs that she was packing."

"She wasn't leaving until tomorrow morning. She was probably putting the packing off until later."

"Where is the videotape she was going to mail to you?"

"Hidden, I suspect."

"Then, we're going to start searching for it. And you'd better pray we find it."

Croghan shoved her in the direction of the dresser. Kay obediently opened a drawer and began her pretense of a search, trying not to look or think about the body lying on the floor just a few feet away.

"I don't understand why you've done all this, Croghan. You're one of the finest courtroom adversaries I've come up against. Surely, with your legal talent, you don't need..."

He stepped over Priscilla's body as though it were nothing but an annoying impediment to his progress as he headed for the nightstand.

"What do you know about what I need? You've got it made, Kellogg. Barely thirty and you're already a partner! I'm thirty-nine. Thirty-nine! Yeah, I've got legal talent. Yet year after year I watched others getting the big breaks and the big bucks. Now I have my chance. This case is making me a household name. I don't care what I have to do. I'm winning it."

"But now that Lee's dead, his testimony that Roy has returned—"

"Will get thrown out of court," Croghan finished as he banged a nightstand drawer shut. "I'll see to that when they find Lee's body where I dumped it and formally charge Steele with his murder. That confession you're going to write saying the two of you set it up will help, of course. Hell, this could take all day. I don't have time for this. I'm just going to have to torch the place. Come on. I've got extra cans of gasoline in my car. You can help."

Croghan yanked her arm and dragged her out of the bedroom.

Kay tried to resist, but Croghan's malicious fingers dug into the sensitive flesh of her arm. She stumbled unwillingly along beside him, biting back the pain.

She had just one ace left. She played it. "I'm not helping you set this place on fire, and I'm not writing a confession implicating myself and Dr. Steele. You won't kill me. You need me to get that mailed tape for you tomorrow."

He stopped in the living room and turned to her, resting the knife just under her chin. "No, I won't kill you, Kellogg. But if you don't do exactly as I say, I'll make you wish you were dead. I have nothing to lose. This is my chance, and nothing and nobody is going to get in my way. Believe it."

Kay did believe it. The man's eyes were cruel and cunning and desperate—a deadly trio. Fear swirled in her stomach.

He dragged her out the front door. His Lincoln was parked behind the visual barrier of the heavy shrubbery on the far side of the circular driveway. He approached the car's back end and flipped open the trunk. He reached in for the two full cans of gasoline stored there and shoved one into each of her hands.

"You'll pour. I'll light. Get going."

Kay looked around, hoping to attract someone's attention. But the heavy shrubbery, which had hidden Croghan's car from her view earlier, hid any other view now. She had no choice but to stumble back up the driveway carrying the heavy cans, as Croghan prodded her in the back every step of the way with the sharp blade of his bloody knife.

She knew he would kill her after he got her to do what he wanted. He couldn't afford to let her live.

She promised herself to resist him, that whatever happened, she must not let him coerce her into writing that confession implicating Damian.

Brave words, but what if she wasn't strong enough to adhere to them? What if she gave in to Croghan's demands in order to ease her pain or buy herself a few more precious seconds of life?

Either from the weight of the gasoline cans or the weight of her thoughts, she stumbled and fell onto the grass.

"Damn clumsy bitch!" Croghan yelled. "Get up!"

Kay rolled onto her side. She didn't hurry. She knew now that death was inevitable. She would meet it as calmly and bravely as it was in her to do.

His furious face glared down at her as he waved the knife inches from her neck. "Move!"

She raised her head slowly. His sneering mouth made a nasty pink twist within his dark beard as he kicked her viciously in the cheek. "Now!"

The pain erupted in Kay's face, pain like she had never felt in her life.

"Get up right now or I'll—" Croghan's threat began. He never got a chance to finish it before a huge arm came out of nowhere. A fist that sounded like the blast-off of a rocket cracked into the side of Croghan's jaw. Croghan's head snapped back just as another fist caught him in the throat. He tumbled backward.

Kay sank back to the ground, swooning from the pain reverberating through her cheek and jaw, the world flapping and waving around her like a white sheet being buffeted by the wind.

She fought to keep consciousness as she squinted into a blurry world. She couldn't see. Still, she knew he was there.

Logically, he should be in jail. Logically, he couldn't possibly be here saving her life.

But at the moment her heart and head were operating on wavelengths far above logic, and they both told her firmly that it was Damian's fists pounding Croghan's face. With that firm assurance, a new fear burgeoned in her heart.

"Don't kill him!" she tried to cry, but she could make no sound. The effort of moving her jaw launched an immediate jolt of excruciating agony that sped her toward the blessed relief of unconsciousness.

Kay fought harder against succumbing than she had ever fought against anything in her life. With all her will, her heart, her soul, she resisted the comforting darkness. She had to face the pain, to remain awake until she could reach Damian. She had to.

"Don't kill him!" her heart cried, because her lips could not.

"I won't, my love," his answer came.

Reassured, she smiled as she gave in to oblivion.

"YOU'VE BEEN IN and out—mostly out—of consciousness for the last two days, Kay. What makes you think you're getting out of this hospital?" Octavia challenged more than asked as she tried to swing Kay's legs back onto the bed.

"Octavia, I feel fine."

"That's because all the painkillers haven't worn off."

"Look, the doctor said I have no broken bones."

"The doctor said you have a concussion."

"He also said I was past the worst of it and on the mend."

"Kay, the operative phrase here is 'on the mend,' not 'mended.'"

"I can't just lie around."

Octavia exhaled wearily. "All right. You fall on your face now, it's your fault. Here, you might as well look your best when they drag you back to the emergency room."

Kay gazed in amazement at the new blue silk pantsuit and matching lacy underthings that Octavia slipped nonchalantly out of her briefcase. There were also heels to match—high heels. Octavia handed them over with a knowing smile and a cosmetics bag full of essentials.

"You did this for me? Even after all the awful publicity I've brought on the firm?"

"What awful publicity?" Octavia asked coolly.

"That business about me and Damian, of course."

Octavia waved a dismissive hand. "Adam and Marc are just being silly with all their growling and grumbling about crossing ethical lines and upholding the firm's reputation. Kay, we're not one of those huge legal corporations with a stodgy clientele. We're a small group of attorneys, who people come to because they're in trouble and want someone who will understand and believe in them."

"Are you saying that all the publicity about my affair with Damian doesn't matter?"

Octavia's smile possessed a pure Cheshire-cat quality. "Oh, it matters. It'll probably increase our client base a hundredfold."

"Increase? But why—"

"Human beings are born male and female first, and whatever professional suit they subsequently put on, they're still wearing that naked flesh beneath. That's why it's the sinners people love in this society—not the saints. Sinners reassure them that those naked-flesh impulses of their own are perfectly normal."

Kay smiled as Octavia flicked her chin with a long, lovely manicured nail.

"And speaking of naked flesh, partner, you'd better get yours covered. Damian will be here soon."

"Bless you, Octavia," Kay said as she gave her colleague a warm, quick hug before grabbing the underthings. "Now, tell me how Damian found me at Priscilla's. I've missed so much excitement!"

Octavia laughed that throaty, rich uninhibited laugh of hers. "She's unconscious for two days and she wakes up complaining about missing the excitement! And to think I once imagined you were just like Adam, all staid and sober."

"I was," Kay surprised herself by admitting. "But this case has had some interesting effects on me."

"Not to mention the client that came with it," Octavia said with a knowing smile.

"So, how did Adam get Damian out of jail so quickly?"

"Well, as soon as Lee Nye came to in the hospital and explained that it was Croghan who attacked him—"

"Wait a minute." Kay paused in putting on her stockings. "Lee Nye is alive? Croghan didn't kill him?"

"Yes, you have missed a bit, haven't you? Okay, let me start from the beginning. When Croghan hit Lee in the face with that brass bookend, he only knocked him out. Thinking Lee was dead, Croghan dumped his body in a ravine off the highway. A couple of joggers spotted Lee just minutes later. An ambulance rushed him to the hospital."

"So Lee's okay?"

"He'll be fine. But his face was bloody and swollen and he was unconscious for a time, so nobody knew he was the missing man. As soon as he came to and the police heard his story, they released Damian. When Damian learned from your secretary that you'd gotten an urgent call from Dr. Payton and you'd gone off to meet with her at her home, he didn't like the sound of it. So he rushed over, and . . . well, you know the rest.''

Kay hoped she did. She really did hear Damian's assurance, hadn't she? It hadn't all been wishful thinking, had it? "Octavia, is Croghan . . . all right?"

Octavia watched her for a moment silently, her sagacious eyes sparkling. "He'll live, but they'll need a wheelchair to roll him into court to stand trial for the murder of Priscilla Payton and the attempted murder of Lee Nye and you. Needless to say, Damian has quite a temper.''

"But a controllable one," Kay said in a relieved sigh.

She was dressed now and wobbled over to the mirror in her high heels. She frowned at her pale reflection. She quickly ran a brush through her hair and collected it to one side to try to hide the very prominent bruise on her cheek. She dabbed some lipstick on her mouth.

"Has Damian been charged for beating Croghan?"

"It was touch and go there for a while, but Adam got the charges dismissed. And speaking of dismissed charges, Fedora Nye called the office this morning and formally withdrew her suit. She had no idea what Croghan was doing, of course. She was just a pawn Croghan was using to try to make a name for himself.''

"Well he's made a name for himself, all right, although it's certainly not the one he was after. I feel sorry for Fedora.''

"Don't. Word is she's selling her story to Hollywood for a very respectable six figures.''

Kay smiled. "Well, good for her. I wonder what Judge Ingle is going to do about the competition.''

"He just held a press conference and announced his own six-figure contract with his publishing house," Damian's deep voice responded from the direction of the doorway.

Kay swung toward him, her heart beating far too fast. "Damian.''

He looked absolutely wonderful, particularly the expression on his face and in his eyes as she said his name. He closed the distance between. She sighed as the closeness of him once again sent that wonderful, warm, lovely streak through her body.

Damian gently took her face in his hands and studied the ugly bruise on her cheek. And then, in a manner so tender she felt it might break her heart, he kissed that bruise and she melted into his arms.

"I WANT TO SHOW you something, Kay."

She rolled over on her back on his black satin sheets, bare and thoroughly beautiful, and looked up into his face, a mischievous smile on her lips. "You've already shown me quite a bit in these last few minutes, Dr. Steele."

Damian chuckled as he gently planted a kiss on the end of her nose. He jumped off the bed and lifted her into his arms. She wrapped hers around his neck and rested her unbruised cheek against his shoulder. "Where are we going?"

"To the den."

She raised her head to nibble on his ear. "Oh, good. As I recall, it does have a very comfortable couch."

He laughed. "What a one-track mind. I'll never understand why nature was so unfair as to give a woman the capacity to experience multiple orgasms while letting a man have only one."

"Just think of it as our due—like closet space."

He chuckled in delight as he navigated the hallway.

"Behave, my beauty, or I won't tell you about the latest in the Lee and Roy saga."

Her voice rose in immediate interest. "Oh, yes! What with everything else that's happened, I nearly forgot. So what's the story? Is Roy back?"

"No. But Lee believed Roy was back because he had begun losing time again."

"I don't understand."

"It wasn't Roy who was competing with Lee for control over his consciousness. Yesterday, I hypnotized Lee and ended up talking to a five-year-old boy named Lyle."

Kay blinked in surprise. "You mean another personality has developed inside Lee?"

"Not developed," Damian said as he negotiated the last turn into the den. "I believe Lyle has been there all the time and that he's the original personality of the child."

"But I thought you said the original personality disappeared with the creation of Lee and Roy?"

"Originally I thought that the most likely explanation," Damian said as he rested her gently on the couch and switched on the TV and VCR, slipping a tape into the latter. He joined her on the couch and pushed the play button.

"This is my session with Lyle yesterday. He took me back in time to the point just before the split into Lee and Roy. Watch this," Damian said as he pressed the button, beginning the tape.

THE LITTLE BOY huddled in the corner of the icy shed with the stiff tarp drawn over his head as the demon bellowed and banged next door in the garage, searching for him.

He shivered with growing terror because he knew that soon the demon would come to the shed. Soon it would find him hiding inside. Soon, it would—

He shut his eyes as tightly as he could. Please, no.

Behind the deepest darkness of his tightly shut lids, a light as bright as the sun suddenly shone on the little boy. A voice, a woman's voice, spoke out of the bright white light.

"Hello."

The little boy was startled. He tried to see who had spoken to him from inside the bright light, but he couldn't. Still, he was curiously unafraid. The light felt warm. The voice sounded soft and gentle.

"Who are you?" he asked in a tentative tone no bigger than the breath of a sigh.

"Why, your guardian angel, of course."

There was something faintly familiar about the way the syllables sung together. But the wisp of memory was misty and so far away.

"My guardian angel?" he repeated uncertainly.

"You don't have to be afraid anymore, little one."

Little one. *The little boy liked the way her voice sounded when she called him that. He liked it very much.* "Are you cold?" *she asked.*

"Yes," *he admitted.*

The bright light wrapped more closely around him like a lovely, warm, soft cloak.

The little boy snuggled gratefully into the comforting folds of the bright light and felt himself being given a warm hug.

"Is that better?" *she asked.*

He sighed. "Oh, yes. Much better."

"Shall I show you something very special?" *she asked in that lovely, soft voice.*

"Please."

"Look there," *she said.*

Her long slim finger extended from the bright light to point at a funny-looking, long gray bug with a hundred different feet and a zillion little toes busily scooting across a sunny sidewalk.

The little boy didn't know where the bug or the sunny sidewalk had come from, any more than he knew where the bright light or the lovely voice had come from. They were just there. And he was glad they were there.

"See how it wobbles?" *she asked and laughed, the sound like the soft tinkle of a merry bell.*

"Yes!" *The little boy giggled in delight to see the funny-looking long bug wobbling along on all those legs and toes.*

"Touch it," *she coaxed.*

"I don't want to hurt it," *he said, unsure.*

"You won't hurt it, little one."

The little boy reached out his finger to gently touch the funny bug on its back. He was startled when it immediately curled into a tiny gray ball and rolled across the sidewalk away from him. He watched in fascination as it disappeared into a deep, dark crack at the very edge of the sunny sidewalk.

"Where did it go?" *he asked.*

The lady's lovely voice came out of the bright light that now fully enfolded him.

"It's gone to a warm, dark, safe place where it can sleep undisturbed and wiggle all its toes whenever it wants."

The little boy sighed from the deepest chambers of his small heart. "I wish I could do that."

"You can," the gentle voice assured. And although the boy could not see her face, he knew that she was smiling.

"When?" he asked eagerly.

"Now," she answered, reaching out her hand to gently touch him on the back.

The demon's pounding boots vibrated the ground as he charged toward the door to the shed. He grabbed the latch, threw open the door, spied the tarp in the farthermost corner with the little boy hiding beneath it and bellowed in vicious triumph.

Only the little boy wasn't there anymore.

Like the funny-looking bug with a hundred little legs, he had curled into a ball and rolled away and disappeared into a deep, dark, safe crack where he could sleep undisturbed and wiggle all his toes whenever he wanted.

"DAMIAN, a guardian angel rescued the little boy from his abuser? These memories can't be real!"

"They are real to the little boy named Lyle. Very real."

"I don't see how—"

"Kay, think about it. You're a little boy who has known a couple of wonderful years with adoptive parents who have shown you love and talked to you about devils and angels. Then you are snatched away from them one night, and you meet a devil in the flesh and are forced to endure its terrible abuse and even accept the blame for that abuse."

Kay nodded. "A devil so real that you end up recreating it in your own mind."

"Yes, Roy was the personification of the devil. And if this child could create a devil with his mind, why not an angel?"

"An angel alter to counteract the devil alter," Kay said, trying out the idea. "Maybe there is a kind of logic to this multiple-personality thing, after all. But if the small child was put to sleep by this angel alter at age two, why is Lyle now five?''

"Lyle's 'guardian angel' woke him up four years ago to tell him that Roy was gone and he could come out if he wanted to. Lyle was hesitant, so he only peeked out occasionally. It wasn't until lately that Lyle has actually come forward and taken over the consciousness at various times.''

"Making Lee lose time again.''

"Yes.''

"Does Lyle understand about Lee?''

"He said his guardian angel explained Lee to him.''

"Damian, have you talked to this personality that thinks it's a guardian angel?''

"No. Lyle's guardian angel told him last night that inasmuch as he was going to be just fine now, there was a little girl in Los Angeles who needed her and that she must leave him and go to that little girl.''

"Wait a minute. A little girl in Los Angeles needs Lyle's guardian angel? But how could a part of Lyle's mind leave to...Damian, you don't suppose that...I mean, this guardian angel couldn't really be...?''

"A *real* guardian angel?'' Damian finished for her.

Kay put her head in her hands. "And to think for a moment there I was beginning to think this multiple-personality phenomenon was almost starting to make some sense!''

He laughed as he hugged her to him. "My poor logical lawyer lost in a free-fall through the miracles of the mind. Hang on, sweetheart. I have you.''

"Great. What are *you* holding on to?''

"The wonder of it all, Kay. The absolute wonder of knowing there's as much lovely illusion in this world of ours as there is logic.''

She sighed as she wrapped her arms around him. "Are all you psychologists so wonderfully mad?''

He grinned at all that delightful chagrin in her eyes. "Are all you lawyers so irritatingly sane?'' he said just before he kissed her parted lips. She sighed into his kiss and lingered in its warmth for several delicious seconds before pulling back.

"Will you tell me *now* what was on those tapes of Roy that you didn't want me to see?"

He touched her bruised cheek gently. "Suffice it to say that when Fedora and Larry Nye testified about Roy beating them, you heard not even the smallest tip of that iceberg of horrendous abuse that Roy inflicted on his wife, his son and, most particularly, his daughter."

"So that's why Croghan couldn't get the daughter to testify. Damian, I hate to admit it, but maybe it's best I didn't see what was on those tapes."

He wrapped his arms more firmly around her and kissed the sweetness of her hair, loving the sweetness of her soul.

"Damian, there's something else I'm dying to know. How did you kill off Roy?"

"Why, I exorcised him, of course."

"What?"

He laughed at the incredulity in her tone as he hugged her to him. "Yes, Kay. You see, Van Pratt was right when he said that only the mind that created a personality can really destroy it. When I finally understood what Roy was, I knew the only way to extinguish him was in a manner consistent with his identity. I also reasoned that if properly approached, the mind that knew Roy was a devil would cooperate with his being exorcised."

"This just keeps getting more fantastic. I wonder what else will come up. Are you going to continue to see Lee and Lyle?"

"Yes. Lee is aware of Lyle now. They've begun to have internal conversations, and I can see some exciting positive changes in Lee. Their future is full of wonderful possibilities for self-exploration. I hope they'll let me be a part of it."

Kay sat up in his arms so that she could look directly into his rugged, charming face. "I love you, Damian. Because of the way you think and feel and the way you make me think and feel."

He brought her to his chest and rocked her as the sweetness of her words rocked him. "Oh, God, I love you, too, my beauty. I think I fell in love with you that first moment

I saw you standing behind all that starched legal formality and knew you had erected it to keep all us beasts at bay.''

She laughed into a happy sigh, thrilled to hear his words. "I'm so glad it didn't keep you at bay."

"No, if anything, it brought out the real beast in me. Kay, you have my heart, always. But you know I can't offer you—"

"Damian, before you say it, first tell me why you didn't kill Croghan."

He exhaled a heavy breath. "I'm...not sure. I wanted to. When I saw Croghan holding a knife at your throat and kicking you, Kay, all the horror of my father's abuse of my mother flashed back. My uncontrollable rage took over."

"If it had, you would have killed Croghan. You didn't, and I know why. Your father may have taught you rage, but your mother and your grandparents taught you love. Love is stronger than rage. The love in your heart, Damian, will never let the rage be in control. What a wonderful legacy that will be for you to pass on to your son one day."

He smiled as he looked into her tender blueberry eyes. She could make him believe it. She could make him believe anything.

"Kay, would you really take such a chance?"

Her chin went up as her spine straightened. "Chance, nothing. We lawyers know a sure thing when we see it. Besides, as long as I've compromised your honor on both local and national news, I figure the least I can do is make an honest man of you."

He smiled at her belief, at her love. "All right," he said in a tone purposely gruff. "But only if loony Aunt Luddie will be at the ceremony so I can congratulate her on giving you such a perfect name."

She wrapped her arms around him, needing all her discipline to put pique in her tone. "You beast."

He held her to him as though he would never let her go. "Your Beast, my Beauty."

He kissed her then, very warm and very long and full of his growing belief in the brightness of their tomorrows.

Outside, it looks like a charming old building near the Baltimore waterfront... but inside lurks danger and romance.

The winner of the 1994 Career Achievement award for Romantic Mystery, Rebecca York, returns with...

PRINCE OF TIME

A devastating avalanche was the last thing Cassandra Devereaux expected while hiking up a mountain in the Alaskan wilderness. Only by ducking into a cave was she able to survive. But when the cave is sealed by the ensuing ice and snow, Cassandra isn't at all prepared for the sight that awaits her deeper in the underground lair....

Don't miss #338 PRINCE OF TIME, in September, wherever Harlequin books are sold. It's Rebecca York's most unusual book ever!

PRIZE SURPRISE SWEEPSTAKES!

This month's prize:

BEAUTIFUL WEDGWOOD CHINA!

This month, as a special surprise, we're giving away a bone china dinner service for eight by Wedgwood**, one of England's most prestigious manufacturers!

Think how beautiful your table will look, set with lovely Wedgwood china in the casual Countryware pattern! Each five-piece place setting includes dinner plate, salad plate, soup bowl and cup and saucer.

The facing page contains two Entry Coupons (as does every book you received this shipment). Complete and return *all* the entry coupons; **the more times you enter, the better your chances of winning!**

Then keep your fingers crossed, because you'll find out by September 15, 1995 if you're the winner!

Remember: The more times you enter, the better your chances of winning!*

PRIZE SURPRISE
SWEEPSTAKES

OFFICIAL ENTRY COUPON

This entry must be received by: AUGUST 30, 1995
This month's winner will be notified by: SEPTEMBER 15, 1995

YES, I want to win the Wedgwood china service for eight! Please enter me in the drawing and let me know if I've won!

Name_____

Address _____ Apt. _____

City   State/Prov.   Zip/Postal Code

Account #_____

Return entry with invoice in reply envelope.

© 1995 HARLEQUIN ENTERPRISES LTD.   CWW KAL

PRIZE SURPRISE
SWEEPSTAKES

OFFICIAL ENTRY COUPON

This entry must be received by: AUGUST 30, 1995
This month's winner will be notified by: SEPTEMBER 15, 1995

YES, I want to win the Wedgwood china service for eight! Please enter me in the drawing and let me know if I've won!

Name_____

Address _____ Apt. _____

City   State/Prov.   Zip/Postal Code

Account #_____

Return entry with invoice in reply envelope.

© 1995 HARLEQUIN ENTERPRISES LTD.   CWW KAL

OFFICIAL RULES
PRIZE SURPRISE SWEEPSTAKES 3448
NO PURCHASE OR OBLIGATION NECESSARY

Three Harlequin Reader Service 1995 shipments will contain respectively, coupons for entry into three different prize drawings, one for a Panasonic 31" wide-screen TV, another for a 5-piece Wedgwood china service for eight and the third for a Sharp ViewCam camcorder. To enter any drawing using an Entry Coupon, simply complete and mail according to directions.

There is no obligation to continue using the Reader Service to enter and be eligible for any prize drawing. You may also enter any drawing by hand printing the words "Prize Surprise," your name and address on a 3"x5" card and the name of the prize you wish that entry to be considered for (i.e., Panasonic wide-screen TV, Wedgwood china or Sharp ViewCam). Send your 3"x5" entries via first-class mail (limit: one per envelope) to: Prize Surprise Sweepstakes 3448, c/o the prize you wish that entry to be considered for, P.O. Box 1315, Buffalo, NY 14269-1315, USA or P.O. Box 610, Fort Erie, Ontario L2A 5X3, Canada.

To be eligible for the Panasonic wide-screen TV, entries must be received by 6/30/95; for the Wedgwood china, 8/30/95; and for the Sharp ViewCam, 10/30/95.

Winners will be determined in random drawings conducted under the supervision of D.L. Blair, Inc., an independent judging organization whose decisions are final, from among all eligible entries received for that drawing. Approximate prize values are as follows: Panasonic wide-screen TV ($1,800); Wedgwood china ($840) and Sharp ViewCam ($2,000). Sweepstakes open to residents of the U.S. (except Puerto Rico) and Canada, 18 years of age or older. Employees and immediate family members of Harlequin Enterprises, Ltd., D.L. Blair, Inc., their affiliates, subsidiaries and all other agencies, entities and persons connected with the use, marketing or conduct of this sweepstakes are not eligible. Odds of winning a prize are dependent upon the number of eligible entries received for that drawing. Prize drawing and winner notification for each drawing will occur no later than 15 days after deadline for entry eligibility for that drawing. Limit: one prize to an individual, family or organization. All applicable laws and regulations apply. Sweepstakes offer void wherever prohibited by law. Any litigation within the province of Quebec respecting the conduct and awarding of the prizes in this sweepstakes must be submitted to the Regies des loteries et Courses du Quebec. In order to win a prize, residents of Canada will be required to correctly answer a time-limited arithmetical skill-testing question. Value of prizes are in U.S. currency.

Winners will be obligated to sign and return an Affidavit of Eligibility within 30 days of notification. In the event of noncompliance within this time period, prize may not be awarded. If any prize or prize notification is returned as undeliverable, that prize will not be awarded. By acceptance of a prize, winner consents to use of his/her name, photograph or other likeness for purposes of advertising, trade and promotion on behalf of Harlequin Enterprises, Ltd., without further compensation, unless prohibited by law.

For the names of prizewinners (available after 12/31/95), send a self-addressed, stamped envelope to: Prize Surprise Sweepstakes 3448 Winners, P.O. Box 4200, Blair, NE 68009.

RPZ KAL